WE'LL ALWAYS HAVE
PARIS

WE'LL ALWAYS HAVE
PARIS

WILLARD ORIOL

Ordering Information:

For orders and inquiries, please contact:
1-888-404-1388
www.goldtouchpress.com
book.orders@goldtouchpress.com

Printed in the United States of America

CONTENTS

CHAPTER 1

In The Beginning

St. Mary's Hospital was a Catholic Institution whose very denomination kept Larry's Jewish Orthodox grandparents from visiting their daughter, his mother, during the 5 days she spent there recuperating from the ordeal of bearing him.

Children of immigrant Russians Larry's parents embraced the United States of America with unquestioning devotion. Only in America could victims of Czarist pogroms and Communist purges find the freedom a democratic Constitution guaranteed them. They were ardent Democrats with a Hallmark Greeting Card view of the world, who ascribed his birthdate as a gift from the patrician orator of Hyde Park, New York, Franklin Delano Roosevelt, the 32nd president of the United States. In the hardscrabble depression year of 1932 he was born in Minneapolis, Minnesota. It was on an early November day, during which Roosevelt won a first term to the highest office in the land, that he entered the world in the maternity ward of St. Marys. His birth occurred about the same time Herbert Hoover, the outgoing Republican, conceded the election over network radio to an audience of millions; 40% of whom were unhappy with the results.

It was a good thing Grandpa Max and Grandma Rose never set foot in St. Mary's. The legions of black shrouded nuns, their bat-like habits accessorized by jangling crucifixes and clicking rosary beads, would have freaked out these first generation immigrants who viewed all crucifixes as crucibles of terror. From early childhood on, he heard about the persecution and hardships his grandparents had to endure under tyrannical rulers of the state and church in the old country.

The self-sacrificing, pinch penny life style of both sets of grandparents enabled his mother and father to attend college and pursue careers that enabled them a comfortable middle class status. Larry's father's career spanned 40 years as a pharmacist in Minneapolis. His Mother, Sara, dropped out of the University Dental School when he was born and remained at home raising his sister and him for the next several years. Larry was four years old when Sara went to work as a dental assistant to a kindly German practitioner named Otto Klein. She could not afford to return to Dental School and rear two kids simultaneously, so she chose to help out family finances in a job for which she was over qualified. They were going through the middle of the depression and even his father's pharmacy felt the pinch of reduced consumer spending.

Dr. Klein was not a Jew, the name could go either way-- Lutheran German or Jewish German--but he was sympathetic to his mother's need to forego Dental School and found her a more than competent employee. He told her of his deep sympathy for Jews living in his homeland. Personally, he thought National Socialism abhorrent and Adolph Hitler an evil man.

People of German descent, who constituted 20% of the population in Minnesota & Wisconsin, were not all as benign towards Jews as Otto Klein. A significant number openly spouted the bile-like rhetoric of their Fuhrer. The upper mid-west was fertile ground for pro-German sympathizers who spread their hate throughout Jewish neighborhoods in the largest cities of Minnesota, Wisconsin and Northern Illinois. It was difficult for anyone to excise memories of the rabble-rousing voice of Father Coughlin, a Catholic Parish priest from Royal Oak, Michigan. Echoes of his virulent diatribes against Jews resonated every Sunday morning over a Detroit based radio station whose powerful broadcasting range covered the entire Midwest. During the prewar years, 1938-1941, every Sunday, mother, father, Larry and sister Elaine all huddled around the family console radio, listening to Coughlin's of vitriol. His relentless screed blamed Jews for every current world problem; the depression and its 25 million unemployed in the United States alone, Godless Communism and its attempt to destroy capitalism, controlling the world's money supply through unscrupulous banking practices. It didn't add up. If Jews had all that money why did he get a second hand Hawthorne bicycle for his last birthday?

It was difficult to comprehend the slanderous attributions about Jewish people he heard on the weekly radio broadcasts until he first encountered them as an eight year old the summer of 1940. One typical afternoon, while playing Monopoly on her screened porch Elaine Skarda accused Larry of killing Christ.

"My mother told me so," she said. You're a Christ killer, "she insisted, repeating the accusation over and over.

Tears poured from his eyes and he remembered protesting, "I did not. I did not. You're a liar."

He turned away and ran back home just down the block. Sara's comforting reassurance that he was no killer, along with a mug of hot Ovaltine, eased the pain of the moment. But over the years that scene often replayed in his mind when his religion or ethnic background was in any way disparaged. The late 1930's heightened the boldness of anti-Semitic acts, continuing throughout WW11 until the Nazis appeared to be losing the war. While the horrors of Auschwitz and Buchenwald had yet to penetrate Larry's caul of ignorance, he was aware of anti-Semitic incidents in the Mid-West. In 1944 he felt more confused than ever reading in the Minneapois Star about German American rallies held in cities in nearby Wisconsin. He knew those that attended such rallies hated Jews but did that have to include him or was it just Jews they met and didn't care for. Amidst all the gloom and paranoia one brief exhilarating incident occurred which allowed Larry to score one for the good guys who saved his people, even though its heros could not, under normal circumstances, be called good guys. Intellectually too young to identify with the concept of 'my People,' he had heard some people call Jews tribal. Not possible. Tribes were for Indians like the Chippewa, the Sioux and the Ojibway. They lived as tribes on reservations. The had leaders called chiefs. Who ever heard of a Jewish chief? The only Jewish reservation he ever heard of was one you made to a restaurant. His lone moment of optimism, in a struggle to understand the basis for anti-Semitism, occurred when the American Nazi, William Dudley Pelley threatened a march on the Jewish section of Minneapolis.

Pelley was the leader of a group called the Silver Shirts who staged anti-Semitic rallies throughout the Mid-West, many of which resulted in destruction of Jewish property and injury to many Jewish citizens.

Pelley had targeted Minneapolis for rally in August. His Silver Shirts marched into the city, stopping at the Minneapolis Elks Club where a big rally gathered to hear the "great man" speak. The place was packed with Silver Shirt sympathizers noisily waiting for him to speak. He climbed the stairs to the podium to thundrous applause. When the room quieted down he began, "Thank you ladies and gentlemen. I think you all know why I'm here. We have a mission. It's an important mission. It's a mission of cleansing. Cleansing you may ask what's that all about? Well it's pretty simple ands pretty obvious. You have an insidious enemy in your midst. They threaten your way of life, your jobs, your patriotism, your religious beliefs and our very system of capitalism which makes our economy strong. Who am I talking about"? The audience roared. Before he could get an answer to his rhetorical question, 12 burly men carrying thick rubber truncheons burst into the room. Several raced towards the podium. The others charged into the audience wildly swinging their instruments of pain randomly, cracking heads, arms, ribs legs, buttocks with joyous abandon, lacerating anyone in reach including those women unlucky enough to accompany their angry collection of fathers, husbands, brothers and boyfriends. The unlikely saviors of the day were a thuggish band of Dave Berman loyalists. Dave Berman, who never graced the polite dinner tables of Jewish society, became an overnight hero to Larry and countless adults who previously looked upon him as a *chanda*, a Jewish pariah, lower than the lowest caste Hindu untouchable. Dave Berman earned his approbrium as top seeded mobster in the upper Mid-West. He controlled every vice known to man; gambling, booze, prostitution, loan sharking and some allege, the occasional 'rub out'. Unknown to most Jews in the Twin Cities, he was approached by a North Minneapolis Rabbi who told him of Pelley's planned rally. He sought Berman's help. The Rabbi wanted protection for Northside Jews who would be put in harm's way when Pelley and his Silver Shirts marched through their neighborhood after the Elks Club rally. The march never occurred. At the following Saturday service the Rabbi offered a special blessing to Dave and his men for their heroic acts of mercy, when his congregation was most at risk.

Months later the Silver Shirts attempted another march on Minneapolis. It turned into a charnel house of blood and broken bones, courtesy of "Berman's Army," a sobriquet bestowed upon Dave and his group for their victories on the battlegrounds of anti-Semitism. Pelley scheduled no more rallies in the unfriendly city of Minneapolis.

Larry's life lesson from all this, although flawed upon reflection years later, was; fight back physically if necessary. Moral victories and martyrdom were not his cup of tea. His template for living, constructed by a conflicted teen ager, utilized a flawed trial and error strategy to gain social acceptance. It was an acceptance he never fully achieved, in a continuing battle of me versus them, until the age 35. Before that advanced age that he never learned that acceptance had to begin with accepting oneself. When his mother went to work for Dr. Otto, she hired a live in maid, Mildred Lynch, a seriously observant Catholic. She would return from 12:00 mass at St. Mathews Cathedral after a sermon filled with love and religion, aglow with virtue. Hard working but inarticulate, psychologists at he time might have termed her "slow".

Immediately after moving into the Miller household, Mildred hung a two foot long crucifix above her bed. It scared the hell out of Larry every time he saw it. Mildred's presence in young Larry's life provided him first hand evidence of the rigidity of blind faith. There was no questioning the gospels. He learned early in life to beware of the person who describes an opinion as "the gospel truth." In her tight assed inner world goodness never seemed to be rewarded. Mildred wasn't a lot of fun. If he did something unseemly like farting and laughing she would warn he'd wind up in hell for such behavior.

A voracious reader of SILVER SCREEN and other star-filled magazines, mostly consisting of posed pictures, she reveled in the brief tidbits about the royalty of Hollywood she revered from afar. Robert Taylor was her favorite. His noble profile, which she showed to Larry on many occasions, would bring tears to her eyes. This 45 year old virgin--his assessment years later about her sexual history--had a serious crush on Taylor nee Skyler Arlington Brew. On reflection he'd bet that she confessed her 'dark feelings' about Taylor every Sunday to a forgiving parish priest. Every Saturday, her day off, she would attend the WORLD Theater downtown Minneapolis, a forty five minute street car ride from the Miller house. Unfortunately new Robert Taylor movies numbered but two per year, each with a three week run at the WORLD. That left Mildred with 50 non-Taylor Saturdays. She seemed to adjust to cinematic replacements in the void left by Taylor. Soon her room was filled with Film Magazines featuring John Payne, Tyrone Power and Errol Flynn.

In late August 1943, mid war, real life sex intruded on Mildred's pristine life. He was too young to understand what happened at the time but one Saturday evening well after her movie going afternoon, Mildred returned to The Miller house. Tears streamed from her eyes. Her stockings were torn. Her dress was in disarray and the meticulous marcelling of her hair left its tight curls loosely spiraling downward.

"He did things to me," she sobbed. His mother quickly assessing the situation hustled Mildred out of the living room into her room at the back of the three bedroom house, before Larry or his eleven year old sister could get involved. She knew there would be more to explain that she was prepared to offer.

An hour later mother Sara came into the kitchen to boil some tea for her new charge. The house was quiet all the next day. Mildred remained in her room until late Monday afternoon when a stiff-walking matron wearing a military style dark blue suit appeared at the front door. When Sara opened it Larry could see a white van parked out front. The lettering on the vehicle read: HENNEPIN COUNTY SOCIAL SERVICES. Larry's last view of Mildred was leaving the house, propped up by the blue suited matron, walking in a daze, mumbling incoherently as the two navigated the six step descent to the sidewalk. 20 years later watching the final scene of Tennessee Williams STREETCAR NAMED DESIRE on Broadway, Larry replaced, in his my mind, the image of a broken Blanche Du Bois with that of an equally broken Mildred Lynch.

Mildred's departure was followed by a couple of really good years, enriched by the golden presence of Anna Hansen her replacement whose arrival made every day seem brighter in the Miller household; the colors, the food, the conversations at dinner. Exchanged kicks under the dinner table between his sister, Elaine, and Larry were replaced by stories of their day with Anna. Under her sunny tutelage they learned to draw with charcoal, pastels, and crayons. They learned Christmas Carols—though never sang them when their grandparents were around—and they learned to play killer MONOPOLY which forever changed the rainy days of summer.

Best of all she introduced them to peanut butter and banana sandwiches and chocolate covered Malomars.

Anna was a head taller than Larry, around 5'4". She always wore trim fitting cotton dresses which hugged her athletic build and discreetly revealed her perfect breasts.

Is there anything more pathetic than an 11 ½ year old falling in love with an older woman of 26?

The next year, the dark side of his 12th birthday, was a mandate from Orthodox grandfather Ben that he immediately commence a crash course in learning the *haftorah* for his Bar Mitzvah, a ritual every Jewish thirteen year old boy must perform to authenticate his fealty to Judaism.

The next 52 weeks of his life a small yellow school bus picked him up, promptly at 3:00 pm, along with 6 other bar mitzvah boys in training. The bus bore large black letters emblazoned on both of its sides which read: ST. PAUL JEWISH CENTER. Each day it boldly informed his Christian classmates—mostly Catholic or Lutheran—who constituted 98% of the school's enrollment, that Larry Miller was a Jew.

On the second day of Hebrew School Larry's social life dramatically changed. The familiar names of George Hough, Bob Luban, Don Moore, Tony Phillips and Dick Johnson were slowly replaced by those of Dave Ginsberg, Ted Abrahamson, Milton Glazer, Walter Fishman and Sheldon Belkin. Overnight he became a Jew, not only by birth but by social stratum.

During the period of social metamorphosis he developed a mindset of psychic armor which prevented trust from penetrating its protective shield. He trusted no one. His invisible shield held both young men and women at bay.

Regardless how intense or superficial his friendships were, it took nearly 25 years for the consequences of witholding inner feelings from all interpersonal relationships to become apparent. It was an epiphany at the outset of his divorce many years later.

The upside of his social transition was an introduction to seriously competitive basketball on the Jewish Center's Intermediate team, which prepped him for a spot on the South High Junior Varsity his sophomore year. For two happy years he was immersed in playing both JV and JC Intermediate basketball. An ability to score points and dish out assists to teammates put Larry on a plane well beyond the reach of anti-Semitism. Or so he thought.

CHAPTER 2

The Scrimmage

On November 9th a notice was posted on the South High School bulletin boards. Varsity basketball tryouts would begin on Tuesday the 11th. Larry, who had a productive tenth grade junior varsity season, was pretty confident of his chances to make the varsity team.

He had worked well under JV coach, Frank Gallanos, but varsity coach Huntley was a different breed of cat. He had a reputation as a hard assed individual who played favorites and bullied those players he didn't like.

The first day of tryouts was nervous making. You had to start off strong to survive until coach's final decisions two days later.

There were 13 JV players competing for 6 slots on the varsity. If you didn't make the cut, your high school basketball career was over. Juniors were not allowed to play JV and also not eligible to try out for the varsity as a senior. There were no second chances at South High.

Larry and his pal Shel Belkin performed well the first two days. His jump shot was on target and he dished out several assists at point guard. On the second day he led all scorers with 13 points.

Belkin at forward also played well hauling in 6 rebounds both days and scord 9 points on day one and 7 on day two.

Coming off the court on day two, Larry passed Coach Hundley looking for some sign of approval, maybe a nod or even a smile. Instead, Hundley turned away abruptly as he walked by, avoiding eye contact.

On day three, cut day, Larry saw he would be playing against an all varsity team including Jim Duffy, second team All City the year before.

At 5'10" Duffy was an inch taller than Larry but out weighed him by 20 pounds.

At tip off Duffy began to play Larry one on one, a departure from Coach's usual zone defense. Something wasn't kosher he thought. Duffy played too close him, a couple of inches from in his face. Larry clearly saw his pock marked face matched the faint red indentations on his shoulders.

As Larry brought the ball up court Duffy matched him step by step, his sweaty arms waving wildly, almost touching as Larry crosshanded his dribble to shake off his smothering opponent.

Past midcourt Larry faked a pass to Ray Gunnar in the right corner, then pulled up sharply to attempt a jump shot clear of the windmill of Duffy's arms. He settle his left hand on the lower side of the ball and let loose with his right.

As the ball left his hand, Duffy's finger tips caught a piece of it. It landed in the hands of Perry Proctor, starting varsity forward, who streaked down court for an easy lay up. Oh, fuck he muttered to himself. He knew he had looked bad in any bystander's eye. Hustle he told himself. Coach likes hustle.

Larry brought the ball up court again. Closely pursued by Duffy, he whipped the ball to Dave Hubbard, then made a dash into the free throw lane where Hubbard fed him the ball. He leaped up for an easy lay up, that didn't happen.

Duffy appeared from nowhere and slapped the ball away the moment Larry jumped.

Larry looked over at the side line. There he saw a smile on Hundley's face. Why the smile?

Larry's team continued to play a zone defense, one they were not familiar with. On the next possession Duffy slowly brought the ball up until he crossed the mid court line. Then with a quick burst of speed he headed into Larry's zone crashing into Larry, knocking him to floor while he continued for an uncontested lay up.

It was clearly a flagrant foul. There was no whistle from the referee. No call for deliberately knocking down an opposing player. What the hell is going on Larry thought? Coach Hundley was actually smiling.

Angry he got up to address Duffy.

"This is a physical game, Jew boy," Duffy said with a laugh.

Larry turned to face Coach Hundley. Their eyes met. He was still smiing as he beckoned to Larry.

"Had enough, Miller?"

"No, but why wasn't a whistle blown on that play? That was a flagrant foul by any standard?"

"Get used to contact. It's part of the game."

"Bullshit."

"Did I hear you right you little son of a bitch? You people are not much for physical contact. You're outta here, NOW."

Shel Belkin didn't fare any better.

It was a bitter pill to swallow when he read the bulletin board results the next day. The Gunnar twins and Ed Gibson, Larry's JV teammates, journey men at best, made the varsity and Coach Hundley got his wish for an all Aryan team that season.

Larry moved on to a new challenge the remainder of his junior year. He joined the staff of the Southerner, the school's weekly newspaper.

He became Sport's Editor of the Southerner his senior year, the year of Coach Hundley's disastrous season. His two All City players Duffy and Markey had graduated the previous spring and three of his starters were Larry's former JV teammates.

His weekly sport's columns refected the shadenfreude of writing about the ineptitude of the team. While Larry made no friends among members of the jock fraternity, Coach Hundley's glares during gym class warmed his heart.

CHAPTER 3

The Young Second Lieutenant
1954-1957

Life in the service was remarkably free of anti-Semitism. Larry's oasis of tolerance was Ellsworth Air Force Base just outside of Rapid City, South Dakota. A bias free three year stint as a Second Lieutenant in the Air Force was of his own making.

At the acceptance of his commission he was asked the routine question, "Religious preference?"

His reply, "No preference", was indelibly etched on his dog tags, a barrier against any Jewish related stigma. Successful denial of heritage became a weapon against any religious prejudice in the Air Force and for most of his early working life.

The first Fair Employment Act to be legislated in America occurred in 1959 in the liberal state of Minnesota. Four years passed before this seminal anti-bias in hiring act was in effect nationwide.

The Fair Employment Act was his passport to a long career in the grey flannel world of Madison Avenue. But that's another story.

Another salient reason why Ellsworth Air Force Base was free of anti-Semitism; there were few or no Jews stationed there, to his knowledge. The statistical anomaly of no Jews among 12,000 men stationed at the base was premised on his daring presumption about the religious affiliation of the 11,500 personnel with whom he never came into contact.

He was, however, sure of the religious identity of the 500 men that comprised his 28th Reconnaissance Squadron. As squadron adjutant he had access to the permanent files of all 500.

Larry enjoyed being treated as an officer and a gentleman by peers and subordinates alike. Deep denial of roots became ingrained in his psyche.

As a horny young 22 year old, Larry explored every avenue to meet girls amidst the barren pickings of Rapid City, South Dakota. His terms for acceptable candidates were women in their early to late twenties; women, unhappily married, engaged, or near ready to move on to greater opportunities outside of the second largest city in the state.

His biggest stretch by far in search of female companionship, was auditioning for a production of the Mikado which ought to have had at least a dozen young women trying out, or so he thought.

His audition rendition, an incredibly off key singing of Gershwin's SUMMERTIME, brought real tears to the eyes of the director, A Yale School of Drama graduate who founded the local community theater group, in hopes of developing a grander regional repertory company. Auditions like that of Larrys and several other airmen must have convinced him that his lofty ambitions might never be attained in this geographic location.

Larry, one of ten men from the Ellsworth AFB vying for a role, was the only officer among them. A young corporal was selected to play the plum role of the Emperor. The others including Larry were assigned to the chorus of 15. Sheer volume would mask their vocal limitations. Female members of the chorus selected were married women in their thirties and early forties looking to lighten the burden of housekeeping and child raising, not romantic liasons.

Although the Mikado caper produced no likely prospects, Larry's luck changed when he met the the younger sister of his exec officer's girl friend, Sheila. She was to be his first romantic involvement at Ellsworth AFB, or so he thought.

Major Bob Trenton, 10 years his senior, was a ramrod straight professional military man who became exec officer of the 28th at the same time Larry joined the unit. His finely starched and pressed summer khakis attested to his gung ho approach to duty. A reservist from WW11, Bob remained in service and was promoted to major when the Army Air Force became the United States Air Force, a separate branch of service in 1947. He also distinguished himself during the Berlin Air Lift of 1951 which President Harry Truman ordered to provide food for West Berlin's beleaguered population. They were, victims of the cold war in a divided Berlin, which limited their access to a steady flow of food and other necessities from West Germany.

After Berlin he served two years in Korea flying B-25's before being assigned to Ellsworth. Bob took a liking to Larry, treating him like a younger brother which made his life easier. A greener than green second lieutenant, he lacked in any real military training.

Not an ROTC graduate, he was a direct commission officer chosen for a needed occupational skill for the Korean war. He never could understand the vital part he had to play in that conflict as a Public Information Officer. He knew squat about military protocol and never let his copy of the US Air Force Manual of Procedures and Protocol out of his sight while in the orderly room, always prepared to address his procedural ignorance.

Major Bob knew he was a recent college graduate with a direct commission who knew nothing about military protocol, but he also knew Larry could be a personal asset to his military and social life. Larry was in a position to do him some good. As the PIO, he had constant contact with the Rapid City Journal and the CBS affiliate radio station, WRCS.

His first favor was getting Sheila a job interview at the radio station. The Gods looked positively on that minor act of influence peddling. She got the job as an executive secretary to the station manager. From then on Larry could do no wrong in his major's eyes. He felt like a 'made' man in the Mafia doing good for his Don.

A brief romance with Sheila's younger sister, Peggy, began at the Officer's Club where Bob and he planned a Saturday night out; dinner and dancing to a good combo made up of members of the AFB's Marching Band.

When the girls arrived they were thoroughly chilled by the gusty winds of October, signaling an early Dakota winter. Sheila's 1946 Ford had no working heater. As Larry helped Peggy remove her too thin cotton trench coat, she was shivering, reflexively he put his arms around her for a few seconds to abate the chill. It was a premature gesture of closeness to someone he'd just met but it enabled him to absorb her athletic body that seemed to perfectly match a beautiful broad face. She was a knockout. Luscious lips, dreamy blue eyes, blonde hair. Peggy was clearly a product of the prevailing genetic make-up in the Upper Mid-

West, a gene pool comprised of Finns. Germans, Anglo Saxons, Swedes and Norwegians residing in Minnesota, Iowa, the Dakotas and Wisconsin which almost guaranteed that the majority of their female offspring would look like some version of Peggy.

Friday night at the Officer's Club Martinis and Manhattans freely flowed at half their mid-week price to encourage total relaxation for those B-36 bomber crews, who lived with the A-bomb, a not too secret on board companion in their daily reconnaissance missions that skirted the geographic edges of the Cold War. Their missions recorded enemy coastlines with powerful oblique cameras which effectively filmed objects up to fifty miles away.

A musical quartet of non-coms played mostly slow dances to accommodate the amorous aspirations of the 25 to 30 bachelors in attendance. Their performance sharply contrasted with their usual parade grounds fare of Sousa marches.

Peggy and Larry fit well on the dance floor. Bodily points of contact offered them a whiff of sexuality, optimistically a foreshadowing of events to come. During the course of the evening,

Larry had five martinis and 15 nutritional olives. He lost track of those consumed by Peggy. Three he thought totally unaware of her capacity for distilled grain with a touch of juniper.

Dinner seemed like an afterthought for Major Bob and Sheila as they hastily picked at their plates of beef tenderloin tips smothered in a viscous brown sauce. They skipped dessert and brought their evening to an end by announcing their plans to leave for town.

"Hate to eat and run," Bob said. "Give you kids a chance to know each other."

Kids? Who the hell is a kid? I'm 22 years old and Peggy's gotta be at least 22.

"Gotcher keys, honey?" Sheila asked her young sister as she got up from a chair which Bob had gallantly pulled aside for a quicker get away.

Peggy, her mouth filled with shrimp cocktail which she apparently had infrequently tasted, if ever, answered with a nod. That was good enough for Sheila who appeared to be in heat. Major Bob, I knew, was always in heat and his apartment in Rapid City was only twenty minutes away. The major once confided to Larry that if he didn't have sex at least 7 times a week he would get severe headaches. He never challenged his theory about sex and headaches. One need not have to justify chronic horniness.

The existence of Bob's digs left Sheila's apartment open to Larry and Peggy. They left about a half hour later, midnight. His 1951 metallic green Chevrolet carried them back to Rapid City in less than half an hour. Peggy moved closer to him. She was a cuddler. All to the good, he thought.

After midnight the town of Rapid City slept. Night life was mainly an improvised entertainment at home; radio, records, sex. Television had not yet come to this bleak outpost in the Black Hills, a new technology as yet unable to scale the 8,000 foot elevations of their peaks.

They entered Sheila's apartment, a bit wobbly. Peggy was just beginning to feel the diminishing motor skills that alcohol induced.

It was a one bedroom unit, tidily furnished with perky chintz curtains and several tarantula-like sling chairs popular in the late fifties and early sixties. The sling chair, an artfully engineered multi-arced wrought iron frame draped in bright colored canvas, resulted in an inviting pocket in which to lounge.

A pull out sofa, a circular slab of cedar, finished in clear acrylic lacquer, set on conical metal legs, and a rectangular Navajo area carpet that covered most of the living room completed the grounded décor. Two overhead Noguchi lamp shades hanging from slender black cords provided the room's illumination.

As Larry sat down on the sofa, Peggy collapsed into his arms. It was not an amorous move, more an act of passing out. Just his luck. Any thoughts of romance faded as quickly as the light from the Noguchi's which he extinguished before taking his leave, but not before tucking the catatonic Peggy into her bed. He discreetly removed her shoes, leaving the major stages of undress to her hung over self when she woke.

He called Peggy the next morning to inquire of her health. A moan and a grunt gave a precise description of her condition. In addition to sympathy he offered his nearly fool proof hangover remedy, Ice cream; you desperately need the sugar; a tuna fish sandwich with loads of mayonnaise—don't laugh it works, followed up by an extra spicy bloody Mary.

Peggy and Larry dated but two more times. Each time he judiciously tempered the quantity of alcohol she consumed. One of those dates, after a movie on Main Street--which was "Singing In The Rain"--ended on the wood framed sofa in Sheila's living room.

They a kissed gently at first, then a little more aggressively, to that point when he slowly slipped a hand under her skirt. She quickly placed both of her hands on his tentative one hand and apologetically said, "I can't. It's that time. You know."

"No problem," he said, releasing her from his diminishing grasp

After one beer and one side of his Benny Goodman Carnegie Hall Jazz Concert album, a 33rpm disc, he left the apartment.

On the drive back to Ellsworth he found himself keeping an irregular beat on the gas pedal to the sounds in his head of Lionel Hampton's vibes, Gene Krupa's drums, and Benny Goodman's clarinet throughout the entire seven minutes of SING SING SING.

It was strike two that night but he promised himself the next time would be different. It wasn't. Next time in Sheila's apartment his khaki uniform pants, sporting a sharp crease along the entire length of each leg, hung smartly from the closed top drawer of Peggy's dresser. His matching uniform shirt was neatly folded on a chintz covered chair.

She lay on the bed wearing nothing but a sheer tea rose pink slip. He crawled in bed beside her. After a few moments of caressing her firm young body, which she seemed to invite and enjoy, she pulled back and said, "There's something I have to tell you."

Oh, God, he thought. What? She's a virgin? Forgot her diaphragm?

"What's that?" he asked.

"I am only seventeen years old."

Saved by her honesty, sweetness, or maybe she knew she just wasn't ready yet. The relationship ended on that note, although he had the decency to send her a dozen roses the very next morning. They contained a short farewell note of apology and wished her a happy life with many kids and a loving husband.

She acknowledged his lame and abrupt break-up strategy with a card, which shamed him to his guilt ridden Jewish soul. It read: "You're a very nice man. There will always be a place for you in my heart." The note was signed with a kiss, a red print of closed mouth lips, which to him read DO NOT ENTER. There it was an imprint on the card like some magisterial seal of finality, which it was.

Some might not consider his calling a second girl he dated a girlfriend, a fair designation of their relationship. Her tenure with him; three weeks, three meetings, and prolonged sweaty frustration—quickly evaporated.

Hilda was of German stock and Hilda might as well have been Brunhilde, possessed of Olympian passion but restrained by the iron curtain of her Catholic upbringing that seemed to place chastity on a higher pedestal than the majority of the U.S. population.

The brief relationship was more like three undercard matches of the World Wrestling Association; lots of cheap theatrics, many twisted holds, frequent thumping take downs and one clear winner.

She might have considered herself the winner of their unofficial grapplings as he acknowledge being the loser. Clear eyed judges of the human condition, with its pleasures and disappointments, however would call their bouts a double defeat. No winner was possible under the ground rules Hilda seemed to improvise and impose.

After the strenuous workout of each match they looked like rumpled, out of breath participants in an extreme sport version of adult pillow fighting; bright red cheeks, damp and distressed clothing--both inner and outer garments.

A D- cup brassiere hung limply over Hilda's right arm, a wrestling trophy he richly deserved, but was denied by this daughter of the Valkyries. Three bouts and Larry retired from the ring and his mid-west Brunhilde.

Bucky Olsen was Larry's third and final attempt at building a relationship with any Rapid City woman. Her name really wasn't Bucky. It was Suzanne Olsen. His friend, Captain Jim Conway, tagged her with that name, though never to her face. The name was his graphic description of one facial characteristic she possessed. Suzanne was dealt an overbite, which had yet to be corrected although the metal braces she wore made her appear younger than her 26 years. Mouth closed she was extremely attractive. She was to become Larry's friend and lover for the last 11 months of his tour of duty in Rapid City.

They were the happiest months of his service career. It was a real relationship, one of sharing music, poetry, jokes, skiing, cooking together, just being in the same room together.

At his request Captain Conway stopped with the ugly nickname.

Suzanne smart and ambitious had a degree from the University of South Dakota. She wanted to better herself. Although Rapid City was her home, long range it was not for her; too limiting. She was administrative assistant to the President of the Alex Johnson Hotel, the finest hotel within a 200 mile radius. Tourists flocked to the Black Hills every summer, spring and fall to see the great American icons of Mt. Rushmore, 60 foot sculptures of four great American Presidents, Washington, Jefferson, Lincoln and Teddy Roosevelt, carved onto the side of a mountain.

More affluent visitors scrambled for reservations at the stylish Alex Johnson. Mt. Rushmore, the life's work of a sculptor named Gutzum Borglum, was a magnet for visitors from all over America.

Suzanne wanted to capitalize on her hotel experience to try her luck in New York; to find a job with one of the nation's top hotel chains, like Sheraton, Hilton or Radisson. Her career goal was to manage a prestige hotel. Career aspirations such as hers were not widely held by the women of that generation. At this point in her life marriage and children were not part of the equation.

"You once told me you were headed for New York when you got out," Suzanne unexpectedly said, one Saturday evening, at the officer's club a couple of months before he was to be released from active duty.

"That's the plan. I've saved a few bucks and I'm going to look for an entry level job in advertising. New York is where the action is."

"Maybe we can meet for a drink in New York when I get there next year."

He never thought of a continuing relationship with Suzanne, although theirs was far more than a sexual affair. She was a delight to be with but he was not in love with her. Is it possible she might be with him? God I hope not, he thought.

The night before his discharge he spent with Suzanne, in her small apartment in the Alex Johnson Hotel. Before leaving early next morning he stopped for a minute, looking at the empty bottle

WE'LL ALWAYS HAVE PARIS

of Moet Chandon champagne she bought as a celebratory farewell. She was still sleeping, the sleep of good booze and good sex.

Larry left a note with the name and telephone number where she could reach him. It was that of his fraternity brother, Harold Freiman, living in New York City, with whom he would stay until he landed a job. Suzanne had become an important part of his life. She deserved his friendship in a new city.

Freiman was a Jewish name but Suzanne, free of prejudice, wouldn't give it a second thought. They never discussed religion and he doubted if she knew he was Jewish. The note also read in capital letters: SEE YOU IN NEW YORK.

Larry's last act before release from active duty was a sad one. He oversaw the demise of a friend who made the rigidity of military life seem less overbearing. He was a friend who helped make off duty time come alive with laughter and bonhomie. Joe Robbins was a theater major seeking a career in theater when the Korean War began and he was drafted into the Air Force. His good cheer and intelligence made it possible to often cast aside the pomp and regimentation of stateside military life.

Sunshine pored over the vast flatlands of South Dakota, as far as he could see from his car. Larry's mission this day, two weeks to the day from his scheduled departure from the USAF, was to unobtrusively squire his friend Joe Robbins around the 8 military stations of the cross required to process his "undesireable discharge" from the service.

He was caught in the homophobic net that seined Strategic Air Command, successfully snaring over 90 airmen. Swift administration of military justice quietly papered over the proceedings far from the eyes of prying media reporters. This epidemic of man love spread throughout the realm of SAC from its headquarters in Omaha to 8th Air Force Headquarters in San Antonio, Texas.

He was about to drive Joe around the base, each stop a bureaucratic removal of Corporal Joe Robbins military identity.

"Do you suppose they'll cut the buttons off my uniform?" Joe said upon entering Larry's car for a farewell lap around Ellsworth AFB.

He laughed half-heartedly knowing Joe's inner agony always masked itself with a tart riposte.

"You know it had to happen sometime but I never lied to you," he said.

"Joe, you were always straight with me. No pun intended," I said.

He smiled. Sergeant Vern Fryer, his closest friend had received his invitation to leave the service of his country two weeks earlier. Lieutenant Ron McHartle, Joe's friend and class mate from Ohio State, an officer and a gentleman, was spared the ignominious departure from active duty. Rank had its privileges. The Air Force kept its officer corps clean from scandal.

Vern, a theater major from Vanderbilt, ran the base radio station. He, along with Joe and Larry, started the base theater group. Fraternizing socially with enlisted men was not encouraged by the USAF. After duty hours were his own Larry insisted to his executive officer, who surprisingly agreed with him.

Nonetheless when the scandal broke Larry's name was tainted in the eyes of many fellow officers. It could have been worse. A homosexual Jew? The worst kind.

He had no complaints about the heat he took after the scandal broke, because Joe and their raggedy theater group made life not merely bearable but exhilarating. It was a sharp contrast to the gray everyday sameness of duty in a non-war zone of the military. Larry's short happy acting career included roles in THE HASTY HEART; he played the fat English soldier, a young playwright in Moss Hart's LIGHT UP THE SKY, and a not too bright Amish youth in PAPA IS ALL. That theatrical experience ignited his life-long love affair with theater, though as a beguiled spectator rather than performer.

Their rounds began with a stop at the Quartermaster's Office where it was determined that Joe possessed no government property.

Check one on the bureaucratic checklist. Next was the Paymaster's Office where the government made sure the departing pariah was paid his due, monetarily. The hospital stop presented him with his last physical report which proved his time in service did him no harm, physically. He signed off at the PX assured he owed no money to that low cost purveyor of booze, cigarettes and condoms, among other discounted consumer goods.

At the Protestant Chaplains obligatory sign off, Joe received a perfunctory blessing and best wishes for a clean Christian life. The sub text shouted; there's no future as a fag.

The Non-commissioned Officers Club gave Joe a clean bill of health, no lingering unpaid chits. At the Squadron Orderly room Airman Robbins was handed his official release to be given to the Wing Personnel Office for signature and verification that he was being discharged as an undesireable. The Wing Personnel Officer of the day happily signed Joe's last hurdle before officially returning him to civilian life. Good riddance was the message.

Last stop was Joe's barracks. Time to collect all worldly possessions. He returned minutes later, duffel bag in hand, all buttons secure on his air force blue uniform as he climbed into the green Chevrolet for the very last time.

They drove in silence to the gates guarding the entrance to Ellsworth AFB. Once outside he could catch a bus to Rapid City, 12 miles away. Larry had hoped to drive him to town but just his luck, he drew squadron officer of the day duty beginning at noon.

Joe got out of the car. Larry did as well. They stood silently for a moment. Joe's huge duffel bag rested on his right shoulder. They shook hands. Real men didn't hug at goodbyes for at least another forty years. It was a lingering handshake. They faithfully promised to contact each other in New York City in the fall.

They never did.

CHAPTER 4

Georgeena Enters My Life

Alex Monheim, a distinguished looking white haired man, pulled Larry aside. His son's wedding ceremony would begin in fifteen minutes. It must be something important Larry thought. Geogeena was off in the reception area talking with friends of the groom most of whom she had come to know during their one year relationship. They met one month from the date he was released from active duty in the Air Force. July 1957.

Arthur Schwartz first introduced him to Georgeena. Schwartz's family owned a children's clothing firm that sold its products through the top chain stores in America. They had recently hired a new designer named Georgeena Bjorkman.

Over drinks at the Viking Room in the Radisson Hotel, he and Arthur celebrated his return to civilian life. Most of Arthur's friends thought him a spoiled rich boy. And he was, but Larry saw his capacity for friendship, generousity and his humorous view of life triumphed over his shortcomings as a young man of excessive privilege.

Two Gin martinis, straight up, each with three anchovy olives stood before them. Beefeater was their gin of choice. He raised his glass as did Larry his, touching gently before downing the first chilled sip.

"L Chaim!" in unison they cried.

"Larry," he began, "before you start thinking about getting a job, let's start with first things first. I'm sure you led a pretty monastic life in the Black Hills of South Dakota."

"Whoa, Arthur, not that bad. Slim pickins the first couple months but once I got the lay of the land…no pun intended…I had my share. And before you say another word about pussy…"

"This isn't just pussy, it's the complete package. Smart, beautiful and she's not just looking for a husband, unlike all the Southside Jewish broads we know who we've learned not to seriously mess with. This woman actually has a career."

"Okay, now that you've offered her credentials, what's the catch? Why don't you give it a go?"

"She works for me. She's a designer. My father always told me you don't shit where you eat. Pithy, huh?"

"What does she design?"

"She puts appliques of little blue and pink bunnies, squirrels and doggies on snap crotch crawlers and elastic waist pants, sizes 3-6X and larger."

"Creative?"

"Very, and not just in the rag business. Her mother was a big time writer and she's smarter than any woman I've ever met. You'd like her. You're a writer. You read a lot. She a reader big time. Knows a few writers too. Her mother pals around with guys like Robert Penn Warren, you know the guy who wrote that book they made into a movie about the crooked Governor of Louisiana."

"Huey Long?"

"Yeah, that's the guy."

"Now you've got me interested. How old?"

"She's 28, divorced and has great apartment on 1763 Linwood."

"I like older women. 1763, huh. That's the year French General Montcalm surrendered Canada to the British General Wolfe on the Plains of Abraham in Quebec. Too bad Wolfe got killed in that battle. Never got to enjoy the fruits of victory."

"Jeezuz, I know you were a history major."

"Can't help it. Cursed with a good memory."

"Wanna see her?"

"Yeah."

"Here's her phone number."

He handed me his card with Georgeena's number written on it.

"You gonna be living home?"

"For the moment, 'til I get a job.

Thursday evening July 1, 1957 Larry made a call that resonated over the next ten years of his life.

"Hi, my name is Larry Miller. Arthur Schwartz suggested I call you. I just got out of the Air Force, a very undistinguished career I must admit. But I did get a chance to catch up on a lot of reading working for Uncle Sam."

"Oh, you're a reader. Like what for example? What kind of books appeal to you?"

"There's a couple of recent novels I particularly liked. LIE DOWN IN DARKNESS – William Styron, CATCHER IN THE RYE, THE ADVENTURES OF AUGIE MARCH, STUDS LONIGAN, THE INVISIBLE MAN, FROM HERE TO ETERNITY, and a couple of Robert Penn Warren novels; AT HEAVENS GATE and NIGHT RIDERS; also some MALAMUD short stories, an early Orwell novel KEEP THE ASPYDISTRA FLYING. Some Grahame Greene and...."

"Whoa, hold it you've convinced me you read," she said with laughter in her voice.

Not mockingly just amused and surprised at his sophomoric outburst he surmised.

"Now what is it you want? What can I do for you? Are you a writer too? Want an intro to my mother? Or is it me? Do you want to take me out? Maybe dinner? Dancing? Love to dance. Movie? Probably not. We should talk before sitting in silence in a dark theater. That is if I choose to go out with you or even more relevant if you ask me."

"I thought we might try dinner tomorrow night and see how it goes. Okay."

"Okay. What time?"

"Seven?"

"Fine."

"It would be a good thing if I knew where you live. Easier to make contact."

"1763 Portland Avenue."

"1763," he said with hope of displaying a bit of erudition, "the year that France lost her North American Empire."

"Really."

He could have gone through the Battle on the Plains of Abraham but she seemed unimpressed with his non-sequitor comment about North American history.

"See you tomorrow at seven."

He wore the navy blue Brooks Brother's style suit he'd just purchased from LEIMANTS, the only store in the Twin Cities that's sold Ivy League cut clothing. Their three-button, narrow lapel jackets with an 8 inch center vent and tapered no-pleat cuffed trousers were complemented by the obligatory button-down white pin point cotton shirt whose collars rolled slightly to ease the formality of a tie and suit. Repp silk ties, which completed the J. Press, Brooks Brothers and Paul Stuart look, bore regimental stripes, patterned after the different colors designated for each regiment in the British Army. Highland Artillery chose red and black diagonal stripes separated at intervals by thin yellow stripes. The Ivy League schools chose school colors for their repp ties; Princeton--orange and black, Harvard red and black and so it went. He chose a navy blue repp with a thin white stripe divider. It signified no school or regiment but it looked pretty slick against his dark navy suit.

He preened in front of the bureau mirror in his old room that still had hanging on its back wall a large red letter S, a memento of his years on the high school varsity track team.

His mother walked in.

"Going somewhere?" she started out innocently.

"Yeah, mom."

"Big date? Look at you all fancied up in a navy blue suit."

"Not too big," I said.

"Anyone I know?" she asked.

Now that was a trick question. What she meant was, "Is she Jewish?" Jewish mothers never ask the question they really want the answer to. They chip away, always indirection.

"Don't think so, mom. Arthur Schwartz fixed me up with some friend of his."

She silently clapped her hands. A big smile filled her face.

"Arthur Schwartz, he comes from a good family."

Translation: The Schwartz's are very rich.

Relieved, his mother said, "Have a good time." She paused. "But be careful."

"I'll drive carefully," he said, knowing he was not addressing the caution she volunteered. Translation: Don't get her pregnant!

Geogeena opened the door at his fourth knock on the door. She stood there softly bathed in the muted light of a twin-bulb overhead hall fixture. Long raven hair draped the bare shoulders of her dramatic black polka dot dress. A touch of décolletage left him wanting more. They eyed each other. After all it was a blind date. They both knew what they were doing and when their eyes met for the first time they laughed simultaneously.

He liked what he saw and could tell the feeling was mutual.

"Come on in," she said.

Unashamedly, he said, "My God you're beautiful."

She smiled, seemingly amused. Had he blown it?

"We can talk about that later," she said as we walked into the compact living room.

A large Noguchi lamp hung from the ceiling. A fragrance hung in the air, one he couldn't quite identify. Was it incense? Where there's incense there's marijuana his brain said. It could become interesting. In service he'd tried it a few times, off base of course. It seemed like a cool thing to do after reading Kerouac.

She led him to a bright orange canvased sling back chair. It was the chair du jour for young people 'starting out' as the expression went. She remained standing.

A small free standing bar separated the living room from her kitchen. She walked over to it, pointing to a bottle of Lloyd's gin, a low cost gin for the sling chair set. It was his gin of choice when he had to pick up the tab.

"Shall we have a roadie?"

"Of course, I never drive without a drink beforehand."

She smiled a perfect white smile. Ah, good. Score one for me, he thought.

"Gin?"

"Of course."

She handed him a large frosty martini, straight up with two olives. They were regular pimento olives. If things go well, must remember to supply Georgeena with anchovy olives.

Pulling up a matching red sling chair close to mine, she raised her glass and said, "Here's looking at you, kid."

Without missing a beat he parried with Bogart's line, "We'll always have Paris."

They both laughed knowing they had made an important connection. Laughter was to become an important component of their relationship. Casablanca's curtain line might have been a little premature that first night but the line, "This could be the beginning of a beautiful friendship," did resonate for the next six months of their tempestuous coupling.

After two more than ample cocktails, Georgeena asked, "Where we going?"

"1 could tell you better after a few more dates."

"Yes, that's true, but what about tonight?"

"Hungry?"

"Starved."

"How does McCarthy's sound?"

"Like an Irish Leprechaun."

"Good. Good." He clapped my hands. "Although the unwashed prefer Harry's, McCarthy's is really the best steak house in Minneapolis."

As he got up a small furry creature leaped across his path. He avoided its slithering tale as it shot by.

"What is that?"

"Sorry 'bout that it's only Pip, my oldest cat."

"There are more?"

"There's Mowgli, and Ricky Tiki Tavi."

"It's a bloody cat house."

"Not exactly," she said frowning.

"How do they respond to strangers?"

"Not too well but perhaps you won't be a stranger in the future."

He liked that. No further comment was necessary.

At McCarthy's they had two more martinis that preceded an enormous New York Cut Sirloin and whatever else was served with it. Although a little hazy on details of their first dinner together he believed they ordered stingers after dinner.

From the haze of an evening he did remember two highlights of the repast at McCarthy's. One was a joke he, told which Georgeena particularly enjoyed, by any standard, a classic. It went something like this.

Three Frenchmen are discussing the true meaning of savoir faire. The first one says, 'Now, madam eez in bed with monsieur when she 'ear a knock on zee door. She turn to her lovaire and says, 'Darling eet eez my husband, would you mind leaving. Zat eez savoir faire.'

The second Frenchman says, "No, No. Picture zee same situation. Madame eez in bed with monsieur, when she 'ear a knock on zee door. Madame turns to her lovaire and says, 'Darling, eet eez my husband, BUT continue. Now zat is savoir faire.

The third Frenchman says, "Not at all. No. No. Picture zee same situation. Madam eez in bed with monsieur when she 'ear a knock on zee door. Madame turns to her lovaire and says, 'Darling, it eez my husband but continue. AND IF HE CAN, ZAT IS SAVOR FAIRE.

The second highlight was remarkably revealing for Larry to utter.

His voice carried a slight slur as he slowly sipped his stinger, "Georgeena this has been a great evening but I think you should know that I am Jewish."

"Big deal. So was Jesus."

Overwhelmed, he leaned over and kissed her.

She then suggested they leave and finish off the evening with a drink at her place. The drive back was a bit wobbly but they navigated the treacherous highway #100 traffic with a heightened sense of survival, and the luck not to encounter a patrol car occupied by two of Minneapolis' finest men in blue.

In her living room they settled comfortably on the only piece of furniture that was padded and could accommodate at least two people. Between sips of cheap brandy they hugged and kissed. His last remembrance, before the sandman got him, was his unsteady hands tugging away at her pantie girdle.

CHAPTER 5

Alex Manheim Offers Advice— Early 1957

"Larry, Larry are you listening?"

It was Alex Manheim, father of the groom, who he had known for 19 years since the time his family moved across the street from the Monheims. His mind had been wandering. Monheim's voice broke his reverie. He knew the lecture he was about to receive. Inevitably It would revolve around *shiksahs* and the terrible mayhem and sorrow they could envoke in a young Jewish man's life.

"Yes, Mr. Manheim, I guess I was day dreaming. Sorry."

He was ready for the onslaught. His son, Rob, had to have told him about Larry's relationship with Geogeena. Rob Manheim, his closest friend, had never commented about the appropriateness or wisdom of a proposed marriage to Georgeena with whom he had been having an 18 month affair.

Alex began slowly. His earnest look was a pained one as he spoke.

"Larry, I don't want to tell you how to lead your life. That's none of my business. You must seek your own path to the future. But as a man who has been around a lot longer than you and seen the consequences of marrying outside the faith, I feel compelled to tell you about some of its perils."

Perils, he thought. What am I the Faye Ray in KING KONG?

"Larry, you're a smart young man with your whole future ahead of you."

Well his future couldn't be behind him, for sure, he assured himself.

"You don't want to find yourself divorced in couple of years, possibly with young children. I've seen that happen. It's a very difficult and painful position to be in."

"No, I don't," he said out of deference to this well-intentioned sermon and non belief in its content.

"There's a lot of anti-Semitism here in the Twin Cities and you and your future wife, as a mixed couple, might be shunned by both Jews and Gentiles alike."

"Mixed couples?" Larry said.

"Yes, I said mixed couples because no matter what religion either belongs to, the problem is still there for both parties. I also want you to know my opinion has nothing to do with Rob's view. We've never discussed your personal life."

Larry had doubts about that but thought Mr. Manheim supposes he is doing the right thing.

"There I've said my piece. Just think about it, okay. Think about how your parents will feel."

He smiled benignly, a truly sincere gentleman but still he had to slip in the parental guilt trip.

"Well, I've got to get back to the reception line."

As he turned and left, Georgeena approached him, looking beautiful, thick raven hair sidling around her shoulders, a striking contrast to the fitted white linen dress she wore. She was smiling. She always smiled just before speaking, flashing white teeth that signaled her readiness for a chat friendly or not. Was it merely a reflex? Or maybe it was planned social warmth. He didn't think the latter. Any speculation didn't matter because that smile always worked, whether to welcome or disarm.

"What was all that about?"

He hesitated. Should he be honest? No because he feared it could damage their relationship. They were in love and nothing should spoil that feeling. Larry could only have dreamed about, his incredible happiness of the past 18 months.

She knew he was Jewish from the outset but they never talked about it. Georgeena was an agnostic having abandoned her Lutheran heritage early on. She found the Unitarians appealing because of their intellectual approach to the spiritual.

"Well," she asked.

"Oh." A momentary silence that might imply he might be withholding something. She had grown to know him well. Speak slowly and carefully hr cautioned himself. "The usual fatherly boiler plate, George."

He called her George when he wanted to change the subject with a faint touch of whimsy.

"How's that?" She seemed unconvinced.

"You know, that paternal protective advice about settling down, concentrating on career and," he paused. "Getting married."

"I like that part about getting married," she said in what he initially thought was a a rather mocking tone but decided it was a slurring of words from too many martinis.

"You would? You seem to enjoy the relationship more than the idea of marriage."

"Maybe number two could be my lucky number."

Georgeena had been married before. Technically it was a hurry-up wartime marriage. Although the Germans had already surrendered, the Pacific War still persisted. This first union disintegrated after 6 months. Game called on account of incompatibility. The 18 year old found she had little in common with her 30 year old GI husband. "Let's talk about it," he said rather lamely.

CHAPTER 6

First Christmas At Georgeena's Family Manse 1957

Christmas in upper class Minneapolis families was a time for extended merriment, lavish gift giving and a ritualistic dress code. Gray suited titans of industry, doctors, lawyers and tweed suited academics on the make all adopted the preening colors of a peacock, Brooks Brother's style.

Larry's initiation into the splendor of the season was at Georgeena's annual family yule tide gathering. The tight knit Bjorkman clan numbered four brothers and one sister all spawned by a crusty Norwegian immigrant whose tenacity and intelligence culminated in a 10 year career as a Federal Judge. His rise to prominence and wealth carved a direct path to entrance into Ivy League Colleges by each of his children.

The name Georgeena, which seemed at odds with the surname Bjorkman, was the result of her mother Harriet's third marriage to an Argentinian Diplomat named Ricardo Duarte. Her Nordic cousins called her George, a habit Larry soon acquired. Harriet was the Bjorkman black sheep, a Bohemian non-conformist whose liaisons with the great and near great in America's literary elite were unspoken entries in the treasury of family lore. For many years she enjoyed modest success as a writer for a more popular print genre, mass circulation women's magazines; LADIES HOME COMPANION, REDBOOK, COSMOPOLITAN, and LADIES HOME JOURNAL. An occasional piece in THE SATURDAY EVENING POST upgraded her credentials as a writer. The last decade, however, was a fallow period for Harriet, reducing her output and income to the point that forced her return to Minneapolis and the largesse of her brothers.

There her literary output consisted of writing movie reviews for THE MINNESOTA LABOR REVIEW, the largest circulation union newspaper in Minnesota.

With a bloody Mary in hand Larry wandered about the cavernous living room, like young Scott Fitzgerald with nose pressed against the window of a neighboring Summit Avenue house, observing the dress, the talk, the body language of those who might someday become his relatives by marriage.

The four Bjorkman brothers were all attorneys though their legal degrees took them in different directions. Lars was President of the Minneapolis Federal Reserve District. Rolf enjoyed a senior partnership in a white shoe law firm while Stefan was Chief Legal Counsel for General Mills. The fourth, Hjalmar, was a specialist in real estate law.

A Lutheran work ethic, coupled with Yale Law Degrees, gave the brothers career success and easy entrée to the power structure of Minneapolis; its top clubs and cultural institutions--The Minneapolis Athletic Club, Minnikada Country Club, the Boards of the Minneapolis Symphony and Minneapolis Institute of Art and as Patron Founders of the Tyrone Guthrie Theater, the nation's most honored regional theater company.

All four stood at the bar set up across from a huge red brick fireplace whose crackling orange fire heated the entire high ceilinged room. In the center of the room a majestic 11 foot Douglas Fir stood, festooned with glittering tinsel which draped around large hanging Christmas balls each bejeweled like Faberge eggs.

A long food-laden table adjacent to the tree teased ones olfactory sense. The festive board groaned beneath the mountainous smorgasbord of both traditional and exotic Nordic foods.

No Norwegian dinner was complete without Lutefisk, a gelatinous textured whitefish and lefse, the traditional soft flat bread. They were the staples of middle class fare in the old country and a badge of ethnic pride for third generation Norskis in America. Bowls of hot Swedish meatball were strategically placed around table like a culinary slalom course, their sweet steaming magic filled the air. Although freed from Swedish rule in the year 1905, Norwegians ungrudgingly appropriated this dish from their former masters.

Silver platters of smoked salmon, geitost (goat cheese), and the popular whole wheat bread, Kneippbrod dotted the blue and red table cloth, the colors of the Norwegian flag. A huge hot porcelain casserole of the national dish, Favikal, cooked lamb and cabbage rested in the middle of the table guarded by twin Poinsettia plants.

The sweet section of the spread was graced by Rommegrot a confection made from porridge, sour cream, sweet cream with a generous drizzle of butter, sugar and cinnamon.

Lukket Valnott was the diva of desserts, marzipan covered whipped cream cake.

Georgeena gave Larry an early tour of the table. Without her guidance his total knowledge of Norwegian cookery would have been the appropriated dish, Swedish meatballs.

Lars the oldest Bjorkman was the host, his columned colonial dwelling being the largest of the brothers four houses, aligned in adjoining two acre plots thoughtfully acquired by their late father during the post-world War 1 housing boom in Minneapolis.

The flagship of the compound was Judge Bjorkman's imposing Victorian house, dark green in color. Its most salient feature was a pointy conical turret like those seen on the castles of Burgundy.

Three stories high, the turret's circular staircase led up to the master bedroom via a discreet side door which magically opened one section of a ceiling to floor bookcase. It silently stored many family secrets in its 70 year existence.

A wrap around open porch encased the house whose perimeter revealed a variety of octagonal and square projecting bays. White trimmed windows eyed the world from their settings in the green clapboard siding. A bower of Scotch pines gave visitors but a dappled look at the original Bjorkman dwelling as they approached its entrance.

Her brothers' generosity gave the profligate Harriet a lifetime pass to live in the Victorian house, passed onto them by the late judge.

100 yards from the original house a 12 foot chain link fence enclosed the manicured family tennis court. High green privet hedge shielded the Har-Tru court from the prying eyes of any passersby on Lake Nokomis Boulevard.

It offered family members eight months of highly competitive tennis. 65 year old parents were as fierce opponents as their sons, daughters, nieces and nephews and one precocious 8 year old grandson.

Georgeena and Larry enjoyed weekend games with all comers.

Larry's 6th man ranking on his South high school team made him a competent performer, steady, a born retriever but lacking the killer instinct put away shot. It was a weakness that extended to his personal and future professional life.

"It's a jungle out there," his commanding officer intoned, several months earlier, while giving his unconvincing re-up speech. The U.S. Air Force seeking an upgrade in administrative officers wanted educated young lieutenants to make the Air Force a career. Without hesitation Larry declined the offer but Colonel Speer was right on one count. He was slowly finding out that indeed, "it is a jungle out there."

And without a killer instinct. Just connect the dots.

In mixed doubles George and Larry usually bested her twin cousins and their less than energetic spouses, although Zeke, the husband of the cousin Jenny, had an excuse, more or less. As an avowed Communist he strongly objected to capitalistic competition in any endeavor. Sharing rather than competing was his mantra.

Tom, the other Bjorkman in-law, married to Joan, Jenny's sister, was a cerebral academic who just didn't give a shit about sports.

At the end of that summer Georgeena and Larry toted up their victories. To the dismay and anger of the sisters, they beat their combined efforts 12 times out of 13 matches.

All summer long Larry tried to perform at his congenial best, everything just short of sycophancy. Despite his efforts the result with some family members was for naught. After one Saturday match, he left the courts for his car parked on Calhoun Boulevard. It was parked on the street facing the privet protecting the courts. Through its porous greenery I overheard Tom say to his mate, Joan, "He's such an unctuous guy. Tries so hard to belong. Not the usual pushiness one might expect."

This late summer evaluation of his persona rang in his head as he timidly passed three Bjorkman bothers in full holiday gear. He eyed them for a moment. All he wanted to do was blend in, trying to heed Georgeena's advice. Just pick a target, she said, then go over and talk to him or her.

Lars, a tall man with a wispy gray mustache wore a Black Watch Tartan blazer and bright green trousers. His middle brother Rolf sported a Tattersall red checked vest that nicely enhanced his two button blue blazer and brick red corduroys. The youngest Bjorkman brother, Stefan, shone the brightest in his lime green blazer and red/green tartan trousers. Hjalmar was not with them.

Larry looked down evaluating his Christmas present from Georgeena, a fire engine red velour vest with brassy gold buttons. It lent a bit of plumage to his traditional charcoal gray flannel suit, nonetheless he felt like a dullish robin red breast amidst a flock of peacocks. Sartorially the brothers seemed too daunting for an opening encounter.

He was beginning to panic. He had to select a target soon or stand like a Hindu untouchable. The Bjorkman sons and daughters, Georgeena's cousins, would be a comfortable choice, but they seemed impenetrable, banded together, as they were, into two groups of three.

Three young men, Ingmar, Sigurd and Erik, the sons of Lars, stood around the fireplace sipping from large tumblers of mulled wine. Ingmar noticed Larry mincing about looking for the right place to place to land.

"Hey Larry, come join us," he said.

He walked up to the warming fire wordlessly nodding to the group.

"Larry, you know Sigurd and Erik?"

"I do. We met on the family tennis court last summer. You guys are pretty good."

They were pretty good at the game and also pretty good at making bad line calls. No one questions a bad call in this gentlemanly group. The honor system in tennis games with the youngest Bjorkmans was thrown out the window. These boys needed to win. It was understandable if not forgivable. After all they were competing fiercely with highly successful fathers from the time they were born.

"I played number three at Blake," Erik offered. "But the freshman competition at Dartmouth is too good. Intra murals are my cup of tea."

It was assumed he'd know that Blake was the best prep school in Minneapolis. There was a pause in conversation. That left the conversational ball in my court.

"When do you guys go back to school?"

Sigurd, the oldest was a senior at Yale and Ingmar, a junior at Princeton.

"We're leaving together on the 12th for a couple of days in New York. Hey, didn't you go to grad school there? Columbia?"

"Yes, I did go to school there but no I didn't go to Columbia. I got a Masters at NYU."

"My fraternity brothers," Erik responded with a smile. "They call it NYJEW."

Chagrined at his gaffe, as soon as he uttered it, Erik opened his mouth to apologize but was interrupted by Sigurd, before he could do any further damage.

"I understand NYU has a good journalism school," Sigurd said. He said it a little too sincerely. Nice try, Sigurd.

"It's not Columbia but a decent program,' he said.

"I understand you might be moving there soon," Sigurd said, continuing to veer 180 degrees from NYJEW.

"Yeah, Georgeena and I are thinking seriously about it."

"You guys really serious, Larry?"

"Yes," Larry curtly responded, not wanting to continue a discussion about possibly marrying a shikse who happened to be their cousin. He took their leave.

"Guys, good luck next semester. I've got a date at the bar. See ya."

He walked to the bar where Georgeena was holding court with her three girl cousins, Joan, Jenny and Clara. They were all about the same age. Four years out of Smith College they each pursued different careers. Joan remained an academic, one year to go for a doctorate in English Literature. Georgeena was a state school graduate, the local U of Minnesota. She possessed all the credentials for an Ivy league school but Harriet was always a little short in the money department.

Jenny was a journalist following in Aunt Harriet's shoes, while Clara chose a career in Social Work in the State of Minnesota's Welfare Department.

Larry always like Jenny and her husband and not just for their politics, liberal democratic, but for their egalitarian view of life. Their privileged backgrounds never intruded on a sincere effort to try and do some good in the world. Jenny was a runner-up Pulitzer candidate for her expose of slum lords in North Toledo. Zeke her husband, yes his real name was Zeke, was a native Kentuckian who left the family horse farm for a career as a librarian in Toledo Ohio. He was as far left as one could get in the USA. His real love was history and he regularly contributed articles to scholarly Quarterlies and American History, a prestigious monthly magazine.

As he approached the girls the booming voice of Jenny asked, "Are we about to be joined by a future family addition?"

"That's for the cat to say," Larry said looking directly at Georgeena.

Georgeena, always up for any situation, cooly said, "Negotiations are in progress and I'm happy to report the parties are making real progress."

He could have kissed her but he was in a social climate that demanded restraint.

"But I'll let you in on a little secret if you promise to keep it so."

"Scouts honor," the three cousins said, holding their palms over their hearts.

"We are going to New York in March. Larry has a job at a small ad agency on Madison Avenue and I will seek gainful employment in my chosen field in the garment industry covering children's asses with bunnies, birdies and Teddy Bears. Shall we celebrate with a real drink?"

Larry examined the offerings of the bar. Ritualistic egg nog was not their celebratory option, nor were bloody Marys or Mimosas. He further scanned the formidable formation of good soldiers at attention for inspection and consumption. An international platoon by name stood at attention. There was Johnny Walker, Jim Beam, Jack Daniels, Jose Quervo and Lord Calvert.

By acclamation the five chose a neighboring bottle, that guardian of the British Empire, BEEFEATER's. When in doubt always go with a dry gin martini.

After several minutes of speculation about their projected life in New York, Harriet, Georgeena's mother joined them.

"Larry there's someone I want you to meet."

Harriet, at age 60, possessed a classic high cheek boned face, but with skin now weathered and worn. Crinkled vertical lines striated both her cheeks. In profile a sharp proud nose gave her the look of a Roman Goddess whose ancient statue, while still majestic, could use a curator's restoration.

A thick head of gun metal gray hair added to her imperious mien.

She wore a maroon velvet dress just below the knee. It was pinched at the waist, a most unsuitable style choice for a woman with a generous girth. A tiny white lace Peter Pan collar framed her wattles completing ones confirmation that Harriet never gave a rat's ass about fashion. She gave up wearing brassieres at age 40 she once told Larry. The pendulous mounds that ended just above the pinched waist gave truth to her story of abandoning the confining feminine garment two decades earlier.

She took his hand and guided him to a gnome like figure in a brown tweed jacket with a worn leather patch at each elbow. His round head was balding, wisps of feathery whiter hair levitating above each ear.

"Max, I'd like you to meet Larry Miller. He's of the Hebrew faith so I'm sure you two have a lot in common."

Max looked puzzled but the look changed to a smile as he shook the hand of an unexpected landsman at this WASP yuletide gathering of Bjorkmans.

"I am Max Kaminsky. I teach Greek Literature at the University of Minnesota."

"What do you teach?" he asked. "I don't believe I've seen you around campus at faculty gatherings."

Condescension oozed from his mouth.

"Max, I'm not a teacher unless you'd call teaching Americans how to achieve cleaner toilets, produce fluffier pancakes, smoke cleaner cigarettes, drive faster cars, teaching."

"I guess you two boys will hit it off just fine," Harriet said as she walked off with a hearty wave of her arm, causing the pendulous mounds of maroon velvet to sway a fleshy adieu.

Harriet was not anti-Semitic just insensitive. He was sure she thought she'd be giving him a respite from the Bjorkmans in the company of a fellow religionist.

"And I thought I was the token Jew," Max said. "Well, young man, it was nice meeting you."

"Oh, Max, before you leave Please tell me how you earned your spot at this convening of Ivy League Cossacks on their best behavior. And what do you teach at the University of Minnesota, INTERFAITH HARMONY?"

"Well, I never."

With that he walked off to spread a little culture at this family festival of fun.

Buoyed by his successful encounter with Max, he decided It was time for him to step up to the plate with heavy hitters, Georgeena's uncles, a triumvirate of far to the right conservatives. Remember start off jauntily, like confrontational lite. Which means, be yourself. What's a good thesis sentence? Minnesota's projected Fair Employment Practice Act. Too easy to finesse. Humphrey's reelection to the senate? Yes, yes, that should get these guys into third gear in less than sixty seconds.

"Gentlemen," he said. "I'm trying to work the room and this is one stop I egregiously missed."

With a slight hesitation in his voice Larry thought, Lars said," Come join us for a quick drink."

The emphasis seemed to be on the word "quick" but maybe he was just feeling paranoiac.

"What'll you have?

"The mulled wine would be good." He didn't trust himself with a third martini, lest he morph into a cackling free spirit like Georgeena and her cousins across the room.

"I was just wondering, you guys unhappy with our senatorial election last month?"

He had boldly initiated a political discussion, a distinct no-no at Bjorkman social gatherings. They might as well be discussing the KAMA SUTRA.

"If you mean the reengaging of that quasi pinko Hubert by a thoroughly uneducated electorate, I'd say it's pathetic. This country doesn't need a man who advocates class warfare. Mark my words he's danger to all of us in this room. Don't get me started," Stefan said.

Goody, Larry thought, I got him started. If things get heated, they'll blame the poor bastard not me. He snatched the bait and is firmly on the line.

Ignoring Stefan, Rolf said, "Larry, I think the man will spend us into bankruptcy. All those welfare programs cost money and most aren't even needed. Too many people are living off the federal government and who pays for it? We do. Taxes will go sky high."

Lars returned with my mulled wine.

"What's got you so hot under the collar Stefan, I could hear you half way across the room?"

"Larry here wants to know what we think about Hubert Humphrey. And what kind of a name is Hubert, anyway? Sounds like a cork tipped cigarette. He's a South Dakota Socialist that what he is."

"Larry, I can understand why you people like him. He's the strongest supporter of Israel in the whole congress. If I were in your shoes I'd back him to the hilt. But as for America I don't think he's the right man for the job."

Okay, Larry thought you've succeeded in getting these guys started now it's time to switch gears, okay. No sense in handing the ball to Stefan again. He's easy pickings. No scenes. Although I am the good guy in all this. Yes, he thought it's time.

"You guys think the Twins can put it all together this year," he asked.

47

The Bjorkmans had a box at Metropolitan Stadium for the past five years since the Twins joined the American League. Before that the family box was at Nicollet Park when the AA level team was called the Minneapolis Millers.

The ensuing baseball discussion, though intense was never partisan. They all loved the Twins especially their two All Stars Harmon Killibrew and Bob Allison. After fifteen minutes of assessing the home team's chances for a pennant in the coming season, Larry departed to say goodbye to his beloved Georgeena and thank you to Lars and his wife for a delightful afternoon.

Chapter 6 A

The Holidays At Larry's House

Larry returned to his family Hannukah celebration which overlapped Christmas the year of 5117. His parents shared the holidays with his aunts Ruth, Betty, and Etta and uncles Saul, Harry, their respective wives, and bachelor uncle Ben. A trio of first cousins; Louis, Margery and David filled out the guest list. This celebration Larry sincerely enjoyed because it was commemoratrion of an event in which Jews prevailed, at least symbolically.

"I'm glad you could make it," my mother said as he entered her pink carpeted living room where everyone had gathered.

As usual the fireplace looked lonely, in need of a fire which it never got. A shiny brass stand and fireplace tools looked as though they had never been used. They hadn't. The fireplace was only for show. A fire in the fireplace could produce ashes, smoke and a staining of pristine ecru drapes that shielded one from the cold outside.

"Greetings one and all and A Happy Hannukah," Larry said. "Do people really say Happy Hannukah? Or did I just make that up to get into the spirit of the season?"

He looked over the gathered *mishpukah*. Someone was missing.

"Where's my beloved sister, Eleanor?"

Surely, he thought she could make the 160 mile drive from Kenosha, Wisconsin to Minneapolis for her twice a year visit.

"Big snow storm coming our way. Now over Lake Michigan. Too treacherous a drive," his father, Leonard, explained.

Eleanor had been married for two years. It was a happy marriage--for at least my parents. Her husband, Walter Marcus, was a man with *yichus (prestige)*in their eyes. He was head of the family retail shoe business, consisting of a chain of stores in the states of Iowa, Minnesota and Wisconsin. The business was started by Walter's grandfather in Kenosha in 1916.

"And Larry, just for the record, you did not invent the phrase, Happy Hannukah."

His bacon eating father could tell when he just wanted to stir up a controversy among the observant ones in the family. His personal lack of faith was tempered out of respect for his observant mother's fealty to all Jewish holidays and traditions. Theirs was a kosher house.

"Come," his father continued. "Have a drink."

"I'll skip the Manischewitz wine and have what you're having." He pointed to Leonard's drink. "A gin martini."

His father enjoyed a drink before dinner much to the chagrin of maiden Aunt Ruth, who, behind his back, referred to him as a *gonsa shiker.* (a drunk)

After paying respects to Betty and Etta, the prettiest of the three Miller girls, he went over to join the men. Etta was married to Uncle Harry who owned a liquor store in the North side of Minneapolis. Her sunny smile and astute bookkeeping skills accounted for much of the success of their thriving business, Weiskopf Spirits and Wines. Etta, who couldn't have children, devoted six days a week to the store.

Conversations of men and women in the family always seemed to be divided by gender. Men would talk to men and women would talk to women. The only exception was at the dinner table where free for all exchanges were open to all participants. Larry's cousins, old beyond their early teen years, hung together the entire evening as if talking to an adult might be infectious.

"What's happening with you Ben?" Larry said to his uncle who was named after Grandfather Ben Miller. Whenever he saw Uncle Ben Larry always went back in time, when he was 7 years old visiting him in Le Sueur, Minnesota the summer of 1940. Father and Larry drove there to help Uncle Ben.

He never knew the purpose of the trip or the specific help they could offer Ben.

In 1938 America was still mired in the Depression the year Ben graduated from law School. Because jobs for young lawyers in the Twin Cities were almost non-existent, he decided to mine the small towns, within a 60 mile radius of Minneapolis, for clients.

Foreclosings and bankruptcies became the prime source of income for many young Lawyers. Soon Ben acquired a reputation for his integrity and skills in obtaining the best possIble outcomes for foundering small businesses.

The trip to the rich agricultural region 63 miles south of Minneapolis, occurred on a hot 93 degree day. They drove with windows open the entire one and one half hour trip. Air conditioned cars were still 15 years away in the future.

They arrived in Le Seur the home of the Jolly Green Giant, coated with dust from the wind swept fields of parched corn stalks. Ben's client was Gustafson's Grocers, which was undergoing a settlement structured to leave Mr. Gustafson a comfortable income when combined with his first Social Security payments from the federal government.

Leonard Miller parked his black Plymouth sedan in front of Gustafson's 2-story wood and brick building. A man was busy scraping the gold letters: GUSTAFSONS GROCERS from the stores plate glass display windows. He had gotten as far as the letter A. A passerby of the moment would read AFSON'S GROCERS

Inside the store a dozen or so women wended their way around high stacks of card board boxes looking for the closeout bargains being offered. Fat, thin, tall or short they all wore the ubiquitous uniform of rural American women. It was called the house dress.

A house dress was a loose fitting day dress with easy closures in the front. It could be a couple of buttons or a wrap style with two ties. It was a brightly printed cotton sack dress that did little to describe, let alone reveal the shape of the body underneath.

The carton stacks contained canned goods, cleaning supplies, and cereal boxes. Produce, meats and dairy products were no longer offered. The refrigerated display cases had long since been removed.

The tall stacks of cartons were all that remained. They contained cans of beans, tomatos, peas, corn, peaches, beets, pineapple, bottles of catsup and pickles, jars of jams and mayonnaise, boxes of cereals, jello, pancake mix, flour and sugar.

The scurrying print housedresses examined the prices of each case, the minimum purchase required was a case. Prices were affixed to the top case of each stack, a childlike scrawl printed in crayon.

A thin coating of saw dust covered the flooring, an accumulation from the dismantling of light fixtures and the huge refrigeration cases. The butcher's section of the store was easy to spot and smell. A still wet floor contained blood stains and rotting bits of animal flesh, at least 10 days old. Although all doors and windows were left open to obviate the stench, fetid air continued to cloud the store.

A trim man in his early thirties approached us. He wore a natty brown gabardine suit, a tan shirt with detachable white collar and brown polka dot tie. Wing tipped brown and white shoes completed his thoroughly urban look, a misfit sartorially in this small agricultural town where coveralls and plaid shirts set the style.

He smiled at Larry's father and hugged him.

"Thanks for coming, Leonard. I'm sure I couldn't haul my "legal fees" back to the city alone in my Ford Sedan."

The only legal fees a grateful Mr. Gustafson could afford consisted of 20 cases of edible goods from his dwindling assorted inventory of canned goods; Starkist Tuna, Alaska Sockeye Salmon, Del Monte Peaches, Le Sueur Peas, Del Monte Corn, Campbell's Soup, bottled Heinz Catsup, bottled Heilman's Mayonnaise, boxes of Wheaties dry cereal, and Aunt Jemimah Pancake Mix.

The retail value of Uncle Ben's "legal fee" was $129. Doesn't sound like much but that was a good week's wage in 1940. In the dollars of 1958 it would be $750. Not bad for a small business bankruptcy.

They loaded up both cars with the 20 cases, each trunk tightly filled and back seats with cases piled so high his father and Ben had to use their side view mirrors for any rear view vision on the ride back to Minneapolis.

Uncle Ben's largesse kept Larry's father and mother and all the aunts in canned goods and cereal for the next six months. A bachelor, his needs for canned goods were minimal in the living room Larry turned to Ben, "How you doing, Ben?"

"I'm doing fine, Larry," Ben replied. I just joined the Oakridge Country Club.

"So you're a golfer now?"

"I wouldn't quite claim that. I took it up last year. As a sport its too sedentary for my taste, but it's a great way to meet new people who might someday require the services of a lawyer who's one of their group. People like to do business with someone who they consider a peer. It's just human nature to gravitate to someone who you think is like you. To be a successful real estate lawyer, my specialty, one must have entree to a broad social group. Hence my Oakridge connection."

Ben was a good athlete. He excelled at swimming, skiing and horseback riding, never one who favored team sports. He was an individual who couldn't subordinate his person to a group. Larry identified with him, the only true sportsman in the family. Pinnocle, Gin Rummy and Poker were the three sports in which the rest of them excelled

"No more bancruptcies?"

He laughed at Larry's recall of Le Sueur.

"No. These days I like getting paid in greenbacks rather than green peas. And you know there's a real estate boom out there. All that GI Bill money has created a bonanza for developers and contractors and somebody has to make all those transactions legal."

Hannukah was not a special dress up occasion for most Jews. Uncles Harry and Saul wore their usual business suits. Casual clothing was not yet an accepted from of dress even at home in the 1950's. The only concession made to dress down by a male figure at that time was removal of his jacket, loosening of his tie and rolling up of shirt sleeves to the elbow.

Ben defied most conventions of Twin City Jewry. He enjoyed more than one cocktail, dated more than one woman, and remained a bachelor at the age of 44. His peers were all married with at least one teen age child.

His safari jacket and Wellington Boots starkly contrasted the garb of Harry, Saul and his father. Larry was happy he never brought up Georgeena, who he briefly met at Curly's Bar one night.

He loved Ben because he allowed Larry the privacy he needed.

From the dining room his mother's loud cry announced," Dinner is served." It was a more assertive voice than usual. When it came to dining she was totally in charge.

All 13 of the group, en masse, settled in the dining room. A festive table greeted their arrival. Mother's finest table setting was on display. Gold rimmed glasses and plates rested on a white damask tablecloth which anchored sterling silver platters and tableware.

One platter contained a generous mound of stacked slices of brisket, oozing hot gravy. Another was filled with a deconstructed roast chicken; legs, breasts, wings the savory scent of garlic.

A third platter revealed the artistry of a perfectly formed rectangle of *lochshen kugle,* neatly sliced into 16 equal portions. *Kugle* is noodle pudding, a staple of Eastern European cooking.

It consists of noodles, apples, raisins, and chicken fat baked into a sweet counterpoint to the meat dishes.

Two circular ceramic platters displayed their offerings. One held a circular green jellow mold containing canned peach halves. The other was filled with a generous heaping of *kasha varnishes*, a buckwheat dish garnished with pasta bow ties. Three large bowls completed the spread filled with butternut squash, chopped chicken livers and half sour pickles.

Seating was not pre-planned. First come, first served. The teen age cousins huddled together at the far end of the table, across from Larry at the other end. Unfortunately at his left he found Aunt Ruth. He wondered who would be a more formidable foe she or Aunt Betty. Fortunately, on his right Uncle Ben appeared. Between the two he was insulated from the rest of the group.

Larry was not a snob. He truly loved his family but at arms length with his limited ability for emotional commitment.

Sara Miller did not sit down. When everyone was seated, she said, "Please state your preference. With matzoh balls?

Let's see a show of hands."

She counted off six and in her mind she was able to separate the yeses from the nos.

"Let me help, mom," Larry said.

Her protest was less than vigorous. He joined her in the kitchen and came out with a trayful of the yeses' choice--six with matzoh balls—which he correctly distributed. Mom, followed with seven bowls of plain chicken soup.

During the course of the evening Uncle Ben asked Larry about his plans for the future. "Ben, I'm going to New York next month to look for a job in advertising."

"You sure you don't want to stay here and get into the real estate business with me?"

"Ben, you know I love you like a father. And don't think I'm ungrateful for your offer, but I've got to try my luck where I can work. I like Minneapolis but the ad business is dead end for me.

Sure there's a couple big local agencies but they're not in the market for a Jewish copy writer. I know. I tried."

"And the big corporations also have a no Jews wanted attitude. I was turned down too many times in at least six interviews. Everything went well until they looked at the bottom of my resume which asked for my religion. No Ben there's no future for what I want here in the Twin cities.

I got lucky. Art Philco, the Bauer's ad manager hired me on the spot, first and only interview. No paper work.

Under Art's drill sergeant approach to mentoring I learned how to do layouts, write advertising copy and oversee production of ads for the dozens of Bauers products that appeared in the Minneapolis Star and Tribune.

And my entry level job in Bauer's advertiing department Department this past year has given me a pretty well rounded feel for the ad business."

"I understand," he said. He reached into his wallet from which he produced a check. He handed it to me. It was for $1,000. Tears came to Larry's eyes. He put his arms around Ben.

"Thanks, Ben. I can't thank you enough."

The dinner concluded with mother's special desserts, stewed prunes and apricots and sugar coated dates stuffed with walnuts.

After brief discussions with Uncle Harry and Saul, an insurance agent, Larry bid farewell to all. Ruth and Betty clucked a huffy good night to him but not before he heard their whispered exchange, "that shiksah has him eating out of her hand."

His mother knew better than to advise him 'not to stay out to late.' One last goodbye he delivered to his religious fanatic cousins, "Louie, Margie and David, keep the faith."

CHAPTER 7

New York, New York—January 1958

When his apprenticeship at Bauers ended, Larry booked a one way ticket to New York on the Twentieth Century Limited, the fast train to New York's Grand Central Station.

As part of their master plan, Georgeena was to join him after he had settled in at his job in New York with an ad agency called Glickman-Oliver

Weeks before leaving Bauers, Larry answered an ad in Advertising Age for a junior copy writer, 1-2 years experience needed. Dan Glickman, the agency owner, called him, saying he didn't expect Larry to come to New York for an interview.

Would he mind an extensive telephone interview? They talked for nearly an hour.

Their conversation ranged from his experience at Bauers to that which he gained in the Air Force. Her asked about Larry's University life. Larry said he played intra-mural sports for his fraternity basketball and touch football teams. He was a member of Sigma Alpha Mu, a Jewish fraternity. Dan Glickman allowed that he was also a Sammy from Rutgers University. He didn't mention his class year but he sounded pretty youthful on the phone. Larry completed his telephone conversation bio substantiating the fact that he could write. For two years at the University he had been a sports reporter for the Minnesota Daily.

Glickman concluded the interview with a request for samples of his work including. press releases, ad copy and articles in the college daily. He culled out his best efforts and sent them off to New York the next day.

One week later he was hired via the telephone. Could he get to New York in 10 days? The agency was working a couple of very important new campaigns.

Leaving Minnesota was a release from cultural constraints as well as the slights of unspoken anti-Semitism and the parochial Jewish cliques of the Twin Cities.

At age 27 he was expected to be looking for a nice Jewish wife and a career with great promise. He did neither and was about to get out from under the endless advice from his well-meaning mother's discussions about marriage.

He could never fully understand why most of his peers were already married or engaged. Did they really know who they were or what they wanted to be. Had they no desire to explore themselves amd the larger outside world?

His recollections of New York City, including the fallacious certainty that Manhattan was New York City were a little fuzzy. It had been 5 years since he received his Masters degree from NYU.

He chose the train to New York. A 3 year stint in the Air Force included dozens of flights on the WW11 war horse, the C-47, whose average air speed was 150 miles per hour. That reliable old aircraft, in commercial use until the 1980's as the DC-3, whose average speed meant the 1,500 mile flight from Minneapolis to New York entailed 9 hours in cramped quarters.

The 29 hour train trip offered a comfortable sleeping berth. In the spring of 1958 nothing could compete with it and the train's bar car whose soft revolving chairs and non-stop service encouraged an easy bonhomie among strangers

If you chose to go it alone you could sit and read or listen to music in your compartment, free from any unwanted companionship.

They had just passed LaCrosse, Wisconsin when Larry entered the bar car. A quick visual survey of the car allowed him to superficially assess his travel mates. He first saw four middle aged business men playing cards, probably in sales he surmised. Why that hasty judgement? Superficial maybe but their animated conversation was kind of loud and their style and dress of was not executive.

First of all their suits were varying shades of brown. A brown suit says mid-west or mid-level executive. These guys just didn't sound like mid-level executives. Moreover, the east coast dress code was a suit of gray and blue. Charcoal gray, light gray, dark navy blue or midnight blue, even pin stripes were good as long as the color was correct.

In 1958 the social order of the business world dictated dress codes, speech patterns, physical fitness and an affinity for games like golf or tennis. Softball and bowling? Forget about it.

To his right Larry eyed three women. about 42-43 years old. They all wore tailored Peck & Peck suits, different fabrics of course but the cut and colors were unmistakable Peck & Peck. The shoes were sensible though not matronly.

They're definitely not going to visit Uncle Charlie and Aunt Clara. Their personal style and expensive alligator purses said career women.

At the time mid-level executive positions for women were pretty much limited to the retail field. His maiden Aunt Sara was a department store buyer. He was sure they were buyers, probably in women's apparel, which covered everything from shoes to lingerie to dress and casual wear.

He ordered a Manhattan from the red coated black man who was the server. Against the possibility he might be trapped in unwanted conversation he brought along two magazines; SPORT'S ILLUSTRATED and another which many tight assed religionists considered it pornography.

The magazine, PLAYBOY, on the market for only three years, was a smash success among men of all ages. Truth was it was more than a magazine of tits and ass. It published the best short story writers in the country; Saul Bellow, Bernard Malamud, Phillip Roth, John Updike and many others. In addition to the prurient it also attracted readers with higher intellectual tastes; those who enjoyed Playboy's quality fiction as well as its platform for the most beautiful unclad bodies in the land.

The cover story of SPORT'S ILLUSTRATED featured Bud Wilkinson the youthful coach of the highly ranked Nebraska Cornhuskers. Larry idly flipped through the magazine's glossy pages looking for the lead story on Coach Wilkinson, whose trim body and crew cut suggested he could suit up and play if called upon.

While engaged in his search for the lead story, one of the Peck & Peck ladies sat down on the swivel seat next to him.

"That's Bud Wilkinson on cover. You a Nebraska fan?" she asked in an off hand but friendly voice.

"I am," he said, "except when they play my Golden Gophers."

"Ah, the maroon and gold, we play them every year in a non-conference game which, of course, is for mid-west bragging rights, dontcha know."

He took a close look at this sports knowledgeable woman, a rarity among those women he knew. Her flirtatious hazel eyes seemed to be asking for an introduction.

"Hi," he said, "I'm Larry Miller.

He extended a hand which she gently shook.

"My name is Laurie Ruff," she said. "I hail from Omaha."

"Omaha, Nebraska. I've always been amused by the name of your hockey and basketball arena, AKS SAR BEN. That's Nebraska spelled backwards. What wag dreamed that one up?"

"It is kind of corny, I admit but then we are the Cornhusker State." Shifting gears she said, "You have business in New York?"

This attractive woman with the streaked blond hair revealed little crinkled lines around the corners of her eyes, which became deeper when she smiled. She got to the point of familiarity pretty quickly. The faint scent of gardenias, a perfume whose name he wouldn't possibly know, unobtrusively hovered over their budding conversation. Not at all unpleasant.

He hedged his answer to her inquiry? Was she asking out of casual politeness or did she really want to quickly determine whether he was someone worth her time.

"You might say I'm going there on business."

"You mean you're unemployed and looking for a job in New York, right?"

"No not quite. I accepted a job from a boss I've never met. I start next Monday."

"What sort of employment?"

"Advertising. After I got out of the Air Force, I managed to get an entry level job in the ad department of a local department store. Now I'm ready for the next step up, Madison Avenue."

"You're very young," she said.

He blushed. At 27 he was easily 17-18 years her junior.

"Young enough to believe in tomorrow," I said.

"Good for you. Not too cynical. I like that."

I bet you do, he thought noting her left hand was free of a wedding band.

"Can I buy you a drink," I said.

"That's very kind of you but I have one over there with my friends."

"Leave it. Let's get a fresh one. Oh, waiter," he said as he beckoned to the red coated server who was at their side before she could demur.

"We'll have two more of these," I said pointing to my Manhattan.

"Yes, boss," he said in an overly solicitous voice.

"You're pretty generous for a guy who's not yet officially employed."

"Not for long, Laurie."

When the waiter returned, they clinked fresh glasses and wished each other good luck.

"I've told you my future plans. What about you and yours. What do you do and why the trip to New York?"

She pointed to her two friends.

"We're buyers for Brandeis & Sons, Omaha's largest department store."

"And what do you buy?"

"Intimate apparel. That's a department men and women seem to enjoy equally. You know bras, panty girdles, Merry Widow body shapers and lacey peignoirs."

"What's a Merry Widow?"

She laughed. "It's the latest in 'gotta have' sexy under garments. It's black and it goes from here to here."

She stood up and pointed to her breasts and then her crotch.

"Covers everything but in a provocative, naughty way."

She laughed again.

"I can see why it's called intimate apparel."

Laurie had been divorced for five years, an event that sent her scurrying to find a new career other than housewife and mother of two. Fortunately Brandeis & Sons was looking for retail trainees who could become buyers for the prestigious store founded in 1881 by an industrious Jewish immigrant.

After two more Manhattans Laurie had swung her seat close to his. It was now close enough for her to nestle a tweed shoulder into his left breast plate. Her voice had morphed into a chirpy bleat.

"You comfy Larry baby?"

Was she being cutesy or was it an intended jab at his youth? He'd never know because the next words out of her mouth ended their budding friendship.

"See those four guys over there. You can at least hear 'em, no? Loudmouths. They're "garmentos.""

"What in hell is a garmento?"

"Guys in the garment business. Cloak and suiters. They sell their coats and suits to retailers like us. They're all alike, money grubbing sheenies."

Sheenies, he hadn't heard that pejorative since high school. An ugly word.

Larry extracted myself from Laurie's breast plate maneuver and stood up to face the surprised, sotted, middle aged bigot.

"Please excuse me Laurie, I have some homework to finish."

A dazed Laurie looked puzzled as to his abrupt departure. He left the bar car, retreating to his compartment two cars down. He remained there until the next morning's breakfast in the diner. He sat alone watching the scenery as they passed through Rochester, New York only 250 miles from Manhattan. His table was a safe enough distance from the three Peck & Peck ladies, his view of them blocked by two burly gentlemen at the table in front of him.

He stared out the window admiring the majestic Hudson river which they paralleled for 150 miles. It was the river of Nathaniel Hawthorne's Hawkeye. It spawned an art movement in the late 19th and early 20th century; the Hudson River School which celebrated on canvas the breath taking beauty of the wondrous waterway and its forested backdrop.

Four hours later they reached Manhattan. There he experienced the promise of his favorite Saturday morning radio show, GRAND CENTRAL STATION. In America's legendary railroad station, he actually witnessed the scurry of people depicted in the program's sign off line "crossroads of a million private lives".

CHAPTER 8

Life In Beacon

The job with the small agency Georgeena and he had counted on for her joining him in New York fell through after less than two months. The owner, Dan Glickman, lost his prime two accounts, Gold's horseradish and Levy's bread, to the and coming and Jewish ad agency Coyle, Danov and Bernstein, and was forced to close his doors. His sad round face told him the news that the job no longer existed, because the agency no longer existed.

He called Georgeena with the catastrophic news. She said she would come anyway. "No way," he said.

He had $1,400 to last him until he found a job. They could not settle in until he was employed. Period. His search for a job in Manhattan writer proved fruitless. The lady at Career Blazers Employment Agency told him, "We are in a recession," As a consequence most agencies and companies were shedding staff rather than hiring.

"Don't worry, honey, these downturns are cyclical." She said. "We should be seeing light at the end of the tunnel in about a year. Trust me."

He didn't really trust her, but looking back she was right the advertising job market did turn around in one year. Market analysts euphemistically called 1959 a technical correction of the market, blithely glossing over the 8.2% unemployment rate that threw 2 million people under the bus for 12 months.

"Now for the good news, sweetheart," she continued. "I've got an opening for a junior writer in Beacon."

"Where's that?"

"In Rockland County," she said.

"Is that in the United States?"

"Sweetheart, it's an hour commute from Manhattan or you can live there. It's much cheaper than here. And you're from the "sticks" in Minnesota. You oughta fit in just fine."

He had never quite thought of Minneapolis, Minnesota as the "sticks" before. She described Ace Advertising Agency in Beacon as the perfect stop for a bright young guy to get the experience he needed to make it to the big time of Madison Avenue.

A $120 bucks a week sounded good.

He called Georgeena to tell her of his new job in a town of 30,000. Not to worry in eight months he'd have saved enough to come back to Manhattan with experience and with excellent prospects for employment on Madison Avenue. Then she could join him.

In no time Larry became a competent, sometimes inspired, copy writer for his no name Advertising Agency quite far from Madison Avenue both in distance and in the quality of its clients. Whereas the big time McCain-Johannson agency had the prestigious Buick account while no name enjoyed the billing from Jerry Fleck's Suburban Nash Rambler Dealership. Other clients carried an equally similar cache. They included the Rockland Weekly News, Al's Sunoco Station, Dave & Paul's Appliance Store, Stop 'N Shop Supermarket, Beacon National Bank and weekly classified ads for Employment Agencies in Beacon and Poughkeepsie.

The lady from Career Blazers was wrong about the agency's name, however, it was called ACE COMMUNICATIONS AGENCY, owned by a forty year old man named Jay Bluhorn who was born and raised in Beacon, a town whose Jewish population was made up of Jay and Jean Bluhorn, their children Sara and Donald and a family named Moscowitz, who owned a fifty acre farm. They were the only Jewish farmers he ever met. In Minnesota it was an occupation devoid of members of the Jewish faith. The only reasonable explanation for this phenomenon was; in Europe Jews were not allowed to own land.

Jay was a generous man who taught Larry a lot about the advertising business beyond copy writing, how to; select media, handle clients, enhance advertising with sales promotion and publicity AND how to turn a profit from one's endeavors. He had all the tools for a successful career on Madison Avenue, the major leagues of advertising ; smart, good personality, great presenter, marketing know-how and was a damn good copy writer.

Although he might have taken his question the wrong way, one day Larry asked him why he chose to ply his profession in Rockland County.

"Jay, you are a really great ad guy. In my eight months here you've given me the equivalent of a master's degree in this business."

He smiled, white teeth aglow, "You really want to know?"

"Yes, I'm more than just curious".

"It's a long story. Let's see, I went into service in late 1941 just before Pearl Harbor. They had a national draft then. Everyone knew we would enter the war sooner or later. I had just graduated from Marist College in Poughkeepsie with a major in English. I was editor of the school newspaper. No too bad a writer, even if must say so myself.

Anyway I had the idea I'd like to try advertising as a career but before I even could get started Uncle Sam called."

"You were in service for four years. Wow."

"Well I had it better than most. With my degree the army, in all its wisdom, assigned me to the signal corps, where I spent the war, mostly stateside, writing instructional manuals and training films. I tried to get assigned to Stars and Stripes, the official armed service newspaper but that didn't come through.

I was discharged in early 1946 and ready to conquer the world of Madison Avenue. Well, I didn't even get a foothold. Had a least 8 job interviews with all the top agencies. My resume, as a writer was good but in every case no dice. You want to know why? On second thought you wouldn't understand. You're not Jewish."

"Yes, I am," He said.

"You're kidding, with a name like Miller and a face like the map of Ireland."

"You never asked."

"Well, Larry, you will understand. Now where was I? Oh, yes. There I was in my first interview with a copy supervisor named Jack Stone at J. Walter Thompson. I had even bought an interview suit, a three button one from Rogers Peet. Brooks was a little too pricey.

Mr. Stone was about 40 year's old. He wore a repp striped bow tie. The sleeves of his blue oxford cloth button-down shirt were rolled up to the elbow. They revealed arms covered in thick sandy hair, a color that matched the short cropped hair on his head. He looked at my book of clippings, stories and training manuals as well as a few press releases and a 16 millimeter reel of training films I wrote. TV was in its infancy and I had experience with writing and producing films. I thought I would have a leg up on the job opening.

Jack Stone even played about 5 minutes of one reel on the white roll down screen across the room from his desk.

"Jay, I like what I see," he said to him. "You have a good eye for film. That's a big plus for this job opening."

"We chatted about our overseas experiences. It was most congenial. He felt things were going well, until he picked up my job application form which contained all my personal information.

He scanned each line." See you were born in Beacon, New York. Pretty country right along the Hudson River. Graduated cum laude from Marist in 1941. Single. Four years of wartime service."

He smiled as he ticked off my solid credentials until he reached a line midway down the job application from. The smile slowly dissolved into the scrunching of eyebrows and pursing of lips. Before my eyes Dr. Jekyl had become Mr. Hyde.

I craned my neck to see where he was on the page. From my angle sitting to his right I could see he had stopped at the entry for religion. You, see Larry, in 1947, a Fair Employment Practice law had yet to be enacted. He stood up. I followed his lead. We stood looking at each other. His impassive face was quite different from our previous 40 minutes together. He extended a hand. His limp handshake foreshadowed my chance for any future employment at J. Walter Thompson.

Unfortunately all the seven other job applications I had submitted contained the same information. In all cases the results were the same; collegial chatter and even enthusiasm for my work which morphed into unspoken 'forget about it' upon reading my vital data."

"Jay, do you suppose the job climate for Jews is any better now that it was in 1947?" I said.

"I wish I could say yes, Larry, but honestly I don't think so. It's still a good old boy WASP fraternity. There are one or two decent Jewish ad agencies in Manhattan but they're highly competitive as you could guess. I know you're getting a little antsy here in Beacon after eight months of the boondocks. I've seen you grow and think you're a very creative guy. I knew from the beginning couldn't expect to keep you forever but I assure you I'll write a glowing recommendation."

I stayed on at Ace Advertising for another four months to save a few more dollars before Georgeena came east for good.

It was trying on Georgeena stuck in Minneapolis putting appliques of small animals on snap crotch crawlers for the 3-6x crowd at the venerable garment manufacturing firm of Lippman and Gross. His loss was their gain. They liked what she produced, never aware that she took perverse pleasure in trying to make the animals anatomically correct.

"The little bastards should be thrilled to learn the facts of life early on," she wrote, about her subversive designs, which went unnoticed by her trusting bosses.

Their original plan was for him to stay at Ace for 8 months saving money in a town where dinner was $3 and a studio apartment $80 a month. His salary was $120 a week from which he saved $30. By extending his stay to 12 months he would walk away with about $1,500.

Their raging libidos were partially satisfied by four connubial visits from Georgeena to his less than stylish Beacon pad. She saw the town of Beacon, New York in small increments of time which centered on the intake of food, time they allotted when not in the sack. They dined each night she was in town at a rustic diner run by a couple of Manhattan expats, two talented homosexuals, Rex Ryan and Gerald Brooks. They escaped Manhattan, where the climate for gays was too often hostile, to open a funky/stylish dining establishment, that captured the look and feel of a mid-western 40's road house. The OLD LOG INN became the place to dine in town where coq au vin had never before graced the menus of any of the town eaterys.

The look was rustic but the Continental European menu was not.

Entering the INN you were greeted by honored artifacts of Americana that adorned the restaurant's walls and hung from its aluminum embossed ceiling. The first thing that caught your eye was the red, white and blue striped motion of a classic barber pole. It was authentic Rex told me.

"Came from your home town in Minnesota that's where they're manufactured," he said.

It was a piece of trivia I shared with Georgeena on her first visit when she fell in love with the OLD LOG INN, its proprietors and the main room's exhibit of nostalgic signs, bottles and sculptures from their youth.

A spirited carousel horse, hoofs a flying from the ceiling, greeted you as you entered the, dining room. Those over 6 feet tall had to stoop to avoid the hanging wood stallion's charge. Coca Cola signs from the 20's featured divas and vamps wearing swim suits of the period. Pola Negri, Lillian Gish, and Clara Bow were covered from knee to neckline a couture look that left these Hollywood stars without apparent mammary glands. The 30's and 40's Coke girls, Betty Grable, Esther Williams and Eleanor Holm liberated women. Form-fitting swim-suits revealed every erotic feature of their feminine figures.

On her first visit Georgeena had stopped in front of familiar red signs, mounted on the wall, signs that dotted the highways of America for over 20 years

She giggled, then declaimed, "When I was young and in my prime I used to do it all the time, but now that I am old and gray I only do it once a day." BURMA SHAVE."

She turned to Rex.

"My cousins and I used to sing those Burma Shave road sign lyrics all the way to Lake Minnetonka."

"Gerald and I have been collecting old Americana signs and stuff for years. Flea markets, tag sales even estate sales. Got a cigar store Indian over there by the bar."

She was able to visit the OLD LOG INN two more times before Larry gave Jay notice. Each time her child-like enthusiasm for objects like Shirley Temple pitchers and Orphan Annie mugs only furthered his growing love for this devilish sprite with whom he was about to build a future life.

At their last parting in Beacon he said, "George next time we meet it will be in Manhattan. JEEZUZ, I can hardly wait."

"I hate being away from you." she said before throwing herself into his arms and kissing him so hard and long he could barely breathe.

One month later he left for Manhattan. His old fraternity brother, Harold Freiberg, who was working on a doctorate at Columbia, graciously said he could crash at his place until Larry got a job.

Working in Beacon at Ace Advertising was a good learning experience. Jay Bluhorn taught him well. He knew he was ready. Jay instilled in him the marketing side of copy writing. Clever words were not enough if the underlying message was too opaque.

Harold understood Larry's frustration, 11 months separated from Georgeena; and yes, loneliness. He knew her from their days together in Minneapolis.

Georgeena grew to be a favorite of his, although at first he couldn't figure out what planet she came from. Like mother Harriet, she had a wildly unconventional side that often took complete control in social gatherings small and large.

At their first meeting, in his tiny campus apartment on University Avenue, Harold's date was a young Jewish undergraduate student from Bemidji, Minnesota, a town of 40,000 citizens 140 miles from Minneapolis.

Her name was Beverly Raskin. Beverly appeared intimidated by Georgeena, particularly after George's third martini opened the floodgates of her raunchy, often funny, repertory of stories. That night she was on a Tallulah Bankhead roll, relating several hoary tales of the husky-throated actress from Alabama, whose father had once been Speaker of The House of Representatives.

"Tallulah," Georgeena began," was on a TWA flight to London for the opening of her show, PRIVATE LIVES. She was approached by a smiling TWA stewardess, who inquired, 'Miss Bankhead would you care for a little of our TWA coffee?'

Tallulah looked invitingly into the young woman's eyes and replied, "No, dear, but I'd *love* a little of your T W A T."

Harold roared and Larry laughed in appreciation although he knew her repertory by heart. Beverly audibly gasped but didn't speak.

Needing little encouragement with the knowledge that she had scored a bullseye on little Miss Bemidji, Georgeena piled on.

"And then there's the wonderful story of Tallulah and June Haver, the peaches and cream, goody two shoes actress who once was a nun. They met at a Hollywood gathering. Miss Haver bragged to Miss Bankhead that she was a Hollywood star and was proud to say she still had her maidenhead, whereupon Miss Bankhead replied, "But darling, doesn't it get in the way when you fuck?"

Miss Beverly Raskin reddened, took a deep breath and announced to us that she was leaving. She gave no reason for her departure.

Harold recalled that Bankhead evening the night Larry moved into his pad on Morningside Heights in the heart of the Columbia campus.

Georgeena, who had written to Larry eight times since her last visit two months earlier, was scheduled to arrive in two weeks. He had just 14 days before she arrived to look for a place to live and the way to pay for that place to live, a job.

Picking a neighborhood to live in Manhattan, required a little research for a non-native new Yorker, but he recalled much of his time spent at NYU. There were then and still existed, at least fifteen distinct neighborhoods in the island extending 12 miles long and maybe a two half miles wide at is widest point.

Two major criteria dictated one's choice. First was cost. Second was safety although some would reverse the order. Aesthetics of neighborhood, convenience of public transportation and size of apartment were definitely secondary considerations.

In quick order with a map of Manhattan in front of him, he determined the north south boundary lines would be 96th street on the North end and Canal street on the South end. As to specific neighborhoods he eliminated the following as undesirable because of their dubious safety:

- Hell's Kitchen extending from West 45th street to West 57th street and 8th Avenue to the Hudson River
- Chinatown
- Chelsea from West 14th to West 28th
- Anything below Canal Street
- Anything East of 1st Avenue from 14th st to Chinatown
- On the east side nothing North of 96th Street from the East River to Fifth Avenue
- Nothing North of 96th street on the West side from Central Park West to the Hudson River

Harold was Larry's real estate mentor having lived in the city for more than a year. Ground rules for apartment hunting were based on his tutorials

Several wrong turns on his quest for a suitable nest led to many dead end trips across Manhattan's multi ethnic neighborhoods. Among the many viewed, he checked off three suitable apartments within his price range.

Lunch with Harold at Butler Hall's sky top restaurant was the time set to review his housing selections. They met on a cold October noon one week before Georgeena was to arrive. Cutting it short. Waiting til the last moment was a personal shortcoming. It reflected his optimistic nature.

Their table offered early fall views of Morningside Park midpoint in the leaf season. Bright yellow, orange and red foliage was a tiny corsage adorning the bleak gray Harlem which stretched well beyond the tiny urban oasis of Columbia's campus.

A small waiter, back bent by the toll of aging, hovered over Larry before he even had a chance to glance at the menu. He looked at Larry, his tired eyes semi closed by the puffy bags just underneath them, and asked, "Jewish coffee?"

It was a question to be sure, but why did the waiter think he wanted Jewish coffee. Could he tell just by looking that Larry was Jewish?

He leaned over and whispered to Harold, "What in hell is Jewish coffee? Do they grow coffee in Israel?"

Harold roared with laughter until tears rolled down his cheeks.

"Larry, Larry, the man just asked, "do you wish coffee? At some point you will figure out the classic New Yawk accent. Did it ever occur to you that he thinks you talk funny?"

It hadn't. He had a point.

After they ordered and his *Jewish coffee* was in front of him Larry pulled out a list of the three addresses he had selected.

"120 Prince Street, "Harold said, "that's in the West Village. Good choice and if it's the building I'm thinking about it has an interesting historical background. Is it on the corner of McDougal and Prince street?"

"Yes it is. Looks like an old town house maybe 125 years old. There's a flower shop on the main floor. My apartment would be the second floor and the landlord lives on the third floor. It's a big apartment, two bedrooms, a big living room, and a separate dining room with two sliding doors that closes it off from the living room. Nice old fashioned touch."

"How much?" Harold asked.?"

"$125 a month."

"How much would you be making on that new job you mentioned that looks promising?"

$125 a week"

"Take it."

He did and Georgeena joined him in their new bare apartment two weeks later. It was one day after he accepted a job at STANDCO OIL CORPORATION. It was not Madison Avenue, but a giant step in the right direction.

CHAPTER 9

Finally Made Her An Honest Woman--1959

Five months after he started the job at STANDCO Georgeena and Larry were married in a civil ceremony in the Scarsdale home of Kate and Rod Kahn. A wedding in Minneapolis was not in the cards. Harriet couldn't handle the expense of a wedding and none of the other Bjorkman's would have picked up the tab. They felt their black sheep sister was receiving more than enough of their largesse.

In their eyes Georgeena was a chip off the old block, bohemian, promiscuous, indiscreet and perhaps alcoholic. Besides who was she marrying? A middle class Jew. As for his parents as wedding hosts that was not even an afterthought.

In spite of Kate's competitiveness with Georgeena, she was genuinely fond of her. She may have been Georgeena's closest friend dating back to their days at the University of Minnesota. Kate and Rod met in Hollywood Hills, an enclave for aspiring actors, where she nurtured hopes of a career in film. Rod, a native Californian fresh out of the navy, also sought to forge a career in the movie business.

Kate was a full bodied young woman of Scandanavian stock with large hands and feet befitting her square jawed Valkyrie like presence. Green eyes, red hair and freckles that lightly sprinkled a perfectly formed nose softened her imposing figure.

Sexy she was, but too physically overwhelming to be an ingénue and too young for serious dramatic roles. Her modest success in theatrical productions of Frank Whiting's U of M Drama Department, never transformed a talent that could match her aspirations.

The victim of too many casting couch encounters she quickly said yes when handsome young Rod popped the question. By then he was a promising male "starlet" under contract like Peter Lawford but unfortunately Rod never came close to attaining Lawford's success.

After too many bit parts, too many bills and the arrival of their second child, Kate blew the whistle on Rod's film career.

Larry met Kate and Rod Kahn was over cocktails at the Lombardy Hotel on East 56th Street. The Lombardy bar had no chairs. It was more like a country club lounge; love seats and couches each with their own coffee table. Dimmed light made it the ideal trysting place for aging ingenues seeking a replacement mate. Everyone remained perpetually young within the confines of the bar's forgiving lighting.

The dim lighting also gave cover for the straying business man and his secretary. It was difficult to make out faces 15 feet away. The corner couches promised total anonymity.

Georgeena and Larry arrived first. Having little to hide they chose the sofa closest to the bar. Rod and Kate's entrance introduced a beautiful couple. Rod, the unsuccessful actor was handsome indeed. His jet black hair, neatly combed back with a prominent left side part, was more the look of an early 1940's leading man than the shorter cropped hair style of a late '50s male.

He smiled his 100 watt smile as he shook Larry's hand.

"Hi, I'm Rod Kahn. Nice to see you. And you Georgeena, it's been some time."

He leaned in, gently kissing Georgeena, a brief brush of lips.

Kate, second half of the picture book couple, was radiant in a close fitting white dress. An extra wide smile enhanced her generous red lips. Larry stood as she approached. Her arms embraced him like a long lost brother. No, make that lover.

She held the embrace a few seconds too long. Her bursting breasts rested too long on his chest producing an unwelcome reflexive rise. Unpeeling her arms from his Kate's fixed smile reflected a look of mission accomplished as she watched his attempt to conceal an involuntary erection.

Kate and Georgeena may have been friends from the University of Minnesota but more than friends they were sexual competitors. Each blessed with nature's beauty, they had a fierce love/ hate relationship. Georgeena often patronized Kate, feeling she was her intellectual inferior endowed with marginal acting skills.

At school they often clashed while pursuing the same beau.

But now Rod and Kate were to become the base upon which their social life was to be built. Although they didn't see each other that often Larry's fraternity brother, Harold Freiman, was his only true friend in Manhattan. There was also Barney Goldfine, a classmate from grad school, but he couldn't be classified as someone who might become a true friend. Barney was a social convenience to him.

Georgeena was close to Maria and Teddy Serenghetti who would become friends with both of them in the future. Her connection with Maria went back to their years as roomates at the University of Minnesota.

"Larry," Kate said after choosing a seat next to him, "I'd like to get to know you. Georgeena and I go back a long way and I want to see her happy."

She nestled a little too close. Her thigh rested on his. It was no accident, making her best wishes for Georgeena's happiness seemed a little less than sincere. Not wanting to appear rude, he moved forward ostensibly to bring an ash tray closer to their end of the coffee table.

"Would you care for a cigarette?" Larry said.

"Yes, I would."

He handed her an unfiltered Chesterfield.

"No filter. How macho," she said. Mockingly, he thought, a reproach for rebuffing her advance.

"Not macho. The filters take away a few extra puffs. Get more for your money with unfiltered brands."

She nodded.

They got through a half hour of 'getting to know you' talk before returning to Rod and George. The exchange left Kate with nothing more than a skeletal knowledge of who he was or what he did which suited him fine.

Her bio was that of somewhat bored 28 year old woman from the mid-west who married a man she now deemed a loser. In moving to New York Rod became moderately successful, selling the hottest new consumer product, the tape recorder, for the New York area distributor, but his long-term prospects were iffy. From his very brief intro to Kate; her wiles and exaggerated woes, he conjectured she most likely found satisfaction outside her marriage.

Georgeena later confirmed his suspicion. Kate was more than a flirt. She was by turns; good mother, promiscuous, discreet wife. Good fuck.

Whatever failings he might attribute to Kate, he would be less than gracious if he did not acknowledge and thank her for her generosity in arranging for their Justice of The Peace wedding in her Scarsdale living room less than three months after their first meeting.

Other than the bride and groom 8 people were in attendance at the mid-February wedding; Barney Goldfine and his lady friend Rosemary, Chip Manfreed nee Friedman, a Fire Island friend and fraternity brother of Barney, Kate and Rod, Dave Dreyer and his wife Shirley and a Hollywood has been, a screen writer named

Alan Campbell, twice married to the witty writer Dorothy Parker. Long a fan of Miss Parker, Larry looked forward to meeting him.

Harold Freiman sent regrets at not being able to attend. He was hosting a literary seminar on Ernest Hemingway in Aspen Colorado.

Alan, a neighbor of Rod and Kate while living in Los Angeles, was down on his luck, broke and homeless until the Kahns took him in. He now seemed to be a permanent guest in their Scarsdale Cape Cod bungalow. The couple's extraordinary largesse to Alan could be attributed to their genuine compassion and, unknown to Rod, Kate's short term affair with Alan during their free-wheeling life style in Hollywood Hills.

All the guests had gathered in the festive living room preparatory to the brief wedding vows. Pine wreaths adorned each window. The scent of cinnamon emanating from a bowl of hot gluwein filled the air. Lit red candles were everywhere and hors d oeuvres were being served by 8 year old Tammy, eldest of the Kahn clan. Rod was busy preparing Mimosas while introductions were made all around by Kate. Dave and Shirley wound up talking to Barney and Rosemary. They had much in common; all being members of the close knit publishing community.

An elderly man walked up to Larry. His rumpled tan pants, worn up too high, about level with his rib cage, were held up by a grey length of close line rope tied in front with an indistinguishable knot. His sunken chest failed to fill out a faded blue shirt leaving a bloused effect around his waist. Larry noted his pants rested two inches above his shoe line revealing skinny bare ankles.

His sunken square jawed face left dark blue eyes almost hidden below his creased forehead. Wisps of thin gray hair refused to stay low, moving with his every gesture. When he spoke he revealed the gap toothed mouth of a jack o lantern.

"My name is Alan Campbell', he said. "Congratulations on your coming nuptials. I've been through the drill three times. Hope you have better luck."

He had barely finished telling Alan about his admiration for his screen play of Lillian Hellman's LITTLE FOXES when Chip Manfreed came bounding over to meet 'the' Alan Campbell former husband of Dorothy Parker.

Chip was a name dropper of people he never knew. His insatiable need for attention often made him a social millstone but out of respect for Barney Larry tolerated his fop like persona. Exaggerations and untruths larded his everyday conversations. This day he affected a red paisley ascot the accessory that pulled together his faux British costume; a tweed Norfolk jacket, wide wale corduroy pants and Wellington boots. An empty silver cigarette holder leisurely rested between his the middle and forefinger of his pasty white left hand.

Privately Georgeena referred to him as the "poor man's Noel Coward."

"Alan, if I may call you Alan," Chip began.

I decided to stick around in case his attempt at badinage got too unbearable for the weary looking Alan Campbell.

"I was at the theater last week and I saw Cole. Cole Porter you know. I thought he looked just terrible. Thought you'd like to know," Chip said with a ring of familiarity that never even remotely existed between himself and the famed composer. They'd never even met.

"Looked just terrible. Looked just terrible, you idiot," Alan said his voice rising in fury. "You moronic simpleton he just had a leg cut off in a ghastly riding accident a few months back and YOU, YOU pipsqueak never heard about it. Get lost junior. Before I put my cane to you."

Chip retreated like a chastised pet.

Larry hadn't noticed the cane before. It was a heavy cudgel-like support and potential weapon. For two minutes this fragile relic of a man came to life again.

He turned to Larry and said, "Excuse me Mr. Miller I think I could use a something a little stronger than a Mimosa."

He hurried over to tell Georgeena of the incident.

She laughed a wicked laugh.

"Serves the little fucker right. He's such a pretentious bore. How can you possibly stand him?"

Barney, immaculately turned out as usual, removed the wedding ring from the pocket of his tailored Dunhill blazer and handed it to Larry. Justice Helmut Kronenberg, posture ram rod rigid, graying hair cut short; could have been an extra from a Holocaust film. This sixtyish looking gentleman, who presided over the wedding ceremony, had the look and manner of an SS commandant. Imperiously he ordered Larry to place the ring on Georgeen's finger. Responding to his command he hurriedly did his bidding. Justice Kronenberg did everything but click his heels as he pronounced them man and wife. Could he possibly have known that Larry, the groom, was a Jew. Did he reveal any tell-tale Hebraic signs or origins Larry asked himself?

Chip skulked around the room during the excellent buffet, nervously avoiding the acerbic Alan Campbell, shifting his locations at Campbell's every move.

Nonetheless, at the next party Chip attended, where Larry was present, he was certain he would hear a not too amusing anecdote about his friendship with Dorothy Parker's ex-husband.

Amidst a hail of best wishes accompanied by two bottles of Moet Chandon, George and Larry left for a two day honeymoon at a posh Washington, Connecticut Inn.

While his new bride showered before their first conjugal act after marriage, he wrote short notes to his parents and country club sister, informing them of his marriage. He wrote another to his friend, Rob Manheim, saying it was too late for a discussion about the appropriateness of his partner for life. He probably should have felt guilty about not inviting his parents to even a simple ceremony but it never would have worked. His mother's mournful carryings on would have placed a huge damper on the proceedings. After all

Shiksa is of a Yiddish root which means *detested thing*, a reasonable designation considering Shiksas spelled assimilation.

He couldn't conceive of his mother's response to meeting Georgeena. Would she have wept, dabbing at her caring brown eyes in shame and misery. On the other hand he knew what Georgeena's initial response would have been.

"Hi, Larry's mom, I'm really the good shiksa even though I'm not a virgin. Am I welcome?"

Or she might have said, "Hi, I'm the shiksa you heard about. It could be worse. I could have been a shvartze."

His sister would sniff at the Bohemian décor of Rod and Kate's house, fluff a few pillows and pull Georgeena aside for an intimate talk about the inappropriateness of their union and what a disaster it would become. His sister was a self-styled prophet of doom. Optimism was her missing gene. The family Cassandra, her down side view of life became a self-fulfilling prophecy of her gaggle of failed marriages.

CHAPTER 10

Doug Breitling Mentor/Boss --1960

After a brief honeymoon, Larry reported for duty at the imposing 40 story STANDCO Building on East 50th Street. Its intricately embossed aluminum siding, designed to self clean during New York's rainy season, was a great idea at its inception, but in between rainfalls the gritty carbon emissions from the giant smoke stacks of Con Edison Power Company transformed the skyscraper into a tarnished filigreed metal box.

Doug Breitling, his new boss was the seminal figure who shaped his early advertising career until he felt secure enough, a few years later, to out his nonsecular origins. Douglas Breitling was the new Advertising Director of the giant oil company. Doug, as he preferred to be called, was hired to clean house at the 30 man advertising department that management, armed with the counsel of McKenzie Consultants, deemed necessary. Too many. Too old. Too highly paid. Too complacent.

From the moment he walked into Doug's new corner office he knew where he was supposed to stand. Doug was out front with his view of authority and its use. Larry was one of three new advertising brand managers hired after the new broom swept out the incumbent three they replaced.

On Doug's multi-windowed office, you couldn't miss a huge gold framed, sepia-toned lithograph that hung on the wall above his desk. It was a tightly drawn pen and ink rendering depicting a majestic lion, head high, roaring triumphantly over a shredded zebra carcass, its blood soaked black stripes even more graphic in the stark monochromatic picture.

The dramatic visual said to viewers, "Survival of the fittest spoken here."

Doug came out of the mid-west, ad director for a regional petroleum company headquartered in Chicago. Chicago, then the second largest city in America, had a second city mentality which was reflected in the way he dressed. When they first met. Brown was his color of choice.

He quickly learned that navy blue or charcoal gray WERE the first city's colors and that suits were to be cut IVY League style, single breasted with either two or three buttons on the jackets. De rigeur: shoes were always black wing tips; topcoats single breasted in dark gray tweed. The more flamboyant might get away with a camel hair double breasted top coat complete with a back belt sporting two buttons. The buttons on the belt were a design feature, serving no utilitarian purpose.

Tall and rangy, Doug had the swaggering gait of a Division 1 quarterback although basketball was his game in college. Like a game controlling point guard he quickly learned the East Coast playbook ; the mores and dress code of Madison Avenue whose power structure was controlled by IVY League MBA's and English lit majors.

Larry's last meeting with Douglas Breitling, before officially coming aboard, was in the corporate dining room, cheerfully called the Moose and Goose Room. Although moose and goose never appeared on the menu, wild game did. Venison, duck, rabbit, and an occasional offering of boar.

Such exotic cuisine was dictated, or rather influenced by the company CEO, Vernon Tillman, a beefy former All-American football player from Yale.

Tillman, an avid huntsman plied his hobby worldwide; elk from Wyoming, wildebeest from Kenya, wild boar in Bavaria. Their impressive heads adorned the otherwise pristine white walls of his executive suite on the 41st floor of the STANDCO building as monuments to his prowess.

Lunch in the Moose and Goose ended with confirmation of his hiring but not before hearing a simple rule for Doug's new hires. In his good old boy Kentucky twang, which he employed when trying to convey a friendly, disarming manner, he laid down the law according to Breitling. His shit kicking aw shucks mode often forced smiles to the faces of sophisticated Advertising Account Supervisors who serviced the STANDCO advertising account.

"Larry," he said. "Ah have but one rule about the lunch hour. Ah know most the old crowd in the department got used to a 2 and 2 lunch, maybe a 2 and 3."

It was a puzzling moment. Was Doug an old U of Kentucky basketball player talking basketball talk? No way. Before speculating further about his word'd meaning, Doug continued.

"Ah mean 2 martinis and 2 hours for lunch. Those country club days are over. And ah can tell you, a lot of those guys are over too. Now ah think a couple of bourbons after hours are just dandy."

Larry nodded his comprehension of this inviolable ground rule.

His edict about the ground rules for lunch—one hour no alcoholic beverages—encouraged Larry to become a bit more assertive in his conversational end which up to now never slipped into personal feelings or revelations.

"You know, Doug," he started with an authority designed to bolster any early impression he made on his new boss, that he knew his way around the block. "Over at SYDNEY PORTER ASSOCIATES, I was lucky to be assigned to our Seagram's account. I wrote a weekly column they ran in the entertainment section of major market newspapers. I learned a lot about the physiological effects of alcohol on people."

His tenure at SYDNEY PORTER ASSOCIATES was short lived, a duration of only three months. It was his "holding pen" while waiting for the STANDCO job to materialize. He learned a lot from Sydney Porter himself. A former editor of the Atlanta Constitution, he taught Larry how to sharpen his powers of persuasion.

His knowledge of alcohol and its effects on people got Doug's attention.

In a voice which told Larry he had piqued his interest he said, "How so?"

"Chemically speaking alcohol contains congeners, which are the little nasties that give us hangovers."

"What's a congener?"

"Congeners are a toxic chemical that forms during fermentation. Some liquor categories have more than others. Vodka contains the least."

Fascinated, he asked, "What   about Scotch?"

Larry was curious why he asked about scotch. Bourbon was the choice of native Kentuckians. I guess he was catching on to the local mores. The favorite libation in the east for non-martini drinkers was scotch. Bourbon bespoke Harlem to those who gathered at the Yale Club bar and other favorite alumni watering holes.

"Scotch is better off than bourbon when it comes to congeners but it still contains three times as many as a similar quantity of vodka."

"What's that about bourbon?"

"Ten times the congeners."

"Well, I'll be."

Lunch ended on that note.

He reported for work the following Monday. His first assignment from Doug was to help him build a case against Arnie Skyler, the holdover Resale Advertising Manager. Skyler was a relic of the old ad department with all its perks and bad habits;

padded expense accounts, three hour lunches and kickbacks from art, printing and promotion suppliers. Now he reported directly to Doug Breitling. Skyler probably knew he was doomed but he also knew there had to be a good reason to let go a grade 20 employee with 25 years at the company.

The assignment disturbed Larry. Was he supposed to be Doug's snitch, a spy, a collector of a dossier of Skyler missteps? He was very uncomfortable at the thought of the task.

"Doug," he said, "I'd prefer if you gave the Skyler assignment to one of the other new guys."

"That wouldn't work, Larry. You're the guy I hired for Special Events which Skyler is supposed to supervise. And he knows that's part of your portfolio. You're a bright young guy, Larry, with a future. Just do your job."

That ended any protest with clear cut finality. The sub text of "just do it" was "or else."

Like most of the people in the department Larry knew little about Arnie Skyler except that he reported to him for one important item in his portfolio of duties. Larry was the point guy for STANDCO Special Events Promotion including biggies like sponsorships of the Indianapolis 500, Sebring, Daytona Beach Indy Car Races and all other local track Indy Car Racing events.

At these events STANDCO provided its own brand of motor oil and fuel to all racing entrants. The Indianapolis 500 of 1961 was his first assignment under Skyler's aegis. Thirty three cars participated in the race.

His job was to direct the filming of each of the cars being filled with STANDCO products, each driver smiling for the camera secure in his snug rubber-rimmed cockpit. The racing cars of that period, 4 cylindered Offenhausers with engine in the front, could attain speeds of up to 150 miles per hour.

Upon completion of the filming he was to go to a studio in downtown Indianapolis and with a voice over announcer produce thirty three different 2 minute news clips.

Each clip was the same, announcing the winner of the 1961 Indianapolis 500. Now all thirty three entrants were covered. No matter who won STANDCO had a winner on film, the car that used STANDCO Super Motor Oil and racing fuel to keep its engine running smoothly enough to help win the race. Immediately after the race concluded he would plug in 20 seconds of footage of the winner taking the winning checkered flag crossing the finish line. Two hours later his film clip heralding the STANDCO winning car would be shipped to over 200 Television Stations throughout America. That evening local station sportscasters around the country would feature film clips of the race and its winner. That particular year Ted Marchioni, a veteran driver, won the race. The next morning America's leading daily newspapers carried ads with headlines that read:

TED MARCHIONI TAKES CHECKERED FLAG
IN 65TH INDIANAPOLIS 500 FUELED BY STANDCO

The print ads were prepared well in advance by the company advertising agency featuring STANDCO products. They contained everything but the winner and his photo. Once the race concluded the agency completed the ads by adding photos captions about the winner.

Everything went smoothly after the race. Ted Marchioni was their man. Doug called the next day, as Larry was leaving for New York, to congratulate him on a job well done.

During his week at the track, Larry saw little of Arnie Skyler. Early in the week Skyler introduced him to the local district manager who had become his buddy over the years at Indianapolis. The two of them found the flesh pots of the city more pleasurable than the grease and grit of the track not to mention the acrid smell and taste of burning rubber that pervaded the air for miles. May in Indianapolis was like a month of Mardi Gras celebration with the attendant aura of partying round the clock. Parades, marching bands and bars filled with young and old men and women alike, gravitated to the city expecting the excitement of new friends, and one-night stands. A plethora of the state's finest call girls also would flock to the event for its abundance of wealthy older men, race car owners and their entourages with an abundance of free flowing cash.

It apeared that Arnie and his pal had fallen in with a guy named Todd Blackledge, who owned race car number 25, a sleek red Offenhauser that finished 24th in the race. His suite at the Marriott was filled with leggy blondes who seemed fresh off the Eliabeth Arden assembly line. White mini-skirts with fitted Chanel jackets to match were the uniform of the day or night. Obligatory white leather boots anchored each long lean leg. They mingled with the famous and near famous of the racing fraternity. A few fat guys in ill-fitting white linen suits held court in one far corner for a bevy of attentive hard faced professional women. There was a payoff somewhere.

Larry tried to touch base with Skyler to no avail. He felt he owed him the courtesy of reporting on his progress in filming the drivers and their race cars.

The objects of his search finally left him a message to meet them for some fun at the Blackledge suite in the Marriott. Lots of action they promised. Skyler even called his hotel room.

"All work and no play makes Larry a pretty dull boy," was his message delivered in a slightly slurred voice.

Larry returned the call. "Arnie, it's none of my business but Doug Breitling is not too happy with you. I think you ought to call him and tell him things are under control."

"Kid," he said," Breitling can go fuck himself. I can handle him. I've got a rabbi in top management. Come on over the place is jumping."

"Thanks, "I'll see what Marco Manetti is doing."

His photographer, Marco Manetti, did more than photograph 33 racing cars. Unbeknownst to Larry he had snapped a few shots of Skyler and his pal, Ray Bogash, pawing a couple of bimbos in the Marriott Lounge. He was unaware that Manetti had included them in the group of photos he shot for Breitling.

Upon their return to New York, Doug viewed Menetti's photos with pleasure,

Adding to Larry's discomfort with the odious hatchet man assignment, but Skyler was a walking disaster. Shake it off he told himself. It goes with the territory.

No, he, had to give the poor bastard another warning, a man he barely knew, who was playing a losing game. Skyler resented his new boss and like a petulant teen ager showed him no respect. He was thumbing his nose at a man who could get him fired. What in the world he was thinking? With his head in the sand or maybe up his ass, the stubborn Dutchman was self destructing.

What am I supposed to do? Larry asked himself. Become baby sitter to a 45 year old man?

"Larry," Doug said. "Now we'll see what he does when you guys go to the Pikes Peak Hill Climb. I don't imagine a fella could get into too much trouble in Colorado Springs. And remember make damn sure he gets that NBC interview on MONITOR. Baxter Donaldson expects that interview. It's national exposure. That man's got an eye on the number one job in this outfit."

MONITOR was NBC's breakthrough network radio show, proving that medium was still relevant for news and sports in the age of Television.

The Pikes Peak Hill Climb was the second oldest auto race in America, established in 1922. It's a 12.41 mile race course with 154 turns ending at the 14,110 foot summit of Pikes Peak. All types of cars were welcome if they could meet the events safety regulations.

STANDCO, in an ever searching effort to extol the benefits of its petroleum products to the American public, seized the Hill Climb Event as an exemplary venue for exploitation.

The racing specialists of STANDCO supplied all entrants with its racing fuel and motor oil. Thus, allowing no room for error, the winner of the Pikes Peak Hill Climb would be fueled and oiled by STANDCO.

As at the Indy 500 Marco Manetti and he filmed all the race entrants, in their cars emblazoned with a large STANDCO decal, as they were fueled.

Arnie Skyler left it to Larry to get in touch with the reporter scheduled to interview Baxter Donaldson live on NBC's MONITOR program. It was broadcast nationally over 1,000 local stations. Larry knew that interview was important as both an image builder and ego trip for Baxter Donaldson, who was looking ahead a couple of years, Doug's future could improve substantially if Baxter got his druthers.

"You guys have everything under control,' Arnie said to Larry, as he left for the Broadmoor Hotel with Colorado District Manager Rich McGrath. "See you back at the Broadmoor."

"Wait a minute, Arnie. I have to know where you are when I make contact with Ron Neely, the correspondent from MONITOR. You have to be there on a moment's notice to bring Baxter Donaldson to the Broadmoor Lounge. Their management has given me a quiet section of the room where we can do the interview. Neely has a lot of interviews to do today. We aren't his only one, you know. And I'm sure it's not his most important one. Arnie, do yourself a favor and show up on time with Donaldson."

"You worry too much, Larry. I'll be in room 206 at the hotel. Okay. Call me and I'll come jumping with Baxter on my arm."

The Broadmoor Hotel was one of America's iconic hotels. Old world elegance combined with gourmet cuisine made it THE GREENBRIER of the West. A championship golf course, with snow-capped Pikes Peak in the background from every vantage point, added to its popular appeal.

Three hours later, with Neely in tow in the Lounge, Larry called Skyler in room 206. No answer. He never left its premises for 24 hours. McGrath had supplied him with an indefatigable blonde who left the lanky spent Dutchman cockeyed and asleep to the world when he called. After his third attempt calling Skyler, Neely, the man from MONITOR got antsy.

"Sorry, pal, I'll give you five more minutes. I've two interviews to do on the Hill."

Five minutes passed, no contact with Skyler. Neely strapped on his recording equipment and left. Larry tried to imagine what was going on in Baxter Donaldson's mind.

Bottom Line: Arnie left the exec VP holding his cock instead of an NBC microphone for his interview.

Doug called that night about the interview. He exploded when Larry told him of the botched interview that never made it to the nation's top radio network.

"That son of a bitch, he's gone."

Larry did his best to keep the poor bastard on track, watching him dig his own grave. And things didn't go much better for Arnie at the Daytona 500 in Daytona Beach, Florida.

Larry and Marco Manetti had the drill down pat. Just get the shots early, schmooze with the drivers for a bit and wait for the winning car. It was a no brainer.

Skyler figured Larry was doing a good job and certainly didn't need him. His trips were play time with yet another District Manager whom he had traded favors with for over 20 years. The only thing he had to do at this event was appear on the podium post race and present a trophy and check to the winning driver.

Daytona Speedway founder, Bill France, wanted a STANDCO executive to present a trophy and an enlarged check—for the cameras—to the winner of his prestigious 500 mile race.

Arnie Skyler was the only one present in Daytona Beach who qualified as STANDCO Management. Larry was far too junior in age and rank to appear on television to present a STANDCO check and trophy.

Skyler never showed for the presentation leaving Bill France in an embarrassing position alone on the podium, not having his major sponsor on tap to present their $100,000 prize money.

To this day Larry could not understand Arnie Skyler, a guy who seemed to view the world through his pants fly. The term sex addict had not yet been forged by America's psychotherapist elite.

Larry tried to steer him onto the straight and narrow but he just ignored the advice. Before the race Larry outright told him, "Arnie, Doug's after your ass. Don't make it easy for him."

"You worry too much. I told you I've got a rabbi on the top floor. He'd never let Breitling cut me loose. I'm just waiting for Mr. Hotshot from Chicago to fall on his face. When that happens and my guy who's going to the top in the next six months gets in, I'm the next Director Of Advertising. You just wait and see."

It didn't take long for Arnie's rosy prediction to go south.

Six months later his guy didn't make it to the top and Arnie's pipe dream went up in smoke. Neither, by the way did Baxter Donaldson. The board didn't fire poor Arnie, just reduced him in rank to a level where he knew it was time to leave on his own steam. He lasted exactly seven months, having been reduced in grade from a 20 to a 16, Larry's exact ranking. He caught on with a small oil company in the mid-west headquartered in Omaha, Nebraska. Skyler was a decent enough. Middle age boredom must have fueled his uncontrollable libido and his stubborn Dutch ego clouded his judgement. Maybe he will keep his nose clean on the new job.

The Bonneville Salt Flats was Larry;s last his racing assignment for STANDCO. The flats were 30,000 square acres of densely packed salt located in Tooele County, Utah, where adventurous drivers and automotive designers sought fame and glory through record setting speeds.

Located in the northwest corner of Utah where that state met Nevada, Salt Flats drivers and their free spending entourages brought notoriety and economic health to the town of West Wendover in the 1950's and 60's. Gambling and prostitution offered the racing fraternity leisure time pleasure that often extended their stays in

Nevada, long after the record attempts had concluded in success or failure.

In 1962 Larry helped inform the world that Craig Breedlove, the legendary American driver, had set a new world's land speed record. He propelled his "Spirit of America," vehicle to an unheard of 388.47 miles per hour; a remarkable feat in the pre-jet era.

STANDCO, of course, supplied the "Spirit of America" with a magic fuel mixture which powered it into THE GUINESS BOOK OF RECORDS.

Aside from the colorful social life of West Wendover, and the phenomenon of the Pliocene Age offering of the Salt Flats themselves, his most memorable take away was the damage the salt had done to his new leather Adidas tennis shoes. 10 days of exposure to the eroding effect of pure wet salt ate away large sections of the white and green sneakers.

Two years of travel; Sebring, Watkins Glen, Indianapolis, Bonneville Salt Flats and the grueling Indy Car Circuit convinced Larry his days at STANDCO must come to an end. The special events assignment didn't do very much to advance his future advertising career but it was one hell of a ride. He would miss the fun and freewheeling life style of the racing crowd, but it was time to tell Doug Breitling he wanted out of race events promotion.

While his absences from home the past two years, undoubtedly, kept Georgeena and him apart too long, he thought a full time New York assignment might repair some of the marital damage incurred during that period. Optimist that he was, he believed any damage done could be easily repaired. Absence doesn't make the heart grow fonder it just increases the odds of eroding a marriage be it a shaky one or solid. Georgeena was definitely not the sort of woman who would sit home alone pining over his absence.

CHAPTER 11

The Direct Mail Campaign

Three advertising agencies in 7 years under Doug Breitling's stewardship did not produce the kind of results Baxter Donaldson, his boss, had hoped for. Company sales were on a flat line. Donaldson's patience with his Ad Director was growing thin and Doug knew it. It was time for something new and not just another ad agency. He'd already used up his quota. Three failed ad campaigns left Doug in a precarious position with top management.

It was time to try another medium about which Doug knew little. For years direct mail had been an effective producer of immediate sales for the package goods sector. Blue chips like P&G, Lever, and General Foods had great success drawing consumers into supermarkets with direct mail. Money saving coupons were an integral part their marketing strategies. Doug decided to give it a try. Nothing else seems to be working.

Larry's last encounter with Breitling's darker side occurred the day Aggie, his secretary, told him the boss wanted to see him.

"What's up, Aggie?"

She smiled her perky Irish smile, hands on hips.

"What's it worth?"

They flirted often but nothing ever came of it, although she did become an office friend with whom Larry occasionally shared an afterwork cocktail. No big deal.

"Two straight up see throughs at the BULL & BEAR. Say 5:30."

"Deal."

She then explained the boss had tapped him for an important Direct Mail Program.

"What the hell do I know about Direct Mail?"

"Shh. You're an expert, okay."

He entered Doug's lair facing the large painting of the King Of The Jungle munching on a wildebeest. He had learned to handle the 'dog eat dog, watch your rear end' subliminal message without developing sweaty palms.

There was a hint of desperation in Doug's voice when he spoke.

"What do ya know about direct mail, Larry? Ever use it?" he asked

Everyone in the business knew the drill, never deny knowing anything about any subject when asked. You could always do a little research. Carpe diem. Let no opportunity to shine pass you by.

"Doug, I know that with a little guidance from Martin Cohen at R.L. Polk, I could make it work for the service station business," he said with a startling show of self-confidence.

Doug had a strange look on his face. Did he say anything wrong? R.L. Polk was the premier direct mail organization used by General Motors, Ford and Chrysler as well as automotive related manufacturers like Champion Sparkplugs and Purolator Filters.

Polk, unique to the Direct Mail Business, amassed the automotive registration data for every car and truck in the country, including names and addresses for over 80 million owners in the year 1962.

Martin Cohen, the Polk account person serving STANDCO for the last 10 years, had no luck selling Doug a program although he called on him at least 3 times this past year. Martin, who was at least 65 years old, looked older. Sagging jowls and eyelids gave him a look casting directors might cotton to when auditioning for the title role in THE MERCHANT OF VENICE. Apparently Doug's thoughts about Martin ran along those lines. He referred to Martin with undisguised distain.

"No not that little kike. He's off the account but asking questions is what you should be doing because they're the professionals who can guide you.

Ya know Larry, we have a saying in Kentucky about the chosen people. "A Jew is just a nigger turned inside out."

Larry thought he had turned white at this comment. Did Doug notice? Shit. Stay cool. What the hell? This cracker in a Brooks Brother suit is a fucking anti-Semitic, yahoo.

What the fuck am I doing here? I don't belong here. I'm here under false pretenses. This super wasp establishment doesn't know there's a Jewish mole in its ranks. Lousy analogy. I'm on their side, he thought, but I am the great pretender. How does that lyric go? Gotta go. Gotta get my resume up to date. The maelstrom of his mind melded hurt and anger.

His look of dismay did not go unnoticed. "Something wrong, Larry?"

"No, Doug. I just remembered I have a date with Charlie Langford to talk about budgets for 1963."

To confirm the validity of his lie, he looked at his watch, swallowing silently as Doug proceeded to explain his desire for a winning Mail Campaign for STANDCO dealers to increase traffic and sales of gasoline, oil, tires, batteries and lube jobs throughout America.

Polk's synergism with the Big Seven of American Oil Companies was its ability to provide them with lists by street and zip code in every town in America, thus enabling all promotion to be localized for their dealerships nation-wide. Doug hoped R.L. Polk could bring him redemption in the eyes of top management with a mail campaign that substantially increased dealer sales. If they were happy, management was happy. Not to be overlooked was the hard fact that a successful campaign would bolster his now shaky job security.

"The new guy from Polk will be coming in on Monday. His name is James Zimmer. He's smart and buttoned down. Used to play for Seton Hall. Good little college team. Made it to the NCAA's a couple of times."

Doug's infatuation with former college players dated back to his days at the University of Kentucky on a basketball team that won the national college Championship in 1932. His view, oft stated, was that a guy who played competitive college hoops was mentally tough and trained to get things done and on time. Maybe he was right. Couldn't prove it by Larry.

"You and Bob Dewey will be working directly with James. He'll guide you every step of the way. We're gonna pre-test everything. I can't impress on you how important this program is for all of us. But I don't wanna get ahead of myself. We'll all meet in my office on Monday. You get on with your meeting with Charlie Langford. Don't want you to be late on my account."

Larry left his office heading for the bank of elevators. He pushed the down button. In less than a minute the doors opened for my descent to the main lobby which has a direct door to Joe & Rose's Restaurant Bar, a favorite of STANDCO mid-level guys.

Johnny Bonito, the bartender, was stacking newly washed glasses in preparation for the noonday regulars.

"Little early, Larry," he said as Larry sidled up to the bar in search of a settling bloody Mary with extra Tabasco. His watch told him it was a tad early. It read 11:30.

"Had a bad morning," he said. It was a good morning until Doug shared his ugly redneck aphorism. Things were going well up to that point. Legal department approved his seat belt ads without too much bitching. Sal La Rocco, his favorite art studio supplier, left him two tickets for the Knick game. He had been with STANDCO for 4 years and with his racing travel ended for over a year he thought things would improve on the home front. They didn't.

Georgeena was drinking more than usual.

CHAPTER 12

Later That Day

The chasm in their open marriage widened and Larry needed a little TLC. Maybe should call Aggie. She was a good listener and loved basketball, the Knicks in particular. How bad can that be?

He'd call Georgeena. Tell her he had a Saturday morning shoot and it might be best if he stayed in town. at Eddie Callahan's pad. Callahan was his junior Account Executive whose largesse he occasionally called upon. Eddie made every attempt to keep him a satisfied client. He felt sure George wouldn't miss their usual drunken, Friday night sex.

She had to know he was fooling around. She didn't seem to care since his last promotion. It allowed her to quit her job as a children's clothing designer, a position she hated, almost as much as she disliked kids. Now she was free to lunch with the girls and sometimes boys. No one officially viewed their marriage as an open one but reality said yes.

Larry half-heartedly muddled through the afternoon tinkering with next year's budget and updating his r esume. Cutting ties with STANDCO had become a priority.

The BULL & BEAR was noisier than usual that Friday night.

Agnes Doyle sat in a corner booth of the smoke filled bar. A green shaded lamp mounted above the booth cast a soft light on Agnes' dark red hair. Hated being called Agnes, preferred Aggie. Deeply engaged in the DAILY NEWS sports pages when he arrived, she looked up and her green eyes smiled along with her lips. Too bad they were only friends.

"How the Knicks doing?"

"Lost 4 in a row. Bernard King blew out his knee last week."

"Did you order?"

She held up a half empty martini glass, the generous sized ones for which the BULL & BEAR was famous.

"I gotta play catch up. Oh, waiter."

Three martinis later he said, "Aggie, I know you're a Knick fan and I have two good tickets for their game with the Celtics tomorrow night. Want to be my date."

Larry tried to sound jocular, an invite with no suggestion of intimacy. You know, cool. He bit his tongue at the use of the word date.

"What's the matter your wife out of town?"

"No she hates basketball almost as much she hates me. But let's not get into that can of worms."

She laughed, reaching across the table for one of his hands.

"Sure. Love to be your "date". Do people still date?"

"I dunno. One more for the road?"

"Depends which road," she said in a tone that definitely sounded like an invitation.

"I lost my road map which one do you suggest?"

"How about 71st street?"

"Good call. Now that we know the road we can have a night cap at 326 East 71st, I know the owner."

The next morning was Saturday. Aggie was still asleep. He watched her breathing. Red freckled arms matched her hair. At age 34 her look was more girlish than womanly. Her body was lithe as that of a college coed, lean but soft. Why in the world had they waited this long. To paraphrase Hoagy Carmichael's pop ballad, "He still had Georgeena on his mind".

Aggie had Overnight become more than an office friend. Upon leaving he left her a note saying he'd pick her up at 6:00 that evening and that they would be having dinner at the Knick's VIP lounge before the game.

Aggie was the perfect basketball game companion. She loved the game, growing up just three blocks from St. John's University Field House. The Johnnie's hoops success was legendary in the Big Apple. She could name every player on the Knick's roster. She knew Bernard King was their leading scorer and that Dick Mcguire was a splendid defensive player whose unselfish play fed the exceptional offense provided by King. Unfortunately the role players around McGuire and King could not provide the support needed to be a playoff contender.

The Knicks lost that night but in future months that night proved to be a winner for both Aggie and Larry. It was a magical evening watching the sports nut lady, who would become a friend for life, root for the intense young Knick center, Willis Reed.

She patiently explained to him the mechanics of the backdoor pass and at the same time made him feel as though he were 21 again.

Aggie rooted heatedly for McGuire. It turned out Aggie was his first cousin. Mcguire was but one of the many sons of Erin who tutored her in the art and game of basketball.

"Your guy did okay tonight, Red," he said when the game was over. "You don't mind if I call you Red. You're like the sleekest, shiniest most beautiful Irish Setter."

"Oh, I'm a dog eh?"

"No, no, that's not the way I meant it." He turned red. What a goofball I am he thought.

Aggie laughed. "I love the name Red and tonight McGuire was not my guy. You were." She leaned in and kissed him. The faintest scent of camellias lingered in her luxurious auburn hair.

The weekend with Aggie erased the sting of Breitling' s hurtful southern screed. It was something he couldn't share with Aggie but one thing became clear he had to leave STANDCO before all self-esteem disappeared.

But first he had to leave with a clean slate and a good reference. That fucking Direct Mail project with Bob Dewey would last at least three months but he would be able to put together a decent resume in that time and maybe snag a few discreet job interviews.

Dewey was an undersized jock, with a chip on his shoulder, whose military service requirement was fulfilled playing football for Great Lakes Naval Training Station. At 5 foot 6 inches, 175 pounds, it was hard to believe he was a starting middle linebacker for a team which played a big time schedule, competing against top Division 1 colleges.

His football success relied on one dominant character trait. The fierce tenacity of a possible sociopath kept him driving forward toward every person or activity he ever tackled. That quality, if tempered with thoughtful prudence, could elicit outstanding performance in any profession or endeavor.

Unfortunately, Bob's unwarranted certainty about almost any topic or theory about politics, religion, marriage, movies, history or even marketing strategy left no room for the free exchange of ideas or even worse, compromise. For the next three months they battled to the detriment of the mission.

Dewey and Larry were never on the same wave length during their daily creative sessions. Their different approaches to the mail promotion were most often contentious, delaying their final presentation to Doug. Three weeks into the 45 day, schedule Doug stopped Larry in the men's room.

He smiled, a disarming smile, large white teeth, firm square jaw working to project warmth that never quite made it. That look always preceded a serious question.

"Hey Larry, how you and Dewey comin' along?"

"Doug, it's coming but looks like it'll take a bit longer. But we are working closely with Zimmer, who really knows his stuff. I figure our dog and pony show will be ready the end of next week."

"Better be," he said, the white teeth slowly disappearing. Unable to reconcile their conflicting marketing strategies Dewey and Larry agreed to offer Doug the idea of testing two different promotions. The two pronged plan was simple. If both approaches tested well they could combine them into one strong campaign for a nation-wide rollout. The down side was; they would need another month to implement and evaluate both strategies. Except for travel expenses, the two part test would cost about the same as a single one.

After hours in the conference room Bob and Larry quietly posted the layouts for Their respective promotions. Each utilized four color mailing pieces. Larry's concept Plan A, promised the consumer $60 in savings over a 6 month period. In 1962 a saving of $60 represented two and one half days pay for the average American worker. His average weekly income was $150.

"You do the math, Bob. It's solid, money in consumers' pockets, approach," Larry said.

"Larry, there's no romance, no aspirational aspect. It's no fun. Everyone wants a family dream vacation, all expenses paid. How many can afford it? Very few, Larry. It's a no brainer."

Silently Larry agreed it was a no brainer. No brains needed to think offering a consumer a million to one shot at winning a vacation would motivate him to buy STANDCO gas.

Give me a break Dewey.

"My sweepstakes offering a family of four a $5,000 vacation for a week in the Caribbean has real sex appeal. You know what I mean? People live on dreams."

"Bob, first of all, it's a sweepstakes. That means the motorist doesn't have to buy squat to enter. You'll get a shit load of entries but I guarantee you that incremental gasoline sales will be zero and we both wind up with egg on our faces. This Direct Mail test is Doug's love child if we fuck up we better get our resumes up to date.

We're selling a commodity, remember. And with a commodity the consumer will buy at the station posting the lowest price. They'll come to our stations to pick up a free no strings attached entry and maybe use our free air pump but they'll buy at the station across the street if that's 6 cents a gallon lower. Middle income and lower income people want to save money and Bob, you can't sneeze at $60 savings in today's economic climate. Use your head for a change."

"Use my head? Damn right I'm using my head. A Caribbean Vacation for a family is a powerful draw."

Neither of us would budge an inch so the following week Doug was presented with two disparate plans from which to choose. In his Solomon like wisdom Doug choose both plans.

"Combine 'em and ah believe we have a winner," he said.

That statement, rather than praise for a job well conceived, was more an optimistic expectation that he was about to grab the brass ring of STANDCO's upper management group.

Two months spent in Columbus, Ohio, their test city, seemed like a year. Implementing the promotion was easy. Three dealer meetings and they covered the 40 company test stations in the trade area of Columbus. Dealers seemed to like the campaign but then dealers loved anything that was free. They were, after all, independent business owners with a STANDCO franchise.

The first two weeks of advertising, including gaudy but attention grabbing point of sale material at the pump aisles produced traffic but half that traffic bought nothing. Wives and children cheerfully grabbing up as many entry blanks as they could from those pads displayed on easy to reach point of sale cards. The following two weeks produced the same glum sales figures, authenticated by the disappointed STANDCO District Manager. He concluded that the cost of the promotion was not worth the candle. He sent results of their handiwork directly to Doug Breitling. As Larry felt all along, the Sweepstakes component of the Promotion doomed it. It produced bodies but no sales. The results put Fury and himself on

Doug's shit list. He abruptly cancelled their expense accounts and suspended their executive dining room privileges. They became pariahs in the marketing department.

Doug's reference to Dewey and himself as "MR. INSIDE and MR. OUTSIDE, a collegial sports metaphor for the excellence of Army's two great All-American running backs, Glen Davis and Doc Blanchard, came to a screeching halt. If he were to continue with his sports metaphors they now would be known equally as MESSRS OFFSIDE and deserving of a penalty. It was definitely time to leave the chilly climate of STANDCO.

CHAPTER 13

Marital Stalemate Early 1964

The relative tranquility ended with Georgeena's response to Larry's leaving STANDCO. She was less than supportive, even after he told her of Doug's odious depiction of Jews. His plaint fell on deaf ears.

"What the fuck. You're throwing away a great job for what? A chance to face more anti-Semitic boogey men on Madison Avenue. You've been bitching about this for years. What kind of security do we have? Do you expect me to go back to work?"

She may have had a point regarding Madison Avenue but Larry knew it was changing and it was time to capitalize on that change. He felt confident he could compete successfully against the best.

Georgeena's comment about working was not a rhetorical question. She had been pretty adamant in stating her distaste for the adorable, furry creatures she had to create in different incarnations and costumes over and over again.

She had a good case against returning to the garment industry but sitting on her slender ass, she chose not to even explore an alternative line of employment she might find satisfying. Georgeena was smart. There were a lot of new careers out there which she could realisitically pursue. She didn't want kids. What the hell did she want out of life? You could hardly call her a housewife. She would be offended being called one.

What could be going on in her head? It wasn't as if she wanted to start a family. All the family she needed was her two cats, six year old Siamese successors to Pip and Mowgli her Minneapolis felines. They were called Mowgli 2 and Pip 2 reflecting Georgeena's excessively sentimental view of her furry companions.

Their marriage had reached the dangerous seventh year of living together. The "seven year itch" was ascribed to the American male, but few, aside from early feminists, speculated that the "itch" was common to women as well.

The liberating oral contraceptive pill opened new possibilities even to married women who suffered from the sameness of a seven year marriage.

Georgeena needed more than extracurricular sex. Her brain and creative bent needed nourishment. What new career could offer her a challenge she would accept? Was she actually afraid if he quit they would be destitute?

"Look George, I'm just starting to look. I'm not stupid enough to quit before I have another job. You know my Jewish practicality."

"Jewish practicality, my ass. You have small claim to anything Jewish. You've been a gentile wannabe since I met you."

Score one for Georgeena. Her fast ball was right down the middle as true as a Sandy Koufax 97 mile an hour strike. Why did he choose the only Jewish pitcher in baseball for his metaphorical analogy. He could have chosen from at least 10 other fireballers in the Major Leagues. Why not Bob Gibson?

No matter how hard you try, you can never can escape from your heritage. You might try to mask it, put up any façade but it will always come back to bite you in the ass if you try to deny it.

"While we're at it," Georgeena said, "Let's talk some more about your non-Jewish persona. You don't have to wear religion on your sleeve but to hide it is sheer cowardice. It seems I married a guy with no convictions. Who the hell are you anyway? Do you believe in anything?"

She won the point, yes he thought, but at this moment she may have lost the marriage. The rent she inflicted on his psyche was too deep to forgive or forget. Georgeena just didn't get it; not a clue about the deep hurt he'd suffered from overt and covert anti-Semitism. She could not possibly imagine the damage it had done to his sense of self worth.

"George," he said, "regardless of what you say about my being a Jew and how I deal with it, it's none of your damn business. You are not my keeper. You're not even much of a wife. So you can't be my judge. How dare you! Do me a favor and just butt out.

I'm quitting no matter what you say. I can't work for that fucking bigot Breitling anymore. I am leaving STANDCO, period. And while I am in the process of looking for a new job I strongly suggest you start getting a life."

"Is that a threat?"

"No, my dilettante beauty, call it a friendly suggestion. God knows you could use a little order in your louche life; and while I'm at it, your lush life as well. Please note: Too much booze produces too much body fat and too many creases in one's complexion. Even Estee Lauder knows booze is too formidable an enemy to defeat."

"Strange you, an avowed atheist, would invoke God," she sneered.

"It's just an expression, asshole; has nothing to do with one's belief system. This is turning into a ridiculous conversation but I'm kind of glad we're having it. Sort of clears the air. Well maybe it doesn't clear the air, but it certainly lets us know where we stand."

He knew it was time to get out but unfortunately knowing wasn't enough. They were about to enter a new phase of marriage, one which focuses on the most painless exit strategy. Reality and a new sense of Georgeena had emerged. The independent woman; the early women's libber liked not having to work. She enjoyed being in a childless non career mode; dependent on a moderately successful husband.

During the next few months, opposing battle plans were drawn up. In that process a chilled civility prevailed in their day to day relationship, sometimes interrupted by a period of excessive politeness bordering on parody of a scene with Amanda and Elliot in Noel Coward's, PRIVATE LIVES.

Georgeena was drinking more than usual and there's no reasoning with a drunk.

CHAPTER 14

Opening Salvos

What brought about his seemingly spur of the moment decision for a divorce? Hadn't he and Georgeena been trying to paper over the recent past? Honest answer, no.

Beside papering over doesn't extinguish the past. She was drinking more heavily, if that was possible, but a dramatic new side of Georgeena unexpectedly revealed itself one Tuesday afternoon in January 1964.

In his office one morning Larry was feeling crummy; achy bones, pounding headache. Could have been a cold or the beginning of the flu, which was going around that winter.

"Connie," he called as she walked past his open door.

Connie was the secretary that he and Bob Dewey shared. She stopped and stuck her head in the doorway.

'Hi, Connie,' He said, "I've had it for the day. Gotta cold, the flu or something. I feel like shit. Do me a favor and tell Dewey if he hears anything, please call me at home. Okay?"

She nodded and said. "Feel better."

Dewey and he were waiting for the other shoe to drop now that their direct mail campaign had gone south. Their status as lepers in the department drew them closer to each other.

Curious thing about corporations, when the boss dumps on you the troops all keep their distance, as though you were contagious. But they had an enemy in common and shared a similar problem.

Doug didn't fire them, no matter how pissed he was. Both of their prior records at STANDCO had been outstanding with superior performance reviews by Breitling himself. Middle managers with excellent performance ratings are not let go after one poor outing.

They knew that and were both prepared to go to the mat if Doug made any attempt to terminate their employment. At this point in his career he didn't need the negative exposure of a corporate investigation into the merit of two simultaneous dismissals.

Breitling, however, could make life difficult for them in the short run. On the other hand when the next request for their help from a STANDCO District Manager came in, the moratorium on both Dewey's and his expense account would be lifted. Take that you bigoted fuck.

He hailed a taxi outside the entrance of STANDCO which took him to his apartment on West End Avenue. The apartment door was locked. Georgeena must be out. Who knows where? Since she quit her job her afternoons remained a mystery.

He spotted a woman's handbag and a pair of white gloves on their oversized sofa when he entered the living room just off a small entrance foyer. They didn't belong to Georgeena. She didn't own white gloves.

Two empty martini glasses stood on the coffee table like sentinels guarding his News York Giants ash tray. Georgeena hated that particular ash tray. It was so middlebrow. None the less it was now filled, full up, with lipstick tinged cigarette butts.

Puzzled, he wondered where the girls had gone. Their bedroom door was closed as was the door to the den, his office. His head throbbed. He went into the kitchen and took two aspirins from the catchall drawer in the counter bar; then set a pot of water on the range to boil. A cup of tea laced with cognac might offer some relief.

He took off his jacket, hung it on a kitchen chair, loosened his tie and opened an overhead cabinet from which he removed a box of Earl Grey Morning Tea, even though it was now afternoon. From the liquor cabinet he took down a liter of Hennessey VSOP. Everything was in place. Just needed the water to boil. Shouldn't take more than a minute or two.

He walked to the bedroom door, opened it and heard two loud gasps along with the twisted rustling of bed sheets. Before one naked bottom could disappear under the bedding he distinctly identified it. Having viewed that now hidden derriere thousands of times in the past, it unmistakably belonged to Georgeena. But who was her partner? The answer quickly came as two heads peeked out at him from under the covers; Georgeena and Maria Serenghetti.

Opening salvos of the coming war were fired by the opposing lawyers. Hers was a solid professional divorce lawyer aptly named Brightman, for bright he was. And more than just clever and quick he knew where the jugular was located. His lawyer was considered one of the top copyright lawyers in New York City, a small credential for competing in the smarmy world of divorce law.

Saul Grossman was a friend from Fire Island Days, knowledgeable, witty and honorable. The latter attribute was definitely a handicap when engaged in the fierce in fighting of divorce proceedings.

When her lawyer informed his of her alimony demands for freedom, plans for an immediate divorce ended. She had the leverage for sure. He was committed to leaving STANDCO and looking for a new job with an iffy salary left him no option but to continue the contentious marriage for the immediate future.

Economics drove the decision to legally continue the marriage for another long 18 months. Living with someone he perhaps still loved but now could barely stand to speak to, was the price of delay.

His first skirmish in the battle for freedom ended without a winner but definitely produced a loser. Larry.

He paid both attorney's fees and remained married to Georgeena.

Maintaining two apartments was impossible to underwrite, so the irregular trek up his Ho Chi Minh trail to the West Side apartment, 8A left him behind enemy lines.

Living together was a misnomer. Living apart together would be more a accurate depiction of the accommodation. Four nights a week he slept at 428 West End Avenue, although he generally came home after mid-night, long after Georgeena had retired. He left before 7:30 each morning in an effort to avoid fraternizing with the enemy with whom he shared the apartment.

Breakfast routine became a toasted bagel and coffee at the Tip Toe Inn, a large gemutlich restaurant on Broadway whose clientele consisted mainly of blue haired ladies dressed to the nines at 7:30 am and elderly gentlemen wearing ubiquitous beige cardigan sweaters and ties. A swath of tables occupied by several Mr. Rogers look-alikes made the room seem like a geriatric SESAME STREET show.

Ordering bagels and coffee over an 18 month period earned him the friendship of Max, as septuagenarian waiter with palsy; sweet, *hamish* but prone to spilling more of Larry's morning coffee into the saucer than the cup.

Their conversations lacked variety. He seemed to always solicit Larry's advice on, "who do you like in the fifth at Aqueduct?"

A coherent reply he never got from Larry. What the fuck would a mid-western guy who'd been to a track but once in his life have to offer a serious horse player?

He did tell Max about his one time experience at Hawthorne Park in Chicago. His senior year at the University Burt Stromberg, a fraternity brother who never acted his height of 5'3", convinced a group of fraters to take the Burlington 400 to Chicago for a big weekend. They were going to a Northwestern game in Evanston, 15 miles from the Chicago Loop on Saturday. But Sunday Burt had a special treat in store for the group, a day at Hawthorne Racetrack. He would show them how how to bet, nothing fancy like an exacta, just straight up win, place or show or across the board.

"Sounded good, Max," Larry said.

"Yeah, then what happened?" he said.

"We go to the track, buy a couple of programs for the 8 race card. I open one up see the numbers of the horses, their names, their jockeys, their owners and a number before the horses name and another number a few columns over.

Burt sees me trying to figure out the deal and says, "See that, the first number that's the horse's pole position. It's best to be on the inside track. It's the shortest distance to the finish line. Outside horse have run a longer way unless they can cut in close to the rail. Got that?"

"Yes, I gotcha. I say.",

"Now look at the number in the last column. That's the weight of the horse."

"No, no," Max interjected.

"Hold it Max. Now Burt continues to tell us that that last number is the weight of the horse AND here's the kicker."

He says, "It rained last night. The track is muddy. Heavy horses tend to sink a bit in the loam. Light horses have an easier time on a wet track. So who do you bet on? You bet on the light horses today, guys."

"Made sense. I looked at the last column for the first race. Horse #1 was the heaviest 134 pounds. The lightest in the first race was 113 pounds. His name was Foxy Boy. I'll never forget that name. Foxy Boy comes in last in a field of 8 and I'm out $10, a lot of money for a college kid in 1953. The heaviest horse won the race only he wasn't the heaviest horse. It was the heaviest jockey who rode him. It wasn't until the next day that we realized that Burt was an arrogant schmuck who didn't know squat about horse racing"

Max laughed so hard drool slipped down the corners of his droopy white mustache.

"From you, boychik, I'll never ask advice from."

Max started his mornings with a smile each day that broke through the glum aura Larry wore from the bad karma he was getting at 428 West End Avenue.

A brisk walk through Central Park to STANDCO's mid-town office building often was the cure for his excessive alcohol intake of the previous evening. It always surprised him how many people inhabited Central Park each early morning. This was an era before people started running for their health. The only runners he ever saw in the park that early were running for their lives.

Over and over he went wading through the hopelessness of his existence. Money was the reason for the separation stalemate. The unyielding demands for alimony, would have reduced his standard of living to that of an entry level college graduate in the publishing business. We're talking La Boheme poor.

Their private Cold War had them on course that could last for at least another 11 or 12 months. He had to face reality. Reality during the long uneasy truce was to appear at all social functions as a married couple. Few in their circle knew the real modus operandi; only Barney and his lady, Kate and Rod, Georgeena's friends the Serenghettis, his secretary and his fraternity brother Harold Freiman.

Life together was kind a tricky conundrum. In New York State, at the time, the only grounds for a non-mutual divorce was adultery. If either he or Georgeena could prove adultery the "injured" party could obtain a divorce without consent of the adulterer. Their divorce attempt was stymied because neither party could agree to its terms.

The living arrangement they now adopted all but ended their sex life with a few memorable exceptions. Now if either party engaged in sex outside marriage it would be adulterous, with disastrous financial consequences to the one branded with the Scarlet Letter A.

Discretion became the rule for both Georgeena and Larry, as the marriage had now become a real open one.

One of the few mornings they bumped into each other, Georgeena was neatly groomed. There she was in the kitchen her hair carefully combed, fresh lipstick applied, wearing a shortie wrap that left little to the imagination.

He could hardly believe that standing there, fresh coffee in hand for him, giving silent notice that she was ready for a morning quickie. During this period of apartness, he knew nothing about her social life. One thing was certain. She needed to be discreet. She held all the leverage as long as any violation of the 6th Commandment remained her secret. As Larry looked at her he could only surmise the furtive flirting gave truth to a desire for sex.

Self-control disintegrated before the magnetic pull of the shortie wrap and the body inside which he knew so well.

Objectively she was more than desirable and he could not rein in his libido regardless of the consequences.

Although his unofficial state of bachelorhood satisfied his physical needs, Georgeena, he had to admit, was still on his mind and at that morning on his body as well.

Later that day, he spotted an opening In ADVERTISING AGE for a young ambitious creative guy with some automotive experience to work for a division of Mcgill-Johannson. The international advertising giant needed someone for the Buick Account, someone who had automotive special event experience. As Larry dropped his resume in the mail, he knew he was that guy.

Five days passed before he received a call inviting him for an interview in the offices of the Fremont-Richards division of McGill. There he had but two interviews. The first was with Teddy Serenghetti who was married to Maria, Georgeena's "friend."

Teddy and he had met a few months previously at one of the Serenghetti soirees.

They both were pleasantly surprised at this second meeting. In Larry's favor, he was no longer an unknown quantity seeking the job. His marriage to Georgeena added to his cache in Teddy's eyes.

On the other hand that cache could disappear in an instant if Teddy knew of her liason with his wife Maria. His brief bedroom encounter with Georgeena and Maria would never be revealed by his lips. But now looking at Teddy he had an epiphany. Why was he being so hard on Georgeena. She certainly was no lesbian. Nor was Maria. Just two adventurous but bored women experimenting. Time to reevaluate, he thought but now let's just get the job.

Teddy looked over his sample book of commercials, video clips, ads and automotive news stories with serious interest. Their conversation lasted for almost an hour.

Teddy looked up from Larry's portfolio and said, "Larry, let's go in and talk to the boss, Bob Steele. He's president of the agency."

Bob Steele also liked Larry's sample book and down to earth quality. He was a native of Chicago and seemed attuned to his mid western accent.

They asked to be excused for a few minutes. After a short meeting outside Bob's office, they returned.

Bob spoke first, "I have good news. You are our man."

Teddy said, "Congratulations, Larry. "

He was offered the job as Senior Writer for Buick Special Events. With it came a $6,000 raise over his STANDCO salary. There at Fremont -Richards he was to prosper with the blessings of Bob Steele and Teddy Serenghetti for the next 2 years.

Not strangely his first thought was to call Geogeena and tell her they had to celebrate. Did that make sense? Yes, they had to talk about his epiphany about her relationship with Maria and its effect on their relationship. And his impetuous reaction.

It did make sense. Over drinks and dinner at Cote Basque that night George and he agreed to try once more to make the marriage work after she aknowledged his over reaction to finding her in bed with Maria. That thing with Maria? He was right. They both thought it would be adventuresome to explore what lesbian sex was like.

"And what was lesbian sex like?" he asked

"Friction and the same end result without all the sticky fluids. But Larry, darling, let me assure you I go for guys."

"Any guy?"

"Don't be silly. In spite of all the shit we've given eachother you are still numero uno," she said as she tightly grasped both my hands

And she did express genuine enthusiasm for my new job.

In the early sixties the WASP stranglehold on advertising agencies was being loosened by the spectacular creative efforts of an agency called Doyle, Dane, and Bernbach which successfully broke all the staid rules of the business. Humor and irreverence played well to a new generation of consumers and those qualities became a staple in the ads created by the whizzes at Doyle Dane.

Who can forget the loveable Beetle ads—THINK SMALL or the cheeky, YOU DON'T HAVE TO BE JEWISH TO LOVE LEVY'S RYE BREAD which featured Chinese men, Irish cops, and Black jazz men gleefully enjoying their slices of Levy's bread. The creators of these gems of original and effective product selling were Italian art directors and Jewish copy writers or Jewish art directors and Italian copy writers. The old mold was broken never again to be replaced. The floodgates opened for talented ethnics of all colors and persuasions. He thought he might now come out of his private Jewish closet.

CHAPTER 15

Bob Steele--Late 1966

Bob Steele's silver mane framed a cherub cheeked handsome face that configured a dimple inducing smile. He was an immaculately tailored man of 52. His medium sized athletic figure added a few pounds since his football playing days with the Hawkeyes, of the University of Iowa.

Bob Steele was second banana to tailback Nile Kinnick whose athleticism enabled him to effectively pass or run on any given play. He also led the league in punting. Kinnick's myriad skills won Iowa a first time top ten ranking nationally and for himself the coveted Heisman trophy.

His unheralded blocking back, Bob Steele was a reliable team player doing what was expected of him without much glory or many newspaper headlines.

In the world of advertising Steele was the unheralded man behind the creative stars he let shine in the limeight. His supportive role defined his career. He had learned from his football years the importance of teamwork in pursuit of a goal. Stolid, always in the background but always reliable, he ground out every promotion he ever got. Ultimately his loyalty and dedication precipitated his rise up the ladder of success to become president of Fremont-Richards, a small but profitable subsidiary of McGill-Johanson.

Steele could be counted on to get things done without flash or fanfare. He was used to leading the way for someone else to perform with distinction. His mid-western homespun philosophy, a catalogue of bromides and motivational exhortations earned him the not unkindly designation as a guy with a kind of Rotarian cool.

He surrounded himself with account and media people of similar style and temperament. although for over a year he depended on the alcoholic Teddy a unofficial creative director with whom he had a curious relationship. Teddy did not hold the title of creative director although he was in charge of all creative output. Most felt it was Teddy's drinking that kept the prestigious title from his grasp.

Harvard educated Teddy was a wannabe Shakespearean actor who had roomed with Jack Lamont at the elite Cambridge College. He settled for the ad business while Lamont went on to become a big time Hollywood star.

Teddy's acumen resulted in his recruitment of an all-star cadre of creative people. As a result the agency won new clients as well as industry awards. Bob Steele looked good and management smiled on his leadership with impressive bonuses, year after year.

Although Larry was fortunate enough to pass Teddy's demanding interviews to get the job, he couldn't discount the fact that Maria, Teddy's wife was Georgeena's roommate at the University of Minnesota.

"I've always liked the cut of your jib, Larry and you have a great wife" Teddy told Larry when he welcomed him aboard.

"Teddy, cut of my jib, my ass, I can't even tie a half hitch knot let alone explain the difference between a schooner and a sloop."

He laughed, "Neither can I. In fact when I was in the navy, I drove the exec officer crazy by asking him, "what is the pointy part of the boat called?" Larry roared.

Teddy was so Ivy League, in a self-mocking sort of way, Larry never could figure out his relationship with Bob Steele, until one afternoon at Teddy's pied a terre on East 49th street. The apartment was not for Maria's use nor was she even aware of it. When he stayed in the city he would tell her he was saying at the Waldorf just around the corner from his private pad.

"Come on get your coat. Let's go have a pop at my place," Teddy said

That afternoon he spilled the beans. After several cocktails Larry was made privy to his nasty little secret about Bob Steele.

Every time Larry saw them together he would view Teddy and Bob as the ODD COUPLE, Felix Unger and Oscar Madison from Neil Simon's classic comedy; although Larry's casting would have been a reversal of body types for the characters. Bob Steele though meticulous in dress and manner like Felix was built like Oscar Madison and Teddy although slovenly and rumpled like Oscar was built like short, small boned Felix Unger.

Teddy often invited Larry to join him for a pop around 1:00 in the afternoon. Fuck lunch, besides Larry thought, he genuinely liked me. After all their wives were close and they both were outsiders who joined WASP clans with less than a warm embrace; the Italian Catholic Teddy and Larry the Jew. Social exclusion may have been a key component in, their growing friendship.

The pop turned into a three hour gab fest by which time the bottle of Johnny Walker Red was reduced in volume by three quarters. Before the afternoon was over Larry was told the real story behind the odd couple relationship. After a third generous drink, Teddy seemed anxious to reveal the tale which few, if any, had heard before.

Their relationship was forged by an unusual combination of chance and Teddy's opportunism. Before Larry joined Fremont-Richards, it was the agency of record for the New Jersey Democratic Candidate for Governor. Teddy, a newly hired political advertising maven, produced a string of blistering below the belt commercials for Governor John Blanchard's campaign, depicting his opponent, a stable married man, as a sexual predator involved with a female staffer in his office. It was pure bunkum but Teddy's handiwork increased Blanchard's poll rating 9 points in less than a week to 58%, a clear majority just seven days from the November election.

The election results Tuesday night, one week later, resulted in a Blanchard landslide 59% to 41%. over Thad Reisler former State Attorney General.

Teddy flush with the success of his turnaround TV commercial called Bob to join him in a victory celebration in Trenton after Blanchard's acceptance speech.

"Got two hotties to join us Bob. Just a little old fashioned fun," he said.

Bob, who was staying at the Hotel Marriott, agreed to meet them in the Hotel Hamilton Lounge, where Teddy assured him the piano player there might add to the victory celebration. The Hamilton was only two blocks away from the Marriott.

Teddy, with a sure eye for straight-arrow Bob's suppressed desire for sex outside his marriage, arranged for a high class hooker to be in Bob's room at 1:00 pm. At that hour Teddy would make sure their little party, at the Hamilton Hotel ended. This would allow Bob ample time to return to his suite and meet his surprise "guest."

When Bob arrived at the Hamilton's crowded bar he was introduced to two attractive young campaign aides to Governor Blanchard. They had been briefed in advance by Teddy to do a little flirty, flirty thing with Bob but to make damn sure they discreetly took their leave at 1:00pm.

The girls played their parts well and Bob, plied with drink after drink, basked in the female attention he'd probably never gotten before. Teddy matched him Johnny Walker Red for Johnny Walker Red and never felt a thing. Sober as a Carrie Nation acolyte.

At 1:00 pm prompt. Tina, the blonde of the two girls, looked at her watch. She poked her companion and stood up.

"Oh, my goodness," she said, "Betty and I have to leave, Bobby. But how about a lil goodnight kissie? Hmmm. She leaned down cupped his face with her hands and kissed him hard and long.

"There. You are such a nice man. Pleased to have met you," she said with a mock curtsey.

Bob thanked his designated dates for a lovely the evening, then said good night to Teddy before leaving the Hamilton Lounge.

When Bob opened the door of his Marriott suite #704, he was greeted by a young naked Eurasian girl. Couldn't have been more than 21. Before he could express surprise, protest or acquiescence the lithe small boned beauty had deftly removed his jacket, tie and shirt. Johnny Walker had slowed his response time. As she reached to unbuckle his belt, after unzipping his fly with incredible dexterity, Bob gave his silent assent by teetering toward the bed, flopping atop the inviting comforter waiting to be administered to by her inimical style of comfort.

One hour later, mission accomplished Bob's Eurasian "gift", fully dressed in a clinging mini dress, walked towards the door. Before opening it, she stopped to take a last look at naked Bob lying on his back, snoring, his argyle socks now drooping like some wilted Scotch flower. Outside in the corridor she checked her bag making sure her mini Minox camera, which had done its job, was still there.

When Teddy got back to the office a day after Governor Blanchard's victory, he stopped by Bob's office and dropped off a package of six 8x10 glossy photographs. Each revealed a different angle of Bob's enjoyment of the gentle art of fellatio being performed on him.

A notice, sent round the office the following week, announced the appointment of Teddy Serengetti as the official new creative director of Fremont-Richards.

Teddy was Larry's boss, but their relationship was special even before he joined the agency. Of course Teddy knew he was Jewish but Teddy's world included many well placed Jews from his Harvard days.

Chapter 16

The Serengetti Soirees 1967

Larry and Georgeena became regular attendees at the Serengetti's semi-annual bashes that filled their high ceilinged apartment on Riverside Drive with as many as 100 chattering guests.

The guest list was always impressive. One never failed to spot a celebrity or two. Teddy's friendship with Jack Lamont kept him in the Broadway and Hollywood loop and Maria's job at Simon Shuster always guaranteed a literary lion or lioness in attendance.

Edward Albee was the star of the second gathering they attended. The young playwright's drama, "A Delicate Balance," had just won the Pulitzer Prize for Drama. He had been a runner-up three times before and the movie of his best known play "Who's Afraid Of Virginia Woolf" had been nominated for an Oscar.

Teddy's theatrical background made him the perfect host. At this gathering he spent much time with Mike Nichols and Elaine May. Teddy had produced a TV commercial featuring the two before their meteoric rise in the world of comedy and theater. He beckoned Albee over to join them. Nichols first major hit as a director of "Who's Afraid Of Virginia Woolf."

Jules Feiffer, the "Voice" cartoon strip satirist, screen writer, playwright was also a regular at the Serengetti soirees. Larry spotted Feiffer alone in a far corner of the crowded room. He was about to break his iron clad rule; never walk up to a celebrity of any kind for conversation without first being invited.

He wondered should I call him Jules or Mr. Feiffer. Mr. Feiffer didn't seem right. The man was about his age.

"Jules," Larry said. "Forgive me for intruding but I had to tell you how much I enjoy your Village Voice cartoons. You have such an original take on life. I loved your short film "MUNRO". I thought it deserved an Oscar."

Larry nervously shook his hand, thanked him and took his leave. Feiffer never uttered a word. He wondered why he thanked the man, for enduring his presence. What a creep he must have thought Larry was.

He saw that Georgeena was talking to Joyce Fiedler, a Washington Post political columnist who was a close friend of Maria. They were classmates at Columbia's Graduate School of Journalism. Georgeena, the state school graduate, first met Joyce at an earlier Serengetti bash.

Fiedler was a White House press correspondent who regularly gave Teddy and Maria a political insider's look at Washington's behind the scene's doings.

"Johnson will not run again in 1968," she announced to Georgeena and a few others gathered around her as Larry walked over to join them.

"The Vietnam War was becoming a millstone around the neck of the President," she said. "His lack of foreign affairs experience is beginning to show. The best he's been able to do is listen to the Harvard hawks he inherited from the Kennedy administration and now their losing their appetite for continuing the god damn war."

"Whose to stop him?" Georgeena asked. "Not Humphrey."

"Hell no. Humphrey is as tainted as Johnson to the peaceniks,. even though that may be unfair. Eugene McCarthy is going to win the New Hampshire primaries next month with the youth vote. The kids are all behind him, knocking on doors, making phone calls, carrying placards. Even getting their heads bashed in. Johnson knows he cannot win," Joyce went on.

No incumbent president had ever lost his party's nomination before. There's no way his Texas size pride could stand a primary loss."

She smiled and said, "You heard it here first folks." "What about his Civil Rights and Medicare legislation triumphs? Don't they give him political capital?" someone asked drawn to Joyce's audacious prediction.

"The unwinnable war, the killing of our GI's, the costs of it will always triumph over domestic legislation. There's a whole country out there that wants out of Vietnam. Last count 46,000 dead GI's. God knows how many wounded and crippled."

Georgeena could never forget those exchanges with, Joyce Fiedler.

Teddy's and Maria's parties gave her the opportunity to shine. Her interest in politics, her love of classic and contemporary literature was not superficial.

George could quote soliloquies from Hamlet, witticisms from Evelyn Waugh, and the words of every song the satirist Tom Leher ever wrote. He marveled at her ability to enchant the literati in attendance with her conversational aplomb.

Georgeena was smart and retained almost everything she read. She was not just another pretty face, although she was easy to look at and the ageing roués from yesterday's best seller lists also enjoyed her flirtatious attention.

But Larry had to admit he and Goergeena shared the fun of mingling with the great and near great of New York glitterati. This shared enthusiasm brought them closer together for the next several months.

Teddy adopted his philosophy of living the good life from the romantic view of Sara and Gerald Murphy, F Scott Fitzgerald icons of the 1920's ; 'Living well is the best revenge."

CHAPTER 17

Georgeena's Soirees

Emboldened by her success in socializing at Teddy and Maria's grand gatherings Georgeena developed her own coterie of interesting people. Her West End Avenue parties included musicians, writers, minor poets, actors and middle level editorial men and women who toiled at publications from lowbrow to middlebrow.

A letter from her mother's friend Walt Brown, critic at large at the Minneapolis Journal, informed Georgeena she'd be hearing from a man named Snooky Wilson. Snooky he felt was a talented trumpet player. Maybe Georgeena, with all her new connections, could help him jump start his career.

Wilson, soon after his arrival in New York, was invited to one of Georgeena's soirees. She never bothered to ask him his real name, although if his mother consumed as much alcohol as he did, it's possible she actually named him Snooky.

Brown was right. Snooky played a mean TRUMPET. He had the lip and the chops but never rose to the top in Minneapolis. He would open for Billy Eckstine or Sarah Vaughan at the HAPPY HOUR, a glitzy little establishment on upper Hennepin Avenue. He also opened for Joe Mooney or George Shearing at the FLAME, another musical watering hole on Hennepin Avenue. Jazz was on the rise in the Twin Cities through the early 60's until Rock and Roll delivered a near knockout punch to the genre. The advent of the swivel hipped Elvis Presley changed what young folk listened to and, more importantly bought, records.

Snooky, a victim of the decline in jazz popularity, was in a loveless 15-year marriage, and a house filled with two unwanted children. The twin pressures of unemployment and unhappy home life precipitated his flight to New York to start anew. There he envisioned new employment possibilities and a new life with a blonde haired back-up singer Winnie Lynn. Not a man of great introspection, he was able to escape from reality in endless clouds of marijuana.

Fleeing without a plan or enough money to last a month in Manhattan, Snooky relied on, as usual, the largesse of others. Living alone was a state of being he could not endure. The moderately talented Winnie Lynn, nee Knoblauch, fulfilled his twin needs of female companionship and financial support.

Winnie's practical Lutheran upbringing always provided her financial backup to her meager earnings as a vocalist. She was an accomplished typist, who graduated from West High School on the non-college track.

Her secretarial skills belied her public persona as a performer— the dumb blonde stereotype popular in male locker rooms jokes. Winnie's 5 year relationship with Snooky was predicated on his earnest promises of marriage at a never defined future date. Like Adelaide, the sniveling blonde in GUYS AND DOLLS, she trusted her procrastinating lover. But Adelaide's 10 year relationship with Nathan Detroit finally concluded in marriage. Winnie was not so lucky.

Shortly after arriving in the big city she found a job as secretary to an officer in the International Ladie's Garment Workers Union. Unfortunately for Winnie, rather than gratitude from Snooky, she received verbal abuse for accepting such a low paying job. Snooky stopped going to the Musician Unions Hiring Hall after only three months in New York. Most of his days were spent blowing his horn in the solitary confines of their tiny apartment on West 26th street and, smoking weed.

Because Georgeena and Larry had seen him perform at the FLAME and HAPPY HOUR saloons, they thought he had real talent. When he called, Georgeena invited him to one of her early soirees.

Snooky and Winnie's most lasting contribution to the shaky life style of Larry and Georgeena was an introduction to hash brownies. These weed laced treats were an edible ticket to a short term nirvana.

The downside of socializing with them was the nasty bickering and shouting that inevitably followed after their alcohol consumption reached three cocktails. Such contentious behavior ultimately led Georgeena to remove them from her party list.

It was unfortunate she hadn't made that decision retroactive to the last invite she'd sent to them. Alcohol, weed, and indolence left Snooky a slathering, often menacing drunk one soiree evening while Winnie worked overtime at the ILGWU office,

Marlene Rothman, an aging mistress of Sinclair Lewis, the Nobel Prize winning writer who died 10 years earlier, made Georgeena's A list of invitees that night. She enhanced the evening with entertaining anecdotes about the literati of the 1930's when she was an ingénue at the feet of Lewis and his friends who numbered John Dos Passos, Christopher Isherwood, Theodore Dreiser, Dorothy Thompson, young John Steinbeck and many other writers of distinction.

Red, Marlene called Sinclair. She told of Red's legendary prowess, a man 30 years her senior.

"He was a bull in bed," she said.

Snooky who had come alone, sat at the edge of a chair, across from the squeaky leather couch occupied by Marlene. She had just described Red's remarkable ability in the bedroom, the veritable bull.

At the mention of 'bull in bed' Snooky's ears perked up. He stood up as he shouted at Marlene in a salacious slurred voice, "You say bull? You talking bull? Take a peek at this, honey."

He unzipped his pants and pulled out an enormous *shlong, putz*. It was the longest male organ Larry had ever seen. From the look on Marcia's face it was the longest she had seen as well.

She placed her hands over her eyes. Larry couldn't make out if she was peeking.

"Put that thing back in your pants where it belongs," Marlene said to Snooky. It was a no nonsense imperious command.

"Well now, honey, it depends on where it belongs," he said with a sly wink."

Larry quickly grabbed Snooky by the seat of his drooping pants and the collar of his jacket and frog marched him out of the living room to the front door, Snooky offered no resistance but his member remained dangling from his pants.

Before Larry shut the door on him for the last time, he managed to say, "Hey. Larry, you got that lil' lady's phone number?"

The soiree ended ended early that night.

Undeterred by the last disaster, Georgeena's ability to dig up yesterday's litersti and strays continued. One Saturday evening a frail, gay 80 something writer was on the guest list. He'd published a few short stories in the 20's and early 30's. His name was Eugene. Larry couldn't recall his last name as he greeted him. Eugene extended a shaky hand. His shaking produced a tremor in Larry as Eugene held on too long. It was definitely not a flirtatious move. It kept him upright with the support of his strong right hand.

Taking no chances Larry led him to a pillowed club chair. Georgeena had mentioned Eugene. He was a sort of spear carrier for literary expats in Paris of the 1920's; Ford Maddox Ford, John Dos Passos, Glenway Wescott among them. Any fame he achieved was through contact with the great and not his own output of words.

Eugene in polite conversation, seemed shocked that Larry had read Wescott's THE PEREGRINE HAWK or even knew of Wescott, a former lover of his.

What the hell, Larry thought. I read. Who in hell is this guy being shocked that I know a little bit about the expat writers in Paris of the twenties besides Hemingway.

"Excuse me, Eugene, I'm going to get a drink."

He walked over to the crown jewel of Georgeena's cultural repertory, Virgil Thompson, critic, composer, writer whose opera, 4 SAINTS IN 3 ACTS, was still an avant guard favorite. Thompson was introduced to Larry at an earlier party.

Georgeena had respect for Larry's ability to mix at parties. She knew he could be counted upon for passable small talk at any gathering.

Larry thought of himself as a sort of a big city tumler, like those entertainers, who work the lounge crowds in the Catskills; a bit more cerebral but none the less with a mission to entertain. No shaping of balloons into animals, just keep em interested, with humor if possible, and an occasional show of erudition.

Thompson, a pudgy red haired man of 65, had rosy cheeks which matched his wee voice and faint Southern lisp. It was a voice that belonged to a Saturday morning cartoon character, not the iconic lion of modern music.

The perfunctory conversation, initiated by Larry, lasted only a few minutes.

"Mr. Thompson, Larry Miller. I just wanted to get your opinion of the new musical I saw last week, MAN OF LA MANCHA. I rather enjoyed it. "

"Pure treacle, young man. Another of Broadway's kitschy pop musicals.

Nothing resembling art or inspired music."

"Interesting. Thank you for that succinct review."

He looked surprised as Larry walked on to his next social challenge.

Thompson spotted a distinguished white-haired man with a noble beak of a nose one could find embossed on an ancient Greek coin. It was the iconic choreographer/dancer George Balanchine.

Larry had briefly crossed paths with Balanchine the afternoon John F Kennedy was assassinated. He had noisily banged on the door of Larry's neighbor, just a few hours after the shooting, when the nation began four days of mourning for the deceased young president.

Georgeena and Larry had gathered in the living room of the neighbor's apartment, the closest place to share their grief. It was the apartment of Diana Adams, a former wife of the oft married Balanchine, and her husband Lowell. She remained friends with the great man.

His first angry words as he entered the room were, "I can't believe it. I just can't believe it."

"Neither can we," Diana said. "What a tragedy."

Balanchine looked puzzled. "How could you possibly know about it?"

"Why it's on every TV channel and every radio staion. One couldn't possibly miss the story."

"No, No, No," he said impatiently, "I don't know what you're talking about. I just came from New York Dance Building at Lincoln Center. They were installing the wooden flooring of the stage and the fools did it all wrong. The individual wooden boards have to be carefully meshed. If they're too loose or too tight they could throw the dancers off in a most hideous fashion. Can you imagine what would happen on opening night. Dancers springing up too high, missing cues. It would be a major disaster."

After his exhortation Georgeena and Larry hastily excused their selves leaving Diane Adams and her new husband to unfold the magnitude of the day's events to Balanchine.

Larry pondered his next move, looking over the field of eligible female guests, Someone touched his arm. He looked down at John Monahan's wife. John was a Senior Writer at a McGraw Hill

Publication, Oil Daily, the petroleum Industry trade magazine. There was the smiling face of Sheila Monahan. Georgeena had met Sheila at a Democratic Club meeting during the 1964 presidential election. They both had volunteered to man the phones for the month of October. Georgeena, who was always ready to add to her guest list, found Sheila a bright and interesting woman and invited her and husband John to the next gathering.

A year or so earlier, at an afternoon soiree, Sheila and Larry had grappled on the the floor of his West End apartment's walk in closet. Approaching the moment of truth the door opened and there they were in flagrante delicto.

Fortunately it was not John or Georgeena, but whoever it was ratted them out.

"I didn't recognize you in the vertical position," she said.

He laughed.

"Nor I you."

You leaving'?

"Yes, but only if we leave together."

"Deal."

They slipped out of the room together and remained together for the next 24 hours. Larry and Georgeena had remained moderately close friends with the Monahans, a relationship which he encouraged.

CHAPTER 18

A Night To Remember

Georgeena, when sober, was a very good cook. Over the years guests enjoyed the sybaritic pleasure her gourmet dinners afforded them.

One memorable evening dinner guests were Harold Freiman, his wife Dotty, the Serenghettis, and Kate and Rod Kahn. She had made a delicious looking roast duck a l'orange with a thick brown sauce. Everyone commented about its efficacy as George shakily brought the serving platter to the table. Her hands, encased in bulky oven mitts--somewhat limiting her dexterity—further encumbered her questionable hand eye coordination.

Georgeena bent her knees slightly to place the platter of duck on the table in a spot next to Dotty who was wearing a taupe hued silk dress. As she lowered the platter the angle of descent was a bit too steep and the duck rolled off onto Dotty's dress.

Dollops of brown sauce spewed from the duck in its downward fall. They found a home on Maria Serenghetti's white linen dress. The dappled pattern of brown on white Larry thought quite artistic. Maria did not concur.

Dotty looked a disaster. Quickly Larry spirited her to Georgeena's bedroom closet to select a replacement dress after freshening up in the bathroom

Larry offered Maria the same opportunity to change clothing but she gamely refused as she patted down the viscous brown blobs. Making no further attempt to remove them. Maria now resembled a dappled two-legged pony.

That Georeena had consumed more booze than usual, was confirmed by the antics which followed.

Teddy brought them his favorite pastry, hash brownies, a special treat to complement the martinis and four bottles of Chablis they had thus far consumed.

After dinner Georgeena, oblivious to the duck mishap, decided to show off her athletic prowess. It was midnight when she promised them to show the group a perfect cartwheel. She shooshed everyone aside to give herself a long enough runway in their 18' x 30' living room.

There were cries of, "go for it girl" and counter cries of, "you'll break your fucking neck."

Georgeena went with the "go for it" option.

She was wearing a light crew neck sweater, pleated tartan skirt but wore no shoes, having kicked them off before the attempted feat. She crouched, took three quick steps and leaped, legs high, arms reaching to touch the floor for support. When she reached the height of her arc, legs now wide apart, her skirt flared up to reveal the privates of a pantyless Georgeena.

The audience reaction was mixed. Rod and Teddy clapped and whistled. Harold and the women were silent. Dotty looked horrified. Maria crinkled her nose. Kate just rolled her eyes. She had seen Georgeena in action before during their campus days at the University of Minnesota.

"Okay, George," Larry said, hovering over her crumpled body still shaking with laughter, "that's enough for the evening."

"The hell you say. The evenings just beginning."

The words haltingly spilled from her mouth like oozing oatmeal. He grabbed both her arms. Perhaps a little too tightly.

She responded with a punch to his face. His nose responded with an outpouring of blood.

"Fuck you, Larry."

He did not relax the grip, ignoring the blood on his hands and shirt.

"Stop or I'll call the cops," she screamed.

A black cat Mowgli 2, scampered across the room roused from his sleep by Georgeena's piercing scream. He didn't stop, continuing to grip firmly. She twisted and turned to no avail.

She unleashed a torrent of "fuck you Larrys" over and over.

The "fuck you Larrys" repeated ad nauseum convinced the guests it was time to leave. Retrieving coats and hats they quickly departed but not before hastily chorusing a rather lame, "Thank you for an interesting evening."

They couldn't leave fast enough. Dotty muttered in his direction, "I'll return the dress tomorrow. Thanks, Larry."

After they left he released Georgeena from his grasp. She immediately went to the phone and called the police. Minutes later two of New York's finest appeared and listened to their conflicting stories. The blood on his face and shirt convinced the officers he may have been the real victim. They willingly filed his counter charges against her.

Bottom line: She was arrested on Larry's charge of her assault on him. He was arrested for his alleged assault on her.

They were led down the elevator, handcuffed and into a waiting black Maria that took them to New York's notorious Tombs.

The Tombs was a holding pen for pimps, prostitutes, wife beaters, armed robbers, and drug dealers awaiting a preliminary hearing in court. Their arrest fell into the category of spousal abuse; felonious assault on a spouse.

The only consolation from being holed up with 15 other accused men in a dark pen, whose sweating stone walls carried the stench of garbage and human waste, was the knowledge that Georgeena was confined in the women's pen adjacent to his.

Although a thick wall separated them, Larry felt sure her fellow inmates were no less threatening than his. The icy stare directed at him by two of his cell mates left Larry in a state of near panic. They fixated on his jacket and tie as if they were clothing from Mars.

The two wore grease laden coveralls, which covered most of their tattoos. They looked like they came from a JIFFY LUBE changing room. Each had his pants rolled up to the knee exposing legs colorfully decorated with what appeared to be the ridged back of a dragon's tail.

Following a true New Yorker's instinct for survival, Larry never made eye contact with either of them during 10 hours of incarceration.

At 3:00 AM a guard beckoned Larry to the pen's barred door, unlocking it carefully, and then relocking after he emerged, and walked him to a battery of wall phones in the admitting room. It was time for his one allowable phone call to the outside world. He called Harold Freiman, who with Dotty his wife had earlier in the evening witnessed the ugly scene that precipitated the joint arrests.

"Harold, I'm sorry for calling so late but this is an emergency. I need a lawyer. I am in the Tombs as is Georgeena. But she can get her own damn lawyer."

"I kind of figured you might be calling and I do have the kind of lawyer you need. His name's Walter O'Malley. He is one tough son of a gun; mean and lean criminal Lawyer. And, Larry, don't give him any advice. Just listen. Remember he's the lawyer. You'll be out by noon today. I promise."

"I can't thank you enough. Harold and I'm really sorry about Dotty's dress."

"She's just fine. No problem. That was some show you guys put on. Good luck."

"Yeah, yeah. But thanks again. I'll look for O'Malley at the hearing."

He hung up and was escorted back to the pen, determined to make no eye contact with anyone until he was in the courtroom for the hearing.

Eight hours later, at 11:00 AM sharp, he appeared before Judge Harley Karns who listened to Walter O'Malley relate that both parties agreed to drop charges. His astute handling of both Georgeena and himself affected the best possible outcome.

CHAPTER 19

John Leaves On A Low Note

The ultimate break-up of their friendship with the Monahans occurred on a drunken Fire Island weekend. Georgeena invited John and Sheila for a weekend at their beach side rental house in Robbin's Rest, a tiny community abutting the village of Ocean Beach. 40 residential houses comprised the community which officiously had its own mayor and police chief, offices which were more honorary than administrative. It gave those duly chosen officials, whose majority for election might require 25 votes little need for rigorous campaigning.

The total electorate of Robbin's Rest numbered 85 citizens, 35 of whom might be sober enough to vote on Election Day. There were no term limits and the two elected officials were paid in product rather than currency—a liter of Jack Daniels per man.

Local ordinances were loosely defined or enforced. The most stringent one forbade bon fires on the beach after 4:00 pm. Fornication on the beach, spousal abuse, and excessive drunkenness were matters tacitly understood to be adjudicated by the private individuals involved all by themselves. Actions on matters such as fires, hurricane damage, and homicides were wisely ceded to the

Long Island Township of Bayshore whose elected officials had a firmer grasp on dealing with disaster.

The Monahans arrived, their little red coaster wagon in tow filled with two oversized pieces of luggage, which seemed excessive wardrobe for a two-day weekend. The red wagons were clearly utilitarian, not just a charming mode of transporting worldly goods. Their sturdy little frames and wheels neatly traversed the soft sands that led to Robbins Rest.

Sheila was the elegant British voice that answered the phones at Koenig & Sons. a large New York children's wear manufacturer.

Her voice, for starters, was more pleasing to the ear than harsh patois of New Yorkers. Sheila, a well-educated woman and seasoned world traveler liked the easy comradery that Georgeena, the smart young American woman from the mid-west offered her.

At work they gossiped together and in a short period of time they dined together as couples, becoming a congenial foursome, although John left something to be desired as a male friend for Larry. His passion for model railroading and the technology of the latest in lighting modes held little interest for Larry and his preoccupation with sports, politics and books.

Barney Goldfine and his date of six years, Rosemary Janson completed the guest list for the weekend. They were well into the cocktail hour when the Monahans arrived at 7:00 fresh off the 6:40 Bayshore Ferry.

Barney, an editor at a minor children's book publisher, was a casual friend from NYU grad school of journalism in the days before Larry entered the U.S. Air Force. He was born in Brooklyn but quickly adopted the Ivy League style in his first job in publishing.

Larry learned everything he knew about eastern style--the Brooks Brothers look—during the nine months he and Barney spent together at NYU.

Larry hadn't maintained contact with Barney during his years in service. Barney never served in the armed forces. They renewed their acquaintanceship when Larry returned to New York.

Barney's taste in dress and choice of women was impeccable. He was also quite good with new people, offering up a slightly elevated level of small talk, occasionally punctuated with an occasional name drop of a B list writer or actor. He was Larry's only Jewish friend other than Harold Freiman.

Barney desperately wanted to become a part of the WASP establishment in publishing but refused to change his name. Blonde hair and blue eyes could not overcome the name GOLDFINE in defining who he was. His style and dress didn't matter.

His pressed white denim slacks neatly complemented his navy blue Izod polo shirt, with its insouciant green alligator logo...

Barney's brass buckled Gucci loafers revealed golden tan ankles. He sat while acknowledging the Monahan's entrance with a nod. To Barney standing would be a sign of accepting them as equals. Good manners never occurred to him

He was often skeptical of Georgeena's choice of friends, but he was wrong about her tending to set the bar too low. It was a judgement he often made about people from his supercilious perch.

Her floral print dress gave Rosemary, a tall blonde editor at VOGUE, the look of a Georgia O'Keefe print. An O'Keefe was the kind of print you bought, at the Marlboro Art Store on the corner of Eighth Street Larry and 6th Avenue, to add color and a touch of class to your minimalist 3-story Village walk up.

Barney was ahead of his time in posturing as a GQ kinda guy. Larry had seen his cavernous closet of style filled with 5 hanging custom made suits, 4 sport coats, and a myriad of different colored slacks. Larry never had time to count the exact number of hanging slacks. Co-workers, behind his back, derisively designated him, 'the perfect man.'

A black Mercedes 300L confirmed in Larry's mind, that Barney came from money. He was his only friend or acquaintance who owned a car in Manhattan. Although he never spoke of his family, his friend Chip Blumenthal said something about their being in the smelting business.

Editors at Rascali Publishing Kids Book Division, Barney's employer, earned no more than 10K per year in the year 1963, even in the best case scenario.

Larry's conjecture about Barney's affluent background was demolished the day they lunched at Donizetti's, a chic white table cloth restaurant in the East 50's.

He chose the venue. It was the watering hole for upper tier members of New York's Publishing establishment where they gathered to gossip and network. Bennett Cerf, Clay Felker, Gay Talese and Richard Snyder were among the regulars.

Barney was the only representative from Rascali Publishing, too pricey for most of its employees. There he enjoyed the vicarious pleasure of being among the elite of the business.

No direct contact, of course, but enough overheard conversations to be in the know.

Two shrimp cocktails, four martinis, a pair of veal piccata specials and a bottle of Barolo added up to a check for $165 for the two of them ; a week's wages in the editorial middle tier of the book publishing business.

The waiter had set the check on the table equidistant from each of them, as if waiting to see who would claim it. Barney barely glanced at the total. "It's on me Larry. No problemo," he said, as he reached for his wallet, in which Larry saw 4 credit cards and a few bills as he opened it. He didn't protest.

Barney placed his Diner's Club card in the open black leather folder that contained he check, folded it and handed it to a red coated young waiter who looked like a chorus boy from the hit Broadway show, HOW TO SUCCEED IN BUSINESS WITHOUT REALLY TRYING. His name tag read, Ken.

Credit cards were new to the world. The Diners Club plastic card was the first, introduced in 1961 and naturally Barney Goldfine had his for nearly two years, one of the first of its initital 30,000 members.

Moments later Ken returned handing the open black leather folder to Barney, the Diner's Club Card atop the check. Lips pursed, Ken haltingly delivered his ominous message.

"I'm sorry, sir, this card was denied," he said. "Do you have another or would you prefer to pay in cash?"

"Sorry about that, Kenny. Your name is Kenny?"

"Actually it's Ken."

"Well, Kenny, here's my American Express card," Barney said, unruffled with an air of condescension, to the nervous young waiter.

Several minutes later, Ken returned, looking even more nonplussed than before. "I'm afraid the American Express Card did not go through either."

The smile on Barney's fine featured face disappeared. He leaned in me and whispered, "Larry, do you have a card you might use? I'll pay you back this afternoon. I know you don't carry around $165 in cash."

You shit he thought. You're begging and you have the balls to patronize me at the same time. Jeezzuz. Reluctantly Larry reached inside his breast pocket and removed his wallet and its sole card, American Express Green, prestige-wise a rung below the cache of their newer AMEX GOLD card.

Three weeks laterLarry opend his mail box containing a $165 check from Barney Goldfine. With no hesitation he raced to the neighborhood Chemical Bank Branch to deposit it, hoping it would clear. Otherwise his landlord, Joe Bianculli, might be inconvenienced by a late payment, which could jeopardize his status as a rent controlled tenant.

They never spoke again of the credit card incident. Barney's short term memory had no room for shame

Barney liked to be waited on as if deference to him was a given. Naturally it was not in his nature to offer the Monohan's a drink when they returned from their bed room, refreshed and appropriately dressed for the beach. Rosemary stepped up to the task. Georgeena was skewering kebabs in the kitchen while Larry attempted to start the gas grille, Weber's newest model in its ongoing attempt to foil unmechanical English majors.

A cannister of LP gas was attached to the grille. Some knob or other needed to be pushed, twisted or pulled up to get the gas to the grille and achieve ignition, to start a fire needed to cook lamb chunks. Shit, maybe John can do it. He knows all that technical stuff, he thought. He's basically a tech writing journalist. When poof, as though by ESP transmission, John appeared.

"Need any help?"

"Indeed, I do."

With lightning speed John found the starter switch. More than a switch, it was a circular metal disc that needed to be turned to ON except ON wasn't clearly marked. The tech writer for McGraw-Hill had an engineering degree. Liberal Arts degrees couldn't prepare one for the early challenges of Weber.

Meanwhile in the living room, Rosemary admirably took complete charge of bar tending. Larry admired the quiet efficiency she displayed in preparing and delivering drinks with a graceful charm.

"Sheila, what are you having?"

"Do you have Compari and soda?

Smart girl, Larry thought. Compari and soda, not a real drinker's libation, yet it had a cache that transcended its low alcoholic content. One could handle three or four of those without blinking.

"And Barney old dear. I see you're ready for another *see through*."

A *see through* was a clear martini obscured only by two green ovoid shapes stuffed with red pimentos that lay at the bottom of the thin stemmed glass.

John and Larry returned to the living room savoring success in igniting the new Weber Grille.

John, who wore tortoise shell eye glasses, had an eye for Jack Daniels, his drink of choice. Rosemary, God Bless her social acumen, brought him a tumbler of the amber Tennessee Bourbon over ice and Barney his usual *see through*. How did she know his beverage preference? She had spotted a bottle of Jack Daniels peeking through a corner of his partially unzipped brief case. When Larry asked her, sotto voce, how she knew, she revealed her secret.

At this juncture of his marriage, Larry could say Barney and Rosemary were their closest friends. Their long-standing rocky relationship paralleled his, with one major difference. They managed to stay unmarried.

"John, what's a Brit like you drinking Bourbon? I would think Scotch would be your tight little island's choice."

"That's a decent assumption but when I came to the states I saw the label Bourbon on several bottles in the package goods store I frequented. As an unreconstructed Francophile I immediately decided I would exert my contribution to a Bourbon restoration in the form of brilliant Jack Daniels."

"You're a monarchist. But then you Brits really are monarchists. What's your head lady's name?" he knew of course but maybe he could get a rise of this stiff bird. "Elizabeth. Yes that's it".

"Elizabeth 11, to be precise," he said.

"Yes, of course, Elizabeth 11," he said.

John and Larry had little in common. Although he was smart, it wasn't Larry's kind of smart. It was the technical smarts. Aside from oil business, he was probably the foremost expert on the new Xenon gas lamps. Larry didn't. give a shit about Xenon gas lamps.

His eyes would glaze over every time John lectured about the efficacy of this miraculous form of lighting. It was a lecture he endured many times over the course of their tenuous friendship.

He preferred Sheila, 9 years senior to John, for her humor, love of books and sex, preferably not with her husband. He often wondered how in the world did she choose to marry a man so different and so phlegmatic. After their first couple of meetings, the answer became clear.

Her late husband, Adrian, a career mid-level diplomat died suddenly while they were stationed in Ghana. He succumbed to a deadly parasite in the drinking water that invaded his body causing his death within a week. Upon return to England with his body, she discovered from his solicitor that his estate had been severely drained by the upkeep of mother in an assisted living facility recommended by the Department of State. Adrian was under the impression that he was covered under the Department's medical plan and not that of the new National Health Service.

Five years in the facility, before she died, had reduced his savings to almost nothing. At age 39 Sheila, who had not worked in 16 years of marriage, had almost no marketable skills. The life style she was used to made the prospect of working as a sales woman at Selfridges a grim prospect. Fortunately the marriage produced no offspring. Unfortunately her aging middle class parents had just enough to live out their years in modest comfort.

Her desperation led her to the want ads of the INTERNATIONAL HERALD TRIBUNE, which she knew often contained requests by affluent and reasonable affluent men who sought eligible, attractive, educated women as possible prospects for marriage.

As luck would have it, she initially thought, she spotted one ad of interest. It read:

```
31 YEAR OLD BRITISH JOURNALIST
SEEKS ENGLISH WOMAN DESIRING TO LIVE IN
AMERICA PLEASE SEND BRIEF BIO
```

She answered with credentials and attributes that needed little burnishing. Well educated and schooled in the ways of entertaining, she could be an unusual asset to a young journalist on the rise. Sheila did however fudge on one important issue, her age. She opted for the age of 33, six years away from the truth. Her enclosed photo revealed a pretty young woman in her early thirties.

His response, though not excessively self-laudatory left one with the distinct feeling this alleged beat reporter for a New York publication was about to vault onto the fast track of journalism. He nattered on about his real chance to become an editor at a top magazine.

The initial submissions by John and Sheila were followed by a flurry of letters from each detailing their likes in art, food, literature, theater, movies, politics and music. Hobbies, entered into the mix at some point, his being wood working and model trains.

Oh dear, model trains, she thought. Well I suppose I can deal with that. She countered with writing poetry and photography.

They met for the first time at Idlewild Airport in Queens at the British Airways Terminal. John had sent her a round-trip ticket, return open ended in case things didn't go swimmingly.

As Sheila spotted the JOHN MONAHAN HERE sign just outside the customs exit she hurriedly pulled along a large leather suitcase. The streaming sunlight that pierced the terminal's huge glass windows cast a full body spotlight on Sheila as John first viewed her. A radiant red cheeked, ginger-haired maiden right out of an English Tea TV Commercial approached him. Her trim but womanly body and fine pretty face said everything about what John had hoped for physically.

Sheila had little trouble hiding her disappointment in John's physical appearance. This first meeting was too important. John was of medium height 5'10' or so. He wore tortoise shell glasses a bit too small for his round face. There was a touch of tummy protruding from the vest of his open jacket Donegal tweed suit. Never did go for mustaches, Sheila thought giving him the once over, at least two times. His smile somewhat forced, was further marred by yellow teeth, the sign of a heavy smoker.

John liked what he saw, a trim woman about 5'4" tall. Nice fit. Shiny white teeth. No need for dental work there. It was warm in the terminal and as Sheila removed her Burberry raincoat she revealed to John, what American's would say, "well stacked." Yes, very nice breasts.

The courtship was brief. Though his bachelor apartment was too small Sheila knew it would only be a matter of time before his next job would enable them to move to more suitable quarters. Though somewhat clumsy in bed, a bit too quick for her tastes, Sheila regained some of the enjoyment of frequent sex, although missionary was the only position he knew but as some American wag once said, "even bad sex is good."

They met the Monahans five years into their marriage. They still lived in his cramped studio apartment on West End Avenue. It had been part of a larger old style 6 bedroom dwelling built in the early 1920's whose owners were rapidly aging and seriously declining in number. New owners seized the opportunity to break up the elegant old buildings into less than posh efficiency apartments

He never did get that next job up the ladder. But as Sheila loved to say, "It's a better life than working the perfume counter of Selfridges." John, on the other hand didn't find out Sheila's true age until their vacation in Mexico. When he handed both passports to the Immigration person, hers flipped open revealing a birth date 9 years prior to his.

I'm not sure how that revelation impacted their ambivalent marriage but it had to loosen whatever compelling ties that did exist.

Trapped with John at his end of the 6-person table, he would be forced to endure some technical discussion for God knows how long. If it wasn't to be another Xenon lamp tutorial, it had be be one just as agonizing. Go on the offensive he told himself. Set the tone and the conversation. Get through it while those lucky four, Barney, Rosemary, Sheila and Georgeena, giggled and guffawed.

He asked John, "PETROLEUM DAILY, that's your paper isn't it?"

He nodded. PETROLEUM DAILY, a McGraw-Hill property, was the oil industry bible, a favorite ideological as well as technical and geo-political source of information, for The Petroleum Institute, an industry trade organization and lobby.

John could give you the GDP of any oil producing nation, their daily outputs and the future prospects for deep water drilling in the Gulf of Mexico, the North Sea and Alaska.

John's views on the geo-political aspects of international oil production and their impact on key nations foreign policy formulation proved to be a God send that evening. He was astute in his comprehension of the subject and for once Larry listened. If only he could have discovered this corner of the Monahan brain earlier, he could have spared himself hours of Xenon torture.

Larry interrupted their conversation with a quick foray into the kitchen for two more bottles of Inglenook Chablis, the Heublein product that had nothing to do with Chablis, a varietal wine from Burgundy. It, in fact, was a mix of French Colombard, white Zinfandel and God knows what other grape. American laws had yet to prohibit wineries from using names that did not identify what was in their bottles. Most developed countries required a wine labeled Chablis to be produced in the Chablis district of Burgundy.

In order to be designated a varietal today in the US, a wine has to contain 75% of a particular grape. I.E. Cabernet Sauvignon wine must contain 75% of the cabernet grape.

After setting the two bottles of faux Chablis on the table John and Larry continued their discussion of the larger questions of the politics of petroleum and how it affected the shaping of U.S. foreign policy. The Saudis we loved for their oil. Think ARAMCO.

America chose an accommodation with Israel to obtain a buffer against Soviet intrusion in the Middle East. It followed the old Arab saw, "the enemy of my enemy, is my friend."

Two bottles of wine and a round of Stingers later Georgeena chirped, "Anyone for skinny dipping?"

Georgeena's predilection for skinny dipping after a boozy evening, was the opportunity to find a little extra curricular action.

Larry had to admit he also enjoyed the opportunities offered by swimming in the nude.

The guests' response was unanimous, an interesting turn of events. He could envision himself in the Atlantic playing dolphin mating with Sheila Monahan. But what about the others? Georgeena could make a play for Barney in the surf but he doubted if Rosemary would let that happen. And Georgeena would certainly have labeled John Monahan as a non-starter.

A soft breeze gently sprayed a veil of salt air across the broad beach of Robbins Rest. They could taste it as they walked to a launching site for six well served bodies. The final tally was four bottles of wine 13 martinis and 8 stingers—sum total for the group, about equally divided except for Barney who had three martinis, which accounted for the odd number of 13.

They settled on a tiny cove mid-point between Robbins Rest and Ocean Beach. "Perfect spot," Larry announced, "I'll give you 30 seconds to get out of your suits and into the water."

In mock seriousness he added, "No peeking."

A gibbous moon illuminated the white bubbly waves. Six people splashed into the oncoming surf, a welcoming swell of water, not yet 75 degrees in temperature.

Larry followed Sheila's generous bum as it disappeared into an oncoming wave. It was a delicious sea marker, two soft white arcs of flesh shaped like an upside down heart. It was a buoy to pursue.

Sheila, a strong swimmer, headied straight out to sea propelled by well-muscled forearms. Larry gamely followed, though water was not his natural habitat.

She looked back. Seeing he had fallen back, she turned switching to a breast stroke as she approached him. They were now at least 200 yards from the group. The pairing up, if any occurred, was difficult to ascertain from that distance.

As they treaded water watching the four with squint eyed curiosity, they touched, then embraced. Her breasts rubbing against his chest gave lie to the myth that a man cannot be fully aroused in 75 degree water.

What a beautiful place to make love. The bobbing waves of the Atlantic protectively engulfed them. Their heads were the only thing possibly visible to the foursome who had retreated to the beach wrapped in towels.

The promise that nudity offered for those on the beach was nullifierd because the matchups were not there. Game cancelled on account of missing chemistry.

Sheila andLarry knew that two of the unlucky foursome were doomed. The pairings didn't work in John or Georgeena's favor. John and Georgeena? Not on your life. Georgeena and Barney? Possible, but Rosemary left with the prospect of John would never let that pairing happen.

Soon the four departed from the beach for a less intimate get together on the sprawling deck of chez Miller.

After Sheila and Larry swam to shore they lay on the wet tamped down strip of beach that separated the receding waves from its untouched powdery soft part.

They let the waves come and go, their bodies awash in the bubbling foam of pleasure.

Hours later they returned to the house where the total darkness of collective anger resided. Who was mad at whom was not apparent until the next morning.

Larry awoke in the living room, buck naked, squinting at a blinding early morning sunshine which intruded on his aching head. An empty bottle of eau de vie lay carelessly at his feet, as he eased himself from a lightly cushioned rattan chair.

Quickly surveying the room his eyes settled on Sheila's soft white body, au naturel, hugging a floral print cushion from the couch she slept on. The pillow covered her breasts, leaving her lower body fully exposed. Stale cigarette smoke hung in a fine haze over the entire room. As he approached the couch where his Venus lay, something struck him as incongruous in this picture. A square piece of white paper covering her mons veneris.

Hovering over her, he made out the crudely scrawled letters on it.

The informal note read : FUCK YOU BOTH! John

His breathing awakened Sheila. She looked up, apparently from her view, he was staring at her crotch.

"Find anything interesting down there?" she said.

"Yes, my love, you have a marital billet doux affixed to your lovely body. To be more accurate, I should say, we have a shared missive from John. It's brief but it does have a point of view."

I handed her the note. She looked pleased rather than aghast.

Noting her naked state she reflexively pulled a knit comforter around her body.

"A little late for cover up."

She laughed.

"The slug-a-beds should be up soon and I don't want to surprise them."

"You might also want to seek suitable cover," she said as she tiptoed to the bedroom she had been sharing with John.

He followed her advice, quickly slipping on a T shirt and damp swim suit. Good thing, too, as Georgeena soon appeared in the living room wearing her green silk shorty, a floral billboard of Monet's lily pad canvases.

The shorty was a walking come on, long before VICTORIA'S SECRET turned bathrobes into garments of sexual enticement. Imagine what was under that clinging garment which embraced her body in just the right places. It was Georgeena's silent invitation to salacious thoughts and looks.

"You're up early," she said.

"Yeah, went for a quick dip. Cold in the morning," he lied.

"Barney and Rosemary are still sleeping. I thought I heard a door slam an hour or so ago. Must have been you coming back from your swim."

So far so good. There was no mention of last night and thank God Sheila scooted out in the nick of time.

"I guess we ought to get some breakfast ready. I'll do the bloodies."

"That'll be a life saver," she chirped.

A little too perky for 9:00 am, he thought. Georgeena was foxy. She could delay a confrontation for at least 24 hours, catching you unaware. Good tactic. Must try it some time.

Breakfast was muted. Barney and Rosemary had that mussed up, red cheeked look of morning sex while poor Sheila explained that John had to get to the city early. Had a deadline to meet. Some story about trouble in the oil fields of Libya. Wonderful story, Sheila, he silently applauded.

Later, when they had a moment alone, she told him the weirdest story. In their bedroom John had dumped on her side of the bed, a mean spirited pile of fecal matter. His calling card Larry thought. Appropriate, he always considered John a pompous piece of shit.

Shortly thereafter John and Sheila separated. Freed of her stagnant 7 year marriage, she opted for a more interesting job than the one at Koenig & Sons. In a short time she snared an administrative assistant's job with J Walter Thompson. At the time Madison Avenue was enamored of English accents. At a modest price, they could add a little tone to any agency.

John remained a Senior Writer for PETROLEUM DAILY. He never remarried.

CHAPTER 20

The New Account

Wit and irony were not part of Bob Steele's cultural repertory. The creatives often patronized Bob but also genuinely liked him. He never bull shitted the troops and was always generous with praise as well as with bonuses.

Bob's ready smile would brighten his child-like red cheeks. His ever present upbeat mood seemed directed by an internal electronic device with no OFF button.

His expansive smile shone even brighter when Mordechai Hassenfeffer called to say FEFFERCO toy account was his; 10 million dollars in billing was big time money in the late 60's. Larry's ad campaign to introduce America's newest toy phenomenon sealed the deal.

His successful presentation elevated him to the number two creative spot in the agency. An added bonus to the new job: he alone would be responsible for all creative, bypassing Serengetti whose drinking would be a red flag for the Hassenfeffer crowd.

The product was a 12" high doll called SOLDIER MAN.

It was a fully articulated plastic soldier whose flexibility enabled young boys to move its head, arms, wrists, torso, knees, and feet into any combat configuration a creative young mind could conjure.

Like Barbie, the girl doll icon, SOLDIER MAN had a wardrobe that could overload any child's toy chest and reduce any mother's household budget. Soon after the ad campaign would break on network TV during late weekday afternoons and Saturday mornings, the choice times to entice young school children, thousands of 6-12 year-old boys would beseech their parents to buy them SOLDIER MAN.

SOLDIER MAN'S accessories were not designed for fashion, like Barbie's collection of au currant scarves, gloves, stiletto-heeled pumps, hats, dresses and jeweled handbags. They were geared for combat; an array of uniforms, helmets, assault rifles, automatic pistols, knives, hand grenades, rocket launchers, space capsules, deep sea diving suits and sea sleds. They nurtured every boy's dream of starring in his own private war.

Soon the young male population of the country would be immersed in the unthinkable —*playing with dolls.*

Bob Steele, recognizing the importance Larry's role would play in maintaining and keeping the new account, quickly came through with a $6,000 raise, a handsome income bump in 1965, which assured his loyalty to the agency for at least a year or two. Loyalty was an unusually cheap commodity on Madison Avenue. Staffing the new account began immediately. Larry was the creative director and Len Davidoff, the media director, whose job was to tell the client how he would spend his money wisely; choosing the right media at the right cost per thousand.

Davidoff was chosen not merely for his proven acumen but for his religious affinity with Mordecai Hassenfeffer, who might just feel more comfortable having a landsman spend his money.

Selecting an appropriate account supervisor was a different ball of wax. The job entailed managing the day to day administration of the account and required a person with finesse and exceptional interpersonal relations skills. His counterpart on the client side would be a young ambitious man named Howard Politz whose ingratiating manner and parsimonious approach to spending ad dollars made him a darling of the Hassenfeffer family. The requirements for the job made Bob Steele's search doubly difficult because Jewish Account Supervisors didn't grow on trees.

The WASP world of advertising was just getting used to the idea of Italian Art Directors and Jewish Copy Chiefs.

Account supervisors were the skilled and often obsequious men who wined and dined corporate Advertising and Marketing Directors. One had to scour the boonies to ferret out a Jewish one. Although Gentile folk lore promulgated the claim that Jews excel in the world of commerce, few were recruited. Despite the myth of their business acuity, few companies seemed ready to bet on a Jewish MBA'S ability to make nice to the Protestant elite who constituted the majority of Fortune 500 Advertising and Marketing Directors.

There were few training grounds for Jewish account supervisors, even those with MBA's from Harvard or Wharton, except for a handful of Fortune 500's with Jewish management or ownership who occasionally hired Jewish ad directors. There were also a handful of small ad agencies that catered to smaller Jewish owned companies, like Ronson, Manischewitz Wines or retailers such as Ohrbachs, Alexanders or Kleins.

Bob Steele knew the paucity of ideal candidates on the avenue and seeking them out could be too time-consuming. Hassenfeffer wanted Fremont-Richards to hit the ground running.

A search by the top "Head Hunter", Henry Fields, produced one candidate. Steele had to find someone quickly. He scheduled an interview with Field's lone prospect.

He thought he found his man in Mike Olcott, a 200 pound power forward and outfielder for Dartmouth who left school after three years without a degree. Nontheless in Bob Steele's mid-western eyes he was true Ivy League, a jock and to further enhance his credentials he was a graduate of prestigious Choate Prep School.

His jock bona fides would match up nicely with Hassenfeffer's oldest son and heir, Byron, a three letterman in Lacrosse at Duke and the wannabe jock ad manager Howard Politz.

In their final interview Steele pointedly asked Olcott, "What are your feelings about working with Jewish people? They must be handled carefully, no bruising of egos or ethnic pride. Do you think you can you handle the Fefferco account with the finesse it requires? I'll be honest with you. I was looking for a Jewish account supervisor."

Mike Alcott laughed, "I can out Jew anyone. I know how to order Chinese food. I know that Yom Kippur is not the name of a Japanese Admiral from WW11, and I know Byron Hassenpfeffer played Lacrosse at Duke under my old Manhasset High School Lacrosse coach, Bill Radley who left the high school ranks 6 years ago. He's the guy who turned Jim Brown, the Syracuse University football star into all American lacrosse player."

That fortuitous sports epiphany from Olcott sealed the deal. Bob told him his client counterpart was to be a young, ambitious man named Howard Politz.

From the day Mike Olcott walked into Larry's cork board lined office, he knew he was trouble.

"Bob said I should come over and introduce myself."

He extended a large hand. His hearty collegial tone was a turn off. Georgeena's cousins had that drill down cold. Artful friendliness 101.

"Mike Olcott. I'm the new Account Supervisor on FEFFERCO."

"So I heard. Have a seat."

Larry offered him a Marlboro from the supply in his glass cigarette box. They handled a minor brand of Phillip Morris, nonetheless every executive office of Fremont-Richards was supplied with the Marlboro man's favorite smoke.

He lit up. Larry joined him. It was his sixth of the morning which usually added up to two packs a day. Dr. Koop's health warnings about nicotine fell on deaf ears at Fremont-Richardson.

By quitting time a thin blue cloud cover lingered over the agency's open office space much like the air of Los Angeles midday.

Olcott proceeded to describe how closely we would work together. Although Larry had final say on what creative the client would be shown, Olcott had the right to demur at something he didn't like, in which case the final decision would fall to Bob Steele.

"Do you like Chinese food?' he asked.

"It's okay. Prefer Italian. Why do you ask?"

"Have you met Howie Politz? He prefers to be called Howie by the way."

"No, but Bob says he'll be here at agency tomorrow morning."

"Plan for a Chinese lunch."

"You prefer Chinese?"

He laughed, his nose turned up, "Definitely not, but have you noticed how Jews go for Chinese? Like it was their native chow. Do you think Moses wasn't really Egyptian, maybe Chinese?"

Olcott laughed again. Larry. His inner Jew wept.

"I can handle Chinese," he said.

"You'll be seeing a lot more of Politz so let me brief you on him. He's got a beautiful young wife, can't be over 24. Aggressive little Jewess, makes sure Howie stays close with Byron Hassenfeffer.

She's ambitious and not to be trusted. She's a cock teaser but it's all a phony act to make her wimpy husband seem more macho by having a hot babe in the sack. I bet she's put her money on Howie. Don't even think of making a pass at her. Capeesh."

Capeesh? That seemed incongruous for this big Scotch/ Irish macho man to mouth.

"Yeah, I do. What's he like?"

"He's a weasel. Smart, ass kisser. He plays Byron like a Stradivarius. Wants to be one of the guys. Fancies himself a tennis player. You play?"

"Yeah."

"Any good?"

"Not too bad."

"Good. He wants to set up a regular game with you me and, get this, Byron Hassenfeffer himself. That could be good for us. Hassenfeffer was a star lacrosse guy at Duke and supposedly a pretty good tennis player. Howie says it's gotta be a client versus agency game.

Larry nodded.

"Almost forgot. Have you started the creative on follow-up commercials for SOLDIER BOY?"

"I have."

"Good. See you at Hasenfeffer's new product review tomorrow at 10 in their conference room at the Toy Building on 23rd street."

The industry's Annual Toy Fair was six months away in February. That was the time toy buyers throughout the country helped select the likely winning products to be introduced with the support of National and Regional TV ads following fall.

Separated from Georgeena at the time. The marriage was on shaky ground and the probability of an amicable divorce in New York State was slight. Neither would have opted for dividing his income and assets 50-50. It would have left Larry with a standard of living reduced by one half; casusing a move to Brooklyn or Fort Lee for affordable rent; social life drastically curtailed. Georgeena would need to get a job to survive. A condition he was sure she would not accept. No, at that moment divorce was not an option.

Mike liked what he perceived as Larry's unburdened bachelor life. It stood in stark contrast to his married life in Glen Cove which included the raising of two small children, the daily 3 hour commute, maintaining a 60 year old house, and a wife who, with good reason, continually questioned his fidelity.

Larry believed that Mike Olcott was one of those guys who should never have married. He hated responsibility. He really didn't like kids and his antsy, restless temperament was totally unsuited for the family life style of suburban living. As a result he lived a dual existence, neglectful father and husband in suburbia and unfaithful boyfriend of Hilda Franke a 5' 10" blonde in the city.

Hilda was unaware of her beau's extra curricular sex life outside of her purview. She nurtured the fantasy Mike would leave his wife for her.

Hilda toiled in the secretarial pool of Fremont-Richards, sharing an apartment, with a fellow secetary Cindy Gellhorn who only spent weekends there. Her weekdays were reserved for Walter Johnson, Fremont-Richards Chief Financial Officer, who maintained a pied a terre on Park Avenue far from the prying eyes of Mrs. Walter Johnson of Greenwich, Connecticut.

The living arrangements of the two young women offered Olcott the ideal play time and place. Weekdays, not all of them, usually three out of five, were spent in the privacy of Hilda's apartment. The other two days he free lanced his sexual pursuits. On weekends he could play the father and husband.

Walter Johnson had a parallel arrangement, whereby he went home on week ends as well. Larry knew he had no right to judge Olcott by the hoary biblical standard: "let he who is without sin, throw the first stone." His current position allowed him no stone throwing privileges.

Olcott did teach Larry one thing, however, which two years later he forgot or chose to ignore. In the ad agency world trust no one. His credo was, 'there's always some cocksucker who wants your job and the higher you climb, the more you expose your butt.'

CHAPTER 21

How The Mighty Have Fallen

It was a cool Sunday morning in Mashashimuet Park. Georgeena and Larry had rented a house for the summer in the old whaling town of Sag Harbor. His new job enabled them to trade up to the Hamptons, a welcome change from Fire Island.

They exchanged the little red coaster wagon—appropriate for sand and boardwalks--for the automobile which considerably widened one's social and cultural choices.

One weekend Larry drove to the welcoming tennis facility Mahashimuet Park offered—eight Har Tru courts—a vast improvement from the single cement cracked court in back of the Ocean Beach Catholic Church on Fire Island.

That autumn day the faintest tinge of orange nipped at the leaf tips of the park's ancient oak trees, which were surrounded by thick clusters of coniferous evergreens. An adventuresome gull flew overhead, a mile from the bay off course from the fish morsels left on the docks by fisherman from boats moored in the Sag Harbor marina.

Sunday morning at eight was the usual meeting time for a doubles game consisting of four quite disparate individuals. They included Barney Goldfine, a street smart Irish construction engineer, Sean Conners, and the secretive Ben Werner.

Ben always seemed to have money but no one ever knew what he really did. He always had a big deal pending, but none ever seemed to come to fruition. When questioned about specifics it was too hush, hush to talk about.

He never once revealed a consummated deal. Yet money was always there. He never bought a house in the Hamptons but always talked about doing so. He managed to get last minute bargain rentals in Bridgehampton North of highway #27.

Back then North of #27 said cheapo, where house prices were half those of houses south of the highway. In bar conversations at Bobby Vans, Werner always managed to finesse conversations about the address of his rental house with a snappy response that ended any more talk about its location.

"I'm only three blocks from Bobby Vans," he would say. "to me the bar is always open."

The fact is he shared the rent with one of his revolving girl friends, a different one each summer; sweet youngish career girls who thought they had picked a winner.

Sean Connor grew up in Hell's Kitchen, first in his family to get a college degree. His social skills, though friendly, were a little rough around the edges. It took him six years but he did get a civil engineering dedgree from a respectable school.

He was most at home with the hard hats he supervised on construction jobs.

His socially ambitious wife, Kathleen, steered him to the Hampton's.

The foursome met at a cocktail party and a common infatuation with sports bonded them as a group.

The rules of Mashashimuet tennis required two people to sign up for courts. This particular week Barney and Larry were the designated two.

A soft breeze flavored the air with its salty essence. Larry approached the Masashimuet Park Club House and saw Barney standing on its tiny deck, one foot resting on a green plastic webbed beach chair. Everyone called it a club house which one might envision as a reconfigured colonial mansion. In truth it was a 14' x 20' box whose sole amenity was a drinking fountain.

In addition to minimalist facilities the club had low requirements for membership by Hampton standards. If you could prove summer residence, had $200 and owned acceptable sneakers for Har-Tru courts, you were eligible for member ship from May through September. The social climate was most democratic and collegial, a mix of academics, writers, publishers and a few from the lower end of the communications world food chain, ad men and PR guys.

The entrance bar to Mashashimuet was low enough for even Barney Goldfine to clear. He was going through what he called, "a bad patch." Bad patch my ass, Larry thought. Barney was in debt to everyone including a major printing house which he owed $100,000.

His 1967 Honda Civic was on blocks in a neighbor's garage. He no longer possessed the where with all to pay for automobile insurance. Currently he rented a room, year round from a wee septagenerian lady in the old village part of Bridgehampton.

Long gone were the lush furnished apartments he leased in fashionable East Side Manhattan buildings. No none ever questioned the logic behind his moves from one good building to another about every 2 years.

It turns out that whenever he fell two months behind in rent he quietly folded his tent like some Bedouin nomad, hence his preference for furnished apartments. It was only when his life fell apart completely that friends we were able to ascertain his ability to move so frequently without raising a red flag to real estate brokers. His secret? He gave his friends, including Larry as references. Everyone attested to his worthiness as a prospective tenant, out of loyalty rather than conviction.

Simultaneously, when asked about his previous apartment management for references, he blithely stated he was living with friends and paid them rent. The character references ostensibly satisfied real estate agents.

After losing his publishing job Barney gave up on Manhattan. He piled his earthly possessions into the Honda Civic and sought refuge in Bridgehampton, leaving behind a line of creditors with no forwarding address or assets to attach.

His sole source of income was $850 a month from Social Security and three months severance pay. Unlike Blanche DuBois he depended, not on the kindness of strangers, but that of friends.

The house in which he rented a room was close enough for him to walk the mile distance to the tennis courts each weekend. The group offered him rides but he always insisted the walk was his only real exercise.

"Hey, Barney," Larry called. "Whatcha doing?"

"Fixing my sneakers."

And so he was Larry saw as he reached the deck. Metallic gray duct tape was being swathed around a weary looking Addidas tennis shoe. The worn sole with barely a trace of tread had detached from its upper leather top. The tape enveloped the sole as well as the shoe's body.

Larry declined comment, noting the other sneaker had already undergone its rehab, remained silent not wishing to extract an explanation of why he was repairing ancient tennis shoes in a less than artful manner.

When his foot was comfortably settled in its new jerry built home Larry looked closely at Barney's handiwork. The result was a doleful image of the young boy flutist in Washington's army, which had just crossed the Delaware, feet bound in tightly wrapped gray rags for lack of shoes or boots.

As Barney placed his right foot on the webbed chair again to tighten his laces, Barry Daltrey appeared two racquets cases slung over his well-muscled shoulders. His white shorts were immaculate, freshly starched and pressed. A navy blue polo shirt bore the Ralph Lauren seal of approval, the ubiquitous embroidered polo player, a badge of belonging in the Hamptons.

His white Nike shoes glistened in their newness.

Barry was rich. Newly rich, he recently sold his electronics company for 25 million dollars and immediately bought a 60 foot yacht on which he lived the entire summer with his new wife Lydia. Almost everything about Barry was new. His stately Chris-Craft was moored for the summer in Sag Harbor and wintered in Boca Raton the rest of the year.

"You the sign in guys this week?" he to asked knowing it was 7:45 AM. Why else would we be here at that hour after the usual Saturday night Bacchanal? Larry nodded.

Barney was finishing lacing up the other shoe when Barry looked in his direction and asked, "Why bother with those old shoes? Looks to me like they've really had it." He emphasized the word really. Jesus is that duct tape.?"

Baeney cooly responded, "I like old things. You know like friends, records, girl friends but I really have a thing for old shoes. I know its quirky but aren't we all somewhat quirky."

Had to give him credit for his tart response to money bags Daltrey.

Barry was silent for a minute then muttered something about hitting off the backboards for a while.

About giving Barney credit, Larry already had to the tune of $10,000. Georgeena was pissed at his largesse. She was right about the reality of getting paid back.

The duct tape tennis shoes were a metaphor for his plunge into near poverty. Long gone was the elegant haberdashery of Paul Stuart, the posh men's store just a cut above Brooks Brothers, who introduced the trim cut two button suit favored by President Kennedy to Ivy League graduates who hadn't turned to fat after college. The boxy three button Brooks model nicely hid oversized derrieres and expanding waist lines but never could compete with the cache of Paul Stuart. A trim Barney Goldfine wore the two button suit with distinction. Adding the fillip of color, a paisley print pocket handkerchief, contributed to his fashion credentials. And fashion credentials Barney had in abundance well beyond his ability to fully pay for them. He also abandoned Brooks roll collar button down shirts for a trimmer looking sharp pointed collar style that gave more comfort and accommodated the Windsor knot tie with greater aplomb.

The Goldfine pursuit of elegance in dress and equipment extended to the slopes of Mt. Stowe, Vermont. His appearance on the novice blue marker trails of Mansfield Mountain quietly stated that the quality of his White Star Skis, tailored White Stag parka and pants and Salomon snap buckle boots vastly exceeded that of his ability to execute Christie and stem Christie turns.

The tennis that day of the taped sneakers was good and after the four headed to the Club Bar for post-game libation, spicy bloody Marys, as was their custom. It really wasn't a club. It was a in Sean Connor's living room on Lumber Lane. The padded oak bar was a flea market bargain picked up by Sean's wife, Joanne, who regularly mined the yard sales of affluent Southhampton for discarded treasures.

Three bloody Marys really took the edge off Larry's previous night's intemperance but a jarring phone ring interrupted the collegial gathering. He'd been in the Connor's living room for over an hour. Sean picked it up and just from the timbre of the voice Larry could tell it was Georgeena.

"I've gone," he whispered to Sean.

"Oh yeah, Georgeena, he left about 10 minutes ago. Yeah. Okay. Bye."

Georgeena didn't approve of his déclassé friends. Shanty Irish, a deadbeat Jew and boisterous social climber. Fine friends you pick she would churlishly utter.

She seemed to forget their upward mobile surge led them to sell ther house on Fire Island and rent a place in the village of Sag

Harbor with future plans to buy there. It was a quiet little town the first couple of summers, well before the Wall Street Yuppies dramatically altered its low key setting.

One weekend after tennis Larry drove Barney back to the house in which he rented a room. It was located on a small street in back of the local IGA.

"How are things going at East End Press?" Larry asked."You've been there about three months now."

To supplement his modest income Barney had taken a part time job writing for a small Hampton weekly. As an hourly wage employee he was paid $9 an hour for four hours work Monday through Friday from 1:30 to 5:30. He was expected to lock up the office each day at 5:30. At 3:00 the three part time emplyees and the editor would leave for the day leaving him alone from 3:00 on to do his writing and answer the phone if needed. When he first told about the job Larry was genuinely happy for him. The extra income would definitely improve his life style.

Working 20 hours a week at $9 an hour he'd make $180 a week gross and after taxes take home about $150. An extra $600 a month was almost equal to his sole income from social security. He could even afford to buy new tennis shoes.

Earlier he had mentioned the first month went well. His efforts satisfied his editor, Jeanne Waterhouse. Each afternoon before she left, Waterhouse, would assign stories for Barney to write. The assignments included local obits, sports, church social events, new store openings, celebrity sightings, as well as features like Restaurateur of the Month and local high school happenings.

His response took Larry aback.

"It's over, pal," he said.

"What?"

"That snotty bitch editor Waterhouse fired me. Can you imagine that?"

"What happened?"

"Last Thursday I came into the office at my usual time, 1:30 and she's there sittimg at my desk. 'Goldfine,' she says,'you're fired. Clean out you desk and leave, now.'

"What the fuck," Larry said.

She said, "Listen, Goldfine, you've played your last game of hide and seek with me."

"What do you mean?" I said.

She said,"You know what I mean you sneaky self important ego maniac. I've been watching for a week. This is not a spur of the moment decision. I came back here last Friday at 4:00 to get a book I left in the office. Guess what? The office is locked there's no Barney Goldfine. No not, Nothing. I thought about it over the weekend. Somethings screwy. So Monday afternoon I came back to the office at 3:30. Again there's no Barney Goldfine. No note."

"The woman goes on non-stop," Barney continued. She said, 'This is not kosher. So I come back again on Tuesday and it's the same scenario. No Goldfine.'

"Now this is the kicker," Barney said. She screams at me, 'You son of a bitch I'm paying you to be in the office from 1:30-5:30. What the hell was in your mind? I'm suposed to be paying you when you're not even in the office?'

"I'm quoting her literally, Larry. She has the nerve to dress me down. I did my work. I wrote my assigned stories. When I finished there was nothing left to do so I left early. Big deal."

"But Barney, she's paying you for hours that you're not in the office. You are an hourly employee."

"So what. I did my work."

I chose not to prolong this conversation to nowhere.

A little too cheerfully Larry changed the subject. "Hey Barney, let's go have a pop at Bobby Vans before I drop you off. Okay?"

Chapter 22

Olcott Reveals His True Colors

The presentation for the Hassenfeffer advertising account still resonated in Larry's head. He did it. He had created not just an introductory ad campaign for Soldier Boy but a fully integrated communications plan; advertising, public relations, sales promotion and in store events. The client loved the whole package. And for a fleeting moment he was the man.

Now the hard work began; completing the finished product ; the words and pictures for client approval. Bob Steele gave Larry 72 hours in which to produce tight, full color story boards for the first two commercials to be aired. The meeting was scheduled for the up coming Monday at the client's board room in Brockton, Massachusetts.

He looked at his. It watch it was 7:00 pm. He had just finished crude stick figure drawings for an 18 panel story board. It was the first of two 30 second commercials designed to introduce SOLDIER BOY to millions of age appropriate boys and their mothers over the vast reaches of network TV.

He pinned the story board onto the corkboard wall behind his desk, and stood back a few steps to both assess and admire his handiwork.

Individual frames of the commercial revealed medium close-ups of a square-jawed Anglo-Saxon American fighting machine; SOLDIER BOY a blue eyed young John Wayne ready to attack.

That description only existed in his mind's eye. The close up stick figure bore no resemblance to John Wayne. His vision had to be recreated by a top notch free lance art director willing to work the weekend drawing 36 panels in the transformational colors that pastels offered.

He needed artwork for the two commercials that could convey the mythical magic of SOLDIER BOY to the client; a magic that could ultimately magnetize 12 milion young boys to their rabbit-eared television sets.

The essence of the mission was to create scenarios whereby the 12" warrior could be engaged in combat situations limited only by the imagination of his 6-11 year old owner/manipulator.

The sound of a door opening and slamming shut interrupted his transfixed fantasy.

He turned away from the pinned up story boards and walked to my open doorway to see who else might be in the office at this hour.

As he walked the long corridor of offices he noted almost all were open and unoccupied until he reached the office of Executive VP Jack Duncan. There leafing through Duncan's in box was Mike Olcott. He was reading Duncan's mail. What the hell.

"Hey, Mike what's up?" Larry said as he walked into the office.

Olcott looked like a kid with his hand in the cookie jar; but quickly assumed the tough posture of Mike Hammer, the hard-boiled fictional detective who captivated American males of all ages in the early 1960's.

"Never can accumulate too much knowledge," said with an assured smile.

"For Christ sake you're reading his mail."

"That's very observant of you, Larry," he said. "Watch and you might learn a thing or two about survival in this business. It's amazing how much you can learn from personal memos. Like Jack here is planning to recommend Dale Markel for a promotion to VP and two other guys in the agency but not me and not you. Does that mean we have to work harder or kiss more ass?"

"Can't answer that one, Mike. Now, if you'll excuse me I've got to get back my storyboards for the big meeting on Monday."

"Have you got a good free lancer who'll do the boards this weekend?"

"I have and I figure it will run about $5,000."

He had figured four thousand but if he busted his balls for two days, the extra grand was for him. Marona, the free lancer said he be happy to kick back the thousand.

"$5,000? Got to be kidding. Job is worth at least $7,500; working all weekend."

"What'll Bob Steele say?"

"Nothing. This is the biggest client acquisition since he's been here. Trust me."

Trust me Larry thought. Are you kidding? You who was just sneaking around opening your boss' private mail.

"Here's the deal, Larry. We pay your guy five grand, we split the difference. You work out the pay back with him; $1,250 for you and the same for me. Capeesh?"

Compliantly Larry nodded. Yeah, capeesh my ass, unhappy with Olcott getting, $1,250 off the sweat of his back but on the bright side, an extra $1,250 might be a down payment on any future legal fees. Okay, so I'm a greedy whore, he thought. Join the fraternity, but make a note to yourself, pal, lock your office door when you leave at night.

CHAPTER 23

The Trip To Europe

The decision to visit Europe happened most spontaneously. Paris was a must, as was Rome. It would have been his first trip abroad as well as a first for Georgeena.

One month earlier Georgeena and Larry sat down for breakfast, their first meal together in the past four months.

Larry was running late, ready to leave the apartment for work. No time for a leisurely breakfast at the Tip Toe Inn. Max, the waiter, would have to live without his company for another day.

"Larry," Georgeena said as she entered the living room. He had one arm in a sleeve of his Brooks Brothers topcoat.

"Yes," I said, "I'm in a hurry."

"Larry, would you please sit down with me and talk about us. I beg of you."

There was something in her voice, a plaintive plea for a serious talk. The life they now led, strangers, ships passing in the night—and day—was unsatisfactory. Larry knew it. She knew it. There was no finality in their relationship. To be more accurate there was no relationship at all. How long could two relatively bright people continue their pitiful play acting.

"Please, Larry."

"Okay, I'll call my office and tell them I'll be in later this morning."

It was 8:30. His secretary, Connie, would be in by then. He called and told her to cover for him until 11:00.

Georgeena took his hands, her fingers tightly grasping them. It was a grip that seemed to want a response. He responded with an even tighter grip on her taut fingers. A chill coursed through his body, a tactile mnemonic that he was still in love with this woman.

After releasing her hold, she went into the kitchen returning with two mugs of hot coffee. Georgeena's mug bore a picture of Ingrid Bergman, her perfect profile framed by the broad rimmed hat she wore in the last scene of CASBLANCA.

Humphrey Bogart, trench coat collar pulled in back, adorned Larry's mug. They bought them years before at a Hollywood Memorabilia Store on Broadway.

She raised her mug, leaning forward to click it against his.

"Here's looking at you, kid," she said.

He smiled at her inspired framing of the friendly setting for a serious conversation.

She was wearing jeans and a Sag Harbor sweat shirt, no makeup, haired pulled tight in a pony tail. It was a sharp contrast to the skimpy togs she wore on the few occasions she greeted him on previous mornings.

Her sexless mode foreshadowed the gravity of this meeting.

Georgeena set the tone of civility they both adhered to throughout a three hour conversation. Each owned up to flaws and indiscretions; maybe not all of them but enough to engender honest, thoughtful reflections on the problems in the marriage.

In the end their future status boiled down to one big question. Did they want to try, once more, to try to make the marriage work? She said she still loved him and he avowed his love for her.

They agreed upon a new beginning to begin in Paris.

The flight "across the pond", as the Brits referred to the Atlantic Ocean was a smooth ride that lasted 8 hours. Although it was an overnight flight, first class was a luxury they awarded themselves to ease the path to reconciliation. TWA's dinnerware nicely complemented its excellent French cuisine. Larry chose the boeuf bourguignon while Georgeena opted for the coq au vin. Celery remoulade and country pate preceeded the entrees.

The finishing touch, a bottle of Chateau Neuf Du Pape, heightened the amorous mood of the moment. It was a good beginning of an Odyessey to reclaim the love which had lost its way.

In the after glow of good food and wine, Larry turned off the overthead light. He then folded down the arm rest and wrapped them in a red velour TWA comforter. The next four hours in flight they spent in each others' arms, snuggling, groping but mostly dozing in tranquil embrace.

Hours later light slipped through a partially closed window shade. Larry reached over Georgeena to pull up the shade. Below was the English Channel dotted with ant-sized crafts, scurrying to French ports of call.

His sudden motion interrupted Georgeena's slumber. She rubbed her eyes, smoothed her hair back and yawned loudly.

"Where are we?"

"I see the English Channel. We're only 30 minutes to Paris."

"How can you tell?"

"We're high enough to see England behind us and France straight ahead."

35 minutes later they landed at Orly International Airport bordering Villeneuve le Ro, the airfield used as a Luftwaffe fighter base during WW II. They had booked the Hotel St. James & Albany on the Rive Dwoit, across from the Tuileries Gardens, created by Catherine de Medici in 1564.

The streets were quiet. Traffic was thin. Missing were the anxious horns of impatient French drivers. The skies were gray and the heat of Paris drove thousands from the city to escape its oppressive humidity. Leaving for the month of *Aout* was a Parisian custom Georgeena and Larry were unaware of. It was mid morning.

The plane had landed at 9:00 am. It was now 10:45. The taxi Ride, 13 kilometers from the Hotel, took only 40 minutes. The month of August made travel in the City of Lights much easier for tourists.

Fortunately Larry had changed money at the airport and to handle the transaction with their taxi driver with relative ease.

After the dour faced driver placed four pieces of luggage in the hands of a Hotel porter, Larry slowly counted out the fare of 26 francs. Impatiently, the driver listened to the cadence count of his 1 franc notes. By the time he reached 26, the sweat poured down his red face soiling the collar of his wilted white shirt.

Georgeena could hardly contain herself from laughing. Larry had no intention of humiliating the man. He had asked for 100 francs at the exchange and perversely, he thought, they gave him 100 one franc notes.

"Et pour vous, monsieur ici cinq franc," Larry said. He liked that sound; sank franc. "cinq franc," he repeated as he handed over the money.

Without as much as a merci, the angry driver stalked back to his dust coated Renault.

Built in 1672 during the reign of Louis XIV, the St. James & Albany was furnished in replicas from that era of the Sun King. It was a furniture style of ornately rounded forms and curved lines. Their 9 foot high ceillinged room offered 8 foot windows that opened to face the Tuileries Gardens.

"I was looking in our Fielding Guide and we are just a stones throw from the Tuileries. I thought we might have lunch there. You hungry?"

"Starved."

"So am I." Larry thumbed through Fielding and found a restaurant in the Gardens. "George, I've got it. It's called Café Renard, a quiet restaurant right In the middle of the Tuileries."

Georgeena walked over and kissed him. "Larry, This is going to be a wonderful trip."

Café Renard proved to be an ideal choice for a first meal in Europe, its terrace shaded by overhanging plane trees shielded them from both the sun and the din of Paris.

After lunch they walked, hand in hand, through the Gardens filled with sculptures by Rodin, Maillol, and Henry Moore. They stopped, walked around and marveled at the sensual beauty of Rodin's, THE KISS. Back at the Hotel several hours later, the heat had somewhat abated, leaving the fan cooled room a perfect temperature for their enactment of Rodin's KISS. Unlike the statuary's frozen passion, Larry and Georgeena moved on to a more fulfilling conclusion.

Two showers later they entered the Garden Courtyard of the Hotel to celebrate their first day in Paris. It was well past 6:00 pm.

"Martinis? Or shall we try something French," Larry said.

"When in Rome, do as the Romans do," Georgeena said.

"But we are in France."

She laughed flashing a smile of appreciation when something he said amused her.

"Hemingway liked his absinthe shall we try? My Fielding says it's no longer illegal."

"I'm for that."

Absinthe, a spirit made from wormwood and other herbs, is known throughout western Europe as the *green fairy*. It was the choice of American expats of the roaring 1920's.

As Larry turned to hail a waiter he noticed a blue/ grey haired woman sitting by herself at the table next to them. He smiled as their eyes met. She returned his smile. Handsomely beautiful and smartly turned out. She wore a stylish Chanel suit.

When the waiter arrived with the absinthe, Larry proposed a toast.

"To the beginning of a beautiful friendship, Louie," he said, in his best Humphrey Bogart growl, as he raised his glass to meet that of Georgeena's.

"We've barely started but in my heart I know we'll always have Paris," she said in a quavering voice, tears forming in her eyes.

Midway through the absinthe he said, "You like your green fairy?"

"Not much. Too bitter."

"I agree. Let's just bag 'em. Oh, garcon," he said to a passing waiter. "Deux martinis sans vermouth et tres froid, sil vous plait."

He nodded comprehension of Larry's high school French, producing two see throughs in record time.

The elegant woman at the next table watched in amusement at their rejection of their absinthe drinks.

She turned her perfect patrician profile to them, a majestic nose, classic French; no Hollywood flavor-of-the-month nose.

"I gather you didn't care for absinthe. I don't either. It's an acquired taste I've never acquired."

"You sound American."

"I am. I see by your open guide book you might be looking for a restaurant."

"We are," Georgeena said. "Any suggestions would be welcome. Come join us."

She rose, picking up a handbag of delicately patterned Turkish silk carpeting. It silently shouted "tres cher." She chose a seat between them us, not wanting to favor either Georgeena or Larry, a measure of her easy charm.

As she sat her pear shaped opal ring, clustered with unusually large diamonds, sparkled in the last rays of sunshine that swathed the table Georgeena said, "I am Georgeena Miller and my husband, Larry.

"My name is Lindsey Wolcott. I gather you're looking for good French food, though some may say there is no bad French food."

"That's right, good French food. Nothing touristy. Ambiance is nice but food comes first."

"I have lived here in Paris the past six years since my third husband died. I seem to have little luck in permanent unions. I may be of help in your quest for a restaurant that is the "real McCoy" as they used to say in the states."

"What are you drinking?" Larry asked.

After all these years in France, I am still addicted to martinis, thank you," she said.

"Join the party."

He again beckoned to the white coated waiter. This time he abandoned his schoolboy French. "Three straight up extra dry martinis. With olives. Yes, I know we just ordered two martinis. Now I'm ordering three more,"

Lindsey nodded yes.

The waiter said, "Oui Monsieur, Je comprende."

"Ne-ver can have too many martinis," he said.

Madame Wolcott probably had two so far. This might be her third. She was in the garden courtyard when they entered nearly a half hour ago. They toasted each other upon arrival of the frosted glasses.

Robert Benchley, famous American wit, bon vivant, writer and actor of the 1930's, 40's, and 50's allowed that the correct amount of vermouth in a martini should be "just enough to take away that dreadful watery look."

Chatter during martini number three consisted of the players identifying themselves, mini bios covering origins, careers, favorite foods, books, plays and more. Lindsey Wolcott was main line Philadelphia, Merion to be specific, home to several U.S. Open Golf Tournaments. Its phone directory revealed a surprising number of historic American surnames. Among them were at least four signers of the Declaration of Independence. Wolcott was one of the four.

Her trim figure belied her years, a finely sculpted body displayed her black Chanel suit to best advantage. Its pert, close fitting jacket offered the profile of a full breasted woman. A single strand of white pearls set off the merest glimpse of a white blouse beneath. Her tiny black pillbox hat was made popular by Jacqueline Kennedy.

"There's a place you might enjoy called Laperouse. It overlooks the Seine and the lle de la Cite, no more than a 10 minute taxi ride. Most romantic. And the cuisine ; magnifique," Lindsey said.

Laperouse, a gathering place for many of the 19th century giants of French literature; Zola, de Maupassant, Victor Hugo, had retained its original murals and gilding dating back to 1766.

Goergeena joyfully clapped her hands at the suggestion. "Let's all do it. That is if you wouldn't mind joining us for dinner."

Georgeena always welcomed an opportunity to 'trade up' in friends and Linsey was a social cut above their usual circle.

"I'd like that," Linsey said, directing her assent to me, a look Georgeena could not help noticing.

She forced a smile. He detect a wee bit of jealousy? No. But maybe.

"Waiter, could I have our check?"

The thin waiter appeared with the check, enclosed in one of those discreet leather pads that sheltered the eyes of one's companion from the cost of cocktails consumed.

"I insist on my share," Lindsey said, waving a 100 franc note. -

"No. No," Larry said waving it away.

She reluctantly put the note back in her pocketbook. The taxi ride to Laperouse took about the 10 minutes Lindsey had predicted,

Glistening views of the Seine dominated the restaurant's Velvet Bar. The intimate atmosphere of worn gilt mirrors, aubergine velvet sofas and etched glass windows evoked an image of 18th century opulence.

A boyish French waiter appeared, immediately after they were seated by the maître de, to ask for their cocktail order. He couldn't have been more than 19, but handsome he was.

"We'll have the usual," I absently said.

"Zee us u al, Monsieur? Que est que c'est?

"Je voudrais trois martinis avec olivia, sil vous plait." -

179

"Bien, Monsieur."

Georgeena smiled, "Pretty chatty in French."

"Are we ready for this round?" Lindsey asked.

Georgeena and Larry answered in unison, "naturalment."

Upon the arrival of three frosted cocktails they clinked glasses and swore everlasting friendship. When they finally got around to dinner Puligny-Montrachet was Lindsey's wine choice for the table. It was a distinguished white from Burgundy, she explained, that magically had the power to bring new friends closer together.

After a second glass of Puligny, Larry felt a hand on his inner thigh. It lingered there for a few seconds for his acceptance or rejection. The answer came in a slow rise that headed up his inner thigh. Lindsey caught they drift and the hand remained there, a foreshadowing of things to come.

Lindsey raised her glass with her free left hand while her right hand confidently remained perilously close to his full blown erection.

"To the three of us," she said with a pronounced slur that belied her impeccable diction earlier in the evening. "You know the French are more sexually expansive than we Americans. They have no constraining Puritan ethos to live up to. I discovered that soon after I arrived here to live."

She leaned her head in and whispered," The threesome is a favorite."

"The threesome?" I asked.

Georgeena shot me a look that said, "Dummy, a threesome is three people engaged in sex together. Menage a trois, n'cest pas?"

He nodded sheepishly at them both.

"I'll drink to that," Georgeena said. "A threesome it shall be." She then looked at Larry for some sign of approval.

"A threesome it shall be," He repeated after her.

After dinner Larry had the inspired idea to top off the celebratory dinner with a Stinger, the deadly cocktail of cognac and creme de menthe.

When Stingers arrived he unhesitatingly said in a somewhat louder voice than intended," To a threesome. My first."

Georgeena wholeheartedly joined in with, "To a threesome. My second."

He shot Georgeena a look. Not with me he knew, but face it Larry there was a Georgeena before him.

Lindsey was next. She shakily stood up, raised her glass and said, "To a threesome. I hope it's not my last."

She seemed unsteady as she sat down hard on just a small portion of her chair.

Larry was happy to hear her pronouncement. At least one of them had real experience in a threesome before, someone who knew its protocol and mechanics, although he didn't rule out Georgeena's where with all.

Waiting for the check he tried to visualize the many combinations and configurations of an entwined threesome. Creativity and physical flexibility seemed to be major components of this orgiastic collaboration. Think Kama Sutra for three.

Georgeena sensed the excitement of his anticipation as he did hers; to be expected after the many long months of less than enthusiastic coupling.

A line of taxi cabs awaited as they left the restaurant. The elegant Lindsey, body swaying as she approached the lead car, and caught a heel as she attempted to step into its back seat.

Her splayed figure twisted awkwardly as she fell forward smack against the cobblestone street, head first hitting the abrasive surface. Blood dripped from lacerations on the bridge of her nose—broken probably--and both cheeks. The white collar of her Coco Chanel suit soon was saturated bright red. No sense chasing her pill box hat which flew off several yards away. She muttered something he couldn't understand, as he gently mopped the blood from her nose and chin. Strands of matted gray hair clung to her cheeks.

"We shall get you to a hospital right away," Larry said.

"No. No," she mumbled. "Home please."

Lindsey shed no tears. Her embarrassment and pain were neatly camouflaged by a fierce pride, enabling her to maintain a semblance of wobbly dignity. They left her at the elevator of the St. James & Albany to quietly retreat to her quarters before the ravages of two black eyes and two chipped front teeth would soon appear in the privacy of her own bathroom mirror.

The threesome had been reduced to a twosome. They never spoke of Linsey again.

The next two weeks of travel through France afforded them every sensory experience, which they shared with child like glee.

The tastes of the huitres from Arcachon at Pharamond, tarte tatin of Normandy, Bouillabaisse in Marseille, terrine of fois gras in the Dordogne.

The smells. The heavenly aromas; a fresh croissant, steaming café au lait, a warm baguette, the salt air on the beaches of Couleur, the rose garden in the Bois de Boulogne, grilled sardine on the beaches of Hendaye.

The sights. Visual overload; Picasso, Matisse, Monet, Manet, Toulouse Lautrec, Renoir, Maillol, Versailles, Giverny, the Rodin Museum and on and on and on.

The sounds. Mostly pleasing; a chanteuse singing in a Pigalle night club, the lapping waves in the harbor of Honfleur, the sizzle of crepe stands along the Rue Muffetard, the screeching and flapping of sea gulls circling Mont St. Michel, the impatient horns of the taxis of Paris at rush hour.

It was difficult leaving France, but particularly Paris and the shared happy memories would remain with them long after they went their separate ways.

Rome was the next stop on the mission of reconciliation, which thus far had been an unqualified success. They arrived at the crowded Rome Airport via Air France on a sweltering late August afternoon. Their plane, a X64 Mirage designed for short runway takeoffs and landings, accommodated a small complement of passengers; no more than 80.

Its steep ascents and descents were terrifying to Larry and several other white knuckle passengers, but not to Georgeena who teasingly chided his discomfort and that of nearby passengers. Georgeena seemed to have little sense of consequence never experiencing even the remote possibility of disaster.

Ultimately the aircraft pulled out of its steep dive and found companionable contact with the sweating black tarmac. The end game of a safe landing did nothing to assuage the immediate needs of many passengers who quickly sought out the nearest bath rooms to tidy up the consequences of their fear of flying.

Georgeena and Larry made it through the baggage claim area without incident though neither spoke a word of Italian.

Everywhere one looked dark wet patches stained the under arm areas of men and women alike, offered visual evidence of the stifling humidity of Rome.

Before checking into the Hotel De Ville, at the head of the Spanish steps, they needed to stop at the American Express Office just a few paces away from the base of the steps. They needed to cash some American Express traveler's checks in exchange for lira.

They entered the dark minimalist AMEX office which needed a paint job. Broken blisters of ecru colored paint dotted the four barren walls. An unpleasant aura of human presence hung in the air.

Five attractive young Italian women manned the office, each sitting at separate desks equipped with new looking Olivetti typewriters. The heavy aura proved to be body odor. Under arm deodorants were a relatively unknown commodity in Italy at the time.

Larry stopped at the nearest desk and requested 250 dollars worth of Italian Lira. There he signed his travelers checks, pocketing a thick wad of lira made bulkier by the size of each bill; nearly twice that of an American dollar.

Before they left Larry called the Hotel which sent a bellboy to schlepp two oversized Samsonite bags up the daunting 80 stair ascent to the Hotel. Unburdened by luggage they quickly reached the summit, just a few yards from a red-coated doorman who stood under a green canvas awning. It bore a cursive scrawl which read Hotel de Ville. They stopped, looked at each other and burst out laughing. No need to explain.

Telltale wet patches revealed their initiation into the Underarm Fraternity of Rome.

Hotel de Ville's Fielding Guide praise had not been overstated. An assortment of spa like emollients: conditioners, fresheners, oils, soaps and shampoos stood at attention on the grey speckled granite counter top of the the outsized marble bathroom. There was a discreet alcove for the bidet, filigreed gold faucets and adjoining glass enclosed showers. The deep green marble tub could accommodate the entire Trapp family.

Two plush terry cloth robes hung in a cedar scented closet that was large enough to accommodate a desk and chair. The individual showers allowed them to view each other's every motion through the clear glass partition which separated them. Georgeena's body, toned and tan, was still that of a lean college cheer leader, although she would be horrified at his choice of analogy.

In Georgeena's eyes cheer leading, bridge, God forbid--Ma Jong, and professional team sports, were middlebrow pleasures of the unsophisticated. One who had the audacity to call food 'tasty' would quickly drop to her C list of pariahs.

As she donned her hefty terry cloth robe, he again admired the body which had given him so much pleasure and grief. She noticed his silent appraisal and smiled, knowing the trip was continuing to be successful.

She let the robe drop and stood watching his naked body respond. She made the first move toward the bed, pulling back its plump duvet, crawling underneath it with only her face from the nose up in view. Larry needed no further invitation.

They coupled with genuine pleasure, no rote expression of marital duty. The intensity was a throwback to their courtship, if one could call it that, eight years earlier. Larry was aware that

Georgeena shared this magical ignition of passion. Exhausted, they languished for an hour on the plumped up four poster bed, luxuriating in the 600 thread percale sheets that enclosed them. Sleep came, after a shared bottle of Pellagrino water.

Breakfast the next morning arrived promptly at 11:00. Two trays were wheeled in and left bedside for their choosing.

"That looks like a French brioche" Georgeena said, resting a four-legged tray on her lap, her lower body still covered in percale.

"The Italians do have a comparable roll. Don't know what they call it," Larry said. Umm, gorgonzola, berries, melon and my god, fresh apricots. Don't see those too often at home."

He poured crèam in the dark brown espresso, a color never seen in a cup of Chock Full O Nuts. When finished, Larry threw off the covers to admire her body. That can wait she said knowing solo showers were next on the agenda. Bathing together might expend too much energy needed for the full day's tour she had planned.

This was a clue to her seldom revealed practical side which had them programmed to absorb all that Italy had to offer first time visitors.

A six hour whirlwind of visits included the coliseum, ruins of the Roman Senate, and gardens of the Villa d' Este. The day culminated with an ice cold strawberry gelato from a little shop facing the historic Trevi Fountain originally designed by Gian Lorenzo Bernini in 1632.

Exploration of the Vatican's multitude of art treasures would be saved for another day. Melted rivulets of red gelato ran down Larry's fingers as they stepped into the cramped back seat of an unbearably hot Italian taxi.

After a quick shower, refreshed and ready for adventure, they headed for the Hotel's luxurious Emperor's Terrace Cocktail lounge of the Hotel. There Georgeena shared the Guide Book, in search of a festive yet authentically native restaurant for their first dinner in Italy.

A bed of violets lining one side of the restaurant's terrace filled the night with a hint of nature's perfume. Two small finches flitted from hedge to hedge, carefully avoiding the 10 Terrace tables occupied by smartly dressed couples. After two martinis they agreed upon a restaurant just across the Tiber, called Il Boccachio.

It proved to be a great choice. The veal piccata was splendid and Georgeena raved about the spaghetti alle vongole. The waiter's recommendation of Barola, a red Piedmont wine made from the nebbiolo grape, was pricey but, brilliant.

Wordlessly they held hands the entire trip back the Hotel, sated, a bit tipsy but clearly in love.

Larry's assessment of the remainder of their time in Italy was a delicious conflation of aesthetic, intellectual and earthy pleasures. In Florence it was the treasures of the Ufitzi, Ghiberti's doors on St. John's Chapel, Michelangelo's David and haggling on the Ponte Vecchio.

Sienna and Perugia meant a savoring of the hearty hill country cuisine and agonizingly electric sex on the region's copper hued hillsides and in the earthen rows of vineyards whose lush fruit was almost ready to be picked.

Abandoned they were, like children at play, exploring and discovering exciting new adventures and attitudes. Tomorrow never once ever entered their heads.

At the outset of the journey both were apprehensive about spending three weeks together, in unknown territory, considering the fragile state of their marriage. He wondered if the worldly charms of France and Italy were enough to ignite a lost sense of trust and passion. Did a mutual interest in the history, culture, and architecture of the European experience bind them closer? Did it help erase the hurts and cruelties of the past? Or at least shove them into a lock box of untouchable memories?

Looking back, Larry savored the fact that they had demolished a wall between them if only for a few weeks. The time together alone, affirmed most of the things that brought them together in the first place.

On the surface they were a most unlikely matrix for marital success. A middle class young man trying to cope with the confines of Mid-Western Jewish insularity and the ultimate WASP, whose fourth generation Lutheran family produced judges, Federal Reserve Bankers, novelists and marching in the street advocates of women's rights, before women had the right to vote.

That which they truly shared was a woven fabric they uniquely created. Unfortunately, such fabrics wear out, unable to stand the test of time.

Their relationship hinged on four critical intersecting points of view.

Point One: LAUGHTER—Viewing the ridiculousness of life with humor rather than despair or sadness.

Point Two: READING --The sheer joy of reading for pleasure, information, story line, satire, historical relevance.

Point Three: MONEY—Enjoy the things it can open doors to, but making it an overriding need for power, prestige and superfluous material goods, NIX. Point Four: SEX—There's no such thing as too much sex.

To the conventional mind the above four don't amount to much. Traditional mating in the late fifties centered on marriage, procreation, and being an active part of a community, be it church, school or charity. Unfortunately that narrow focus made people like Larry and Georgeena life long outsiders.

Tragically the blissful bonding In Europe was broken less than one year later.

CHAPTER 24

Georgeena Leaves Her Mark

Since their return from Europe the marriage underwent an exciting transformation. Georgeena would often surprise Larry with an unannounced visit to his office on the 28th floor of the Pan Am Building. It became her way of initiating a lunch date with him.

It was imposible to stay mad at George. All thoughts of divorce quickly disappeared in the thrall of her playful wit and artful seductiveness.

"Hi, it's me," she said standing in the doorway of his office while he assessed story boards push pinned to a wall of coffee colored cork board. He was looking at a pair of new commercials for SOLDIER BOY.

On his desk lay a pile of crumpled layout sheets, failed sketches of the little doll in action; rejects, ideas that didn't make his cut.

He kept staring at the story boards that tentatively met with his approval.

"The little fucker is giving me a hard time," He said, holding up a naked SOLDIER BOY figure.

"Look. He's not even anatomically correct," Georgeena said. "Do you want thousands of little boys to grow up thinking soldiers have no balls?"

"Does Barbie have a vagina?"

Playfully she lifted her skirt up revealing an anatomically correct woman wearing no panties.

"This give you any inspiration?" she said.

"Yeah, but not the kind I need at the moment." "No lunch?" she said with a twisted moue of disappointment.

"Only if we order up. I've got a deadline."

"No need to call. I'll run up to the Sky Top and grab us a couple of burgers and bloody Mary's. Sound good?"

"Yes, it does and hurry back."

Half an hour later Georgeena reappeared with the best burgers in town and two bloody Mary's in paper cups she had filched from the agency coffee stand.

"You are a foxy one? How'd you sneak those bloodys out of the bar?"

"Personal charm," she said in her most kittenish manner.

He thought better of asking if she had offered to lift her skirt to ensure safe exit with her contraband.

Lunch together was agreeable. Greedily they scarfed down the burgers slathered in melted blue cheese. Georgeena was at her best, playful, funny and inexorably sexy. She deliberately positioned her chair a feet away from his desk, directly facing his line of view. "Here's to your next campaign for the little military eunuch," she said raising the last of her bloody Mary.

"He pays the rent," he, said knowing she knew her freedom from the burdens of a job, were directly attributable to the 12" doll he worked for.

She kissed him lightly as she departed for whatever activity was planned for that afternoon. He never asked about her comings and goings. Jealousy was never to be a part of their new marital equation.

The presentation to Bob and Mike and Howie went well. They liked his D-Day landing, a scenario he wove into 30 seconds of a fully equipped SOLDIER BOY in action. He, along with his buddies, had the requisite battle gear and equipment; scaling ladders, hand grenades, combat boots, M-1 rifles, gas masks, rain ponchos, trench shovels, flame throwers, bazookas and, of course, their basic battle fatigues.

Another less demanding TV, spot pinned on the conference room cork board, featured heroic warriors decked out in wet suits and diving equipment aboard an recent addition to the SOLDIER BOY line, the sea sled. This impressive water vehicle could propel it occupants at impressive speeds in swimming pools or lakes.

"Good job all around," Howie said. "Ought to consider shooting them in London."

Bob and Larry exchanged puzzled looks which indicated 'we'll talk about this bomb shell of an idea from Howie later.'

Olcott always quick to strike a note of collegiality said, "Hey guys, why don't we talk about London over drinks at the Bull & Bear."

Bob Steele nodded his approval.

"Okay," Larry said, "but only one pop for me. George got us theater tickets for tonight. I don't want to fall asleep on Julie Andrews." He lied rather convincingly. It wasn't for Julie Andrews he wanted to stay awake for this night.

After they ordered a double scotch for Olcott, a beer for Howie and Larry's usual martini, the discussion began. Bob Steele left early for a corporate management meeting that evening.

"I've been talking to Byron about London and he seems to think it's a good idea," Howie began. "Here's the deal."

He outlined a plan whereby they would shoot 6 or 7 commercials in London. They would to be previewed at the TOY FAIR in February when major toy manufacturers gathered to display their new lines to all the top retailers in the America.

Toy Fair was four days of wining and dining buyers and revealing the TV support retailers needed to maximize holiday sales, those 45 days before Christmas. That short period of time represented 65% of yearly sales volume for both toy manufacturers and retailers.

Larry worried about being out of the country for a couple of weeks. George and he were now in a good place. The marriage was gaining strength but it needed nurturing. He didn't want to interrupt the progress they were making. Forever the optimist, he thought the marriage, though fragile, might be viable again.

The shoot might take four weeks, too long to be away from Georgeena. They both were still needy and a break, considering the progress made since Europe, might be damaging to that progress. It could seriously interrupt the new closeness they both were feeling.

Howie's mind was made up. He was eager for a little out of town action. Larry knew he could handle Howie but wasn't sure he could stomach four weeks of Olcott; work, lunch and dinner. Ugh.

Commercial shooting overseas by American agencies had been a neat little windfall for a client's bottom line. You didn't have to pay residuals to the actors in Europe. SAG and AFTRA, the actors unions for movies, radio and television required the talent be paid a shooting fee for each day of work on the set plus a residual payment when a commercial was aired in which one appeared. An actor was entitled to receive a payment each time he or she appeared on screen.

The amount of a residual payment was based on the size of the viewing audience. For example: In 1970 a commercial running on the ED SULLIVAN SHOW in prime time would have as many as 30 million viewers. A commercial run on a daytime soap might have 8 million viewers. The SULLIVAN show residual would, of course, be considerably higher than the one from the soap opera.

In Europe each actor received a one-time payment for his or her performance in a TV commercial. It was called a buyout. At the time Larry would be shooting the amount of a one-time payment ranged from $100 to $200 a day. The result of the overseas loophole meant a less costly commercial.

Howie's cost conscious mind had figured they would need at least 4 actors per commercial. Shooting 8 commercials, paying 32 actors about a $125 a day would cost $4,000. In the US the cost per day would have been $375 a day or $11,900. A 10 million dollar ad campaign could cost the client another $50,000 for talent residual payments.

In addition cinematographers, art directors, carpenters, lighting designers, editors, sound directors, prop people, dressers and makeup artists would be paid less than half of that which their counterparts in America would receive.

A commercial shot in the U.S. costing $16,000, would cost half if produced in London. HEFFERCO stood to save $64,000 by choosing eight commercials in England.

As to personnel traveling to London Larry, Olcott, Howie and a professional director, Hal Weitz. No matter how they might indulge themselves with generous expense accounts the cost would be a pittance relative to the savings of the shoot.

"Howie," Olcott added, "The agency has already sent crews to shoot commercials in London and it was a slam dunk."

"Case closed," Howie said. "We will plan to leave the second week of October."

When Larry returned to the apartment around 10:00. Gerge was sipping a glass of wine, her other hand occupied by J.D. Salinger's only collection of short stories, called NINE. It was a brilliant dissection of his dysfunctional fictional Glass family.

She acknowledged him with the faint wave of a hand after setting down her half filled goblet. Her freed hand pulled down a corner of her shortie, to divert attention from the fact that there was nothing underneath its skimpy folds.

"Gonna take a quick shower," he said.

Don't dawdle."

He didn't' and in minutes they were entwined in a grip which, for the moment, securely held the bonds of their marriage.

When Larry arrived at the office next morning, all members of the steno pool clustered around the Xerox machine. The Xerox desk top plain paper copier, first introduced in 1963, was still an office phenomenon. Before its introduction carbon copies and mimeograph machines were the standard means of replicating copies of originals, a time consuming process.

Fremont-Richards got its first machine at that time, the Xerox 813, which was marveled for its ease of use and sharpness of reproduction.

People gathered around the X813, which had lost most of its magic in the two years since installed. Now interest in the machine was renewed. Above it a 9"x12" black and white reproduction hung, in sharp detail, it revealed the unmistakable portrait of a women's vagina. Yes, but whose was in everybody's mind? Subject matter suppressed any verbal speculation by the mostly under 30 secretaries, at least in ear shot of the gathered crowd.

Who was the audacious model? The question which dominated every conversation the rest of the working day, from office boy to Bob Steele.

After a good laugh Bob thought the perpetrator had to be unmasked. A poor choice of images. "Revealed", an obvious alternate designation, also had a prurient cast to it.

"Bob," Larry suggested, at a hurried meeting in the conference room, "We can't invoke the honor system. No one in her right mind would claim ownership of that private close up. Or I should say close up of privates. Forget that as an option. It also would be impolitic and logistically impossible to ask each female in the organization to: 1. take off her panties 2. Climb onto the Xerox machine 3. Push the print button and 4. Hand in a copy of her privates with her name attached to the document."

"Let me give it some thought," he harrumphed. He was angry, embarrassed and actually shocked; an offense to his puritanical ethos. Privately he knew it was a no win situation. Let a little time heal the problem and it will quietly go away.

In the meantime Bob left the offending Georgia O'Keefe flower look alike posted for a while. Never know who might be foolish enough to show up.

The reproduction remained posted for a week. No responses, though some wag made the vertical vagina a horizontal one which now seemed to be smiling. Bob's secretary finally pulled it off the wall, destroying what all thought was its only copy, not aware that Mike Olcott had made a copy of the copy for his own files. Why? No one bothered to ask. Too kinky to ponder.

Two weeks later George and Larry had a lunch date. She picked him up and they had a 2 and 2 lunch at the Bull & Bear. Where else? She sealed the lid on a most agreeable get together with a display of two tickets to GYPSY given to her by a dancer from her chorus boy coterie in their Fire Island days. Georgeena periodically held reunion parties for the Peggy Fears Hulley Gulley dancers.

The "Hulley Gulley" was a line dance of 12 to 15 gay men who unleashed their closeted weekday life each weekend, a defiant expression of freedom from homophobic Manhattan; their sweating bodies rhythmically gyrating in sync to the music.

In the 60's Georgeena was known as a "Fag Hag." This politically incorrect designation was a term of approbation back then.

Larry generally begged off appearance at the reunions, employing the obligatory client dinner excuse which both knew was a fiction. Yet she appreciated his lack of enthusiasm for being the only straight guy among a gaggle of gays.

George walked Larry back to his office at around 3:00pm. She asked if she could take a pad of layout paper, something she was cooking up for a party and left shortly after. One half hour later he heard a whooping reprise of the vagina picture incident. A crowd once more gathered around the machine. he joined them and quickly saw the cause of the furor was a posted copy of a life size vagina above the Xerox machine.

"It's probably just a copy of the original," one girl said.

"No," Mike Olcott boomed. "I have the original and it never left my hands."

A Freudian slip if ever I heard one. Wonder what else he had in his hand.

Olcott returned with the original and tacked it up on the wall next to the newest addition to the Fremont-Richards female organ collection.

Bingo. A perfect match.

Quickly calculating the date of an earlier in house lunch date with Georgeena, Larry had no trouble identifying the model for this erotic piece of art on display. It was an image he had viewed, up close, many times over the past seven years.

CHAPTER 25

The Mr. And Mrs. Game

Zeke and Jenny, Georgeena's cousin and her husband, arrived for a visit the week before Larry was scheduled to go to London to shoot Heffreco's new commercials. Zeke was a historian and Jenny an award winning journalist.

After an enthusiastic rehash of their European trip over dinner which included Barney Goldfine and his lady, Rosemary, everyone settled down in the living room for an evening of parlor games.

Zeke and Jenny were fun to be with, outrageous gamesters and punners. One of the zaniest word games they created the previous summer was introduced to the family when Geoegeena and Larry visited her mother Harriet in Minneapolis.

They called their outrageous game MR & MRS. It was the game they chose to play that evening.

The rules were simple but creativity was key to the witticism strived for. There were no real winners but the extent of applause and kudos from fellow players unofficially designated the evening's eventual winner.

An example of the game could be explained quickly without a need to analyze its structure.

EXAMPLE:

Larry created the following: Mr. and Mrs. De fois gras and their daughter Patty.

Got it?

It was that evening's game at which he first introduced his French oriented Mr. & Mrs, which almost everyone thought very original.

Jenny held her nose after his French Mr. & Mrs. *mots jus* but admitted later the French twist on the game was original and funny. If one was not into puns, the game was not just boring but stupid.

Jenny followed Larry with 'Mr. and Mrs, Derdoil and their son Stan.' Get it ?

Standard Oil.

This time Larry held, his nose and responded with another Frenchism, even though it was not his turn.

The game was designed for those who exercised their most absurdist creativity along with a sufficient number of cocktails. It never started before each contestant had consumed 3 martinis and continued with consumption of wine throughout the evening's play.

"At least that's wittier than your out of turn, Mr. and Mrs. de Fois Gras and their daughter Patty." Jenny continued.

"Okay, okay children don't fight," Georgeena said. "Barney you're next, Larry took an extra turn. Go."

Barney was not too swift at word games, particularly spontaneous punning. For a Phi Beta Kappa recipient he had the most undisciplined approach to life, a dreamer, a manana guy with a flexible moral compass. Actually no moral compass Larry would find out much later.

He was in the city, temporarily living with Rosemary, a matter of expediency rather than romance. Generous Rosemary pitied his plight and offered him a place to temporarily live during his "bad patch" of financial luck. Her offer was premised on his promise to seriously start looking for a job again. And against all advice from friends, "loaned" him $2,000.

They were no longer lovers.

"Let's see," Barney said tentatively, stalling for more time.

The rest of the group were thinking ahead to have a dandy MR and MRS ready when their turn came around.

One might blame Barney's stalling on the quantity of Beefeater Gin he had consumed during and after dinner. It was 86.6% proof, nearly 10% higher proof than most American gins.

But then they all had consumed equal quantities of alcohol.

Barney a little unsteadily came up with, "How about Mr. and Mrs. Parmigiana and their son Veal."

A chorus of boos and hisses followed Barney's pathetic attempt.

"For Christ sake, Barney, you're missing the point of the game," Jenny said reproachfully.

"Where's the pun? No pun no fun." Zeke chimed in.'

Quick to step in to the breach, before Barney was stripped clean by the circling intellectual piranhas, Larry volunteered, "In the French vein I give you Mr. & Mrs. De Seigneur and their son Dwight"

The boos turned to whistles and clapping from Jenny, Zeke and Georgeena. Barney looked on dazed and unhappy but glad to be off the hook.

Quietly during the shouting, Rosemary had nodded off, into the arms of Morpheus, splayed on the carpet next to a lamp which exuded a comforting warmth.

Barney still looked puzzled while Jenny leaped up and shouted, "Mr. and Mrs. Ordinairre and their son Van."

Those still awake whooped and whistled in appreciation while Jenny collapsed on the floor next to Rosemary. Her last sober breath uttered, 'Van.'

The remaining players played on for another 30 minutes until the big hand on the Feline Faced kitchen clock had a little paw on 1 and an extended paw on the 4. Twenty past one.

Zeke got up unfolding his six foot four inch body and announced, "I have an American Heritage breakfast meeting in the

Hotel at 8:00. Let Jenny sleep over. She'll be okay. I'll call late in the morning. Okay? Thanks for everything and Larry, your French addition to the game added a nice international flavor. Next time we should explore Russian Mr. & Mrs."

He kissed Georgeena on both cheeks, nodded at half dozing Barney and left.

"Should I wake them?' Larry said to Georgeena.

"No need to, let 'em sleep it off. Come on lover the evening's young,"she slurred.

Needing no further invitation, he, stripped off all his clothing, did a quick brush of the teeth and returned to their bedroom.

Georgeena was sound asleep, making odd breathing noises, several octgaves lower than a whistling tea ot, while clutching a large Morroccan pillow to her bosom.

Slipping on a t-shirt and shorts Larry returned to the living room for the book he was reading, Betty Freidan's The Femine Mystique. He felt a need to catch up on the nascent feminist movement which affected every male in America, like it or not.

Rosemary seemed sound asleep, snoring loudly, still huddled in her private corner.

Jenny semi-curled in a fetal position, obviously, unaware her dress had risen up to her pink panty line. Nice legs he thought.

Barney, legs spread out the love seat, looked comfortable. Six empty bottles of wine and a dead liter of gin gave evidence that the group had sunk below the plimsole line of sobriety.

Clutching his book he returned to the bedroom. A reading lamp next to a floral covered chair would suffice until he felt the need for sleep. His capacity to consume alcohol had increased markedly in the past few months.

Georgeena was asleep. She had pulled the covers up too far, fully covering her upper body but leaving her bottom exposed. It was hard to tell whether her bare butt was an invitation or just an accident of fatigue.

His watch said he had read for almost an hour. It was 2:05. Maybe a little scotch would do it. Once more he entered the living room heading for the liquor cabinet. The light from a small standing lamp offered enough light to give one a clear view of the three guests Rosemary hadn't moved an inch, still emanating funny sounds from her nose and mouth. To his left, next to an unlit floor lamp, was Barney on top of Jenny who, eyes closed, was completely out of it.

There he was fucking a sleeping drunk.

"Hey," Larry yelled, "get off of her you clod."

He looked up meekly and dismounted his prey.

"Put on your pants and get the fuck out of here," Larry said.

"But what about Rosemary?"

"I'll stick her in a cab in the morning you necrophiliac creep."

"She's not dead, Larry."

"Get out."

He grabbed his jacket and shoes, shirt tails out and sockless as he slammed the door on departing.

Larry locked the door and returned to the kitchen for a pour of Johnny Walker Red. Georgeena appeared in the bedroom doorway.

"Somebody new come in?"

"No," he said, "somebody totally fucked up just left."

"Whatcha doing?"

"Having a drink. Can't sleep."

"I have a better sleep remedy."

CHAPTER 26

The Break Up

On November 10th Olcott, Politz, Dietz and Larry flew to London. 20 years after WW ll the Brits retained a distinct cultural life style still quite different from that in America. The world had yet to become globalized where middle class people aspired to the same material things and shared the same musical tastes.

Nothing in New York compared to London's Carnaby Street's style incursion into the daily life of those under 35. It influence was everwhere; skinny legged men's trousers, Beatle-like hair styles, mini skirts that defied any sense of propriety, ubiquitous white leather boots—their tassels flying to the Rock beat of the moment. Laughter was everywhere; its contagion beginning to rock the establishment. And above it all there were the young—freed by the pill, distrusting anyone over the age of 30. At the age of 35 Larry knew he fell into the category of those in whom not to place any faith.

The production plan was to utilize local talent ; the actors, cameramen, and all members of the production crew.

The TV spots were shot at Shepperton Studios, the production venue of England's knighted film producer, Sir Alexander Korda. Working on a studio lot next to famed Carol Reed, who was directing the musical, OLIVER, was a heady experience. Larry was able to hire an art director from Stanley Kubrick's film, A SPACE ODYSSEY which had just finished its post production.

In the studio commissary he met one of the stars of OLIVER, Hugh Griffith, the actor whose portrayal of Falstaff in Henry 1V was considered the gold standard for that role.

On weekends the unlikely bedfellows Olcott, Miller and Politz often explored the hot spots of London. There was Annabelles, the IN PLACE in the late 60's on Berkley Square and the Mayfair Hotel Casino where they spotted the likes of Anthony Armstrong Jones and his wife Princess Margaret, the iconic model, Twiggy and fashion designer, Mary Quant.

During the week 12 hour days left Larry ordering up dinner most nights at the Westbury Hotel. Standing all day in the dank studio left him weary and lonely with little motivation to explore London on workday nights. But mostly he missed Georgeena.

The first three weeks he talked to Georgeena every night. She too was lonely, missing him and the warmth of their new found relationship. He would tell her about the details of the shoot. Setting up the individual shots. Making sure the actors were dressed properly, spoke their lines without a British accent and made up to reflect the look of the story board's direction. He complained about temperamental kid actors and their pushy mothers; enduring the maddening mid-morning breaks for bangers and mash by the entire crew and their rush to the nearest pub for a couple of pints at lunch.

She listened with interest and wished he'd get home soon. Only one more week he told her and also about his erotic dreams of her every single night since he left.

The last week, in post production, was a ball breaker. He worked with film and sound editors from 8:00am to 8:00pm, leaving him exhausted when he got back to the Hotel; barely energy enough for a beer and a burger in bed.

Later on reflection he realized he had called Georgeena but once that week before returning to New York.

The London night life shared with Olcott and Politz, did nothing to foster any personal closeness. Working together professionally did not guarantee a personal relationship. A wall between him and his co-workers. Olcott was a dick and Howie was an imperious kiss-ass.

On the plus side, upon reviewing the rough cuts of the commercials, they agreed the end product was very good.

At 11:00 pm, December 10th they returned to the United States, landing at JFK. After luggage retrieval, the hassle of customs and getting a taxi, Larry finally made it back to 430 West End Avenue at 3:00 am.

He chose to bunk out on the oversized sofa in the living room because Georgeena was asleep. With the smell of stale cigarette smoke hanging in the air Larry dropped into his bed for the night. He slept until 10:00 the next morning. Georgeena had already left the apartment. Where to? He hadn't the foggiest. While making coffee in the kitchen he spotted two familiar empty bottles in the mesh covered trash bin, Hanky Bannister Scotch and Lloyd's Gin. Curious, they traded up from those downscale brands at least three years earlier.

The New York Times, which Georgeena left on the kitchen counter was folded to the employment ads. While waiting for Mr. Coffee to complete its slow drip task, he turned to the front page bearing a headline: McNAMARA DEPLOYS 75,000 ADDITIONAL TROOPS TO VIETNAM. The news didn't warm Larry's heart nor did his discovery in the living room.

He settled into the leather chair facing the table upon which he. was about to set his coffee mug. A sliver of light that bounced off a gleaming object caught his eye. It was an 18K gold Dunhill lighter. It looked familiar and it was.

Its three onyx letters were ones he was quite familiar with. He'd seen them many times, over the past couple of years, on the cuffs of custom made shirts owned by Barney Maurice Goldfine. The raised letters, BMG, seemed to stare at him.

When Georgeena returned to the apartment that afternoon, he sat her down for a little talk. He didn't ask where she'd been. He didn't want to know.

They talked about the Dunhill lighter, the Lloyd's Gin bottles, and Barney Maurice Goldfine. Voices were not raised because he did most of the listening. He listened until he wanted to hear no more.

Larry left, without goodbye or see ya later, for a long walk around Central Park.

He must have walked a couple of miles before winding up at the Edison Hotel on 46th street where he checked in for the night.

The next morning Larry returned to the apartment around 10:00 am. Georgeena was sitting at the breakfast counter drinking coffee and poring over the employment section.

Without looking up she said, "You back?"

"No, Georgeena, I'm not. I'm out of here kiddo. No more bullshit. No more lying," he said.

"I haven't lied," she said. "You should talk to me about lying."

"I lied to you twice in 10 years," Larry said, "I admitted those to you a long time ago. It's true I didn't tell you about Alex Monheim' advice not to marry you. I lied because I didn't want to hurt you. I loved you. Does that make me a bad person? And it's also true I didn't answer truthfully if I had ever slept with Sheila Monahan. That was not a defensible lie but its motivation was. I didn't want to hurt you because I still loved you. As for any other dalliances you may have had, I never inquired until now."

"But you did lie and I didn't. You asked and I told you."

"Yes, I asked and you told me, when I found a gold Dunhill lighter with the initials BMG on my night table yesterday morning after an 8 hour flight from London. I'm was tired, confused and curious. I asked you what in hell is Barney Goldfine's lighter doing on my night table? You said he spent the night."

"To be more accurate I said, 'we had sex and he spent the night here.'

"I asked you and you told me you slept with Barney Greenfield, a guy I thought was a friend, while I was off shooting commercials in London."

"But I didn't lie to you."

She hadn't, but then, from his point of view, honesty was one of her only remaining virtues. Providing good sex was not a virtue. Her goofy sense of humor was not a virtue. They're just pleasing physical and personality attributes.

He assessed a 10 year relationship now stripped clean of any romantic illusions. It was a time to cut bait.

"You know, George, I honestly wish you had lied. I've lost you, someone I loved you in spite of all the shit we've given each other. Losing that fucking snake in the grass, Barney Goldfine, as a friend isn't much of a loss.

I'm over. Gonna move out this weekend. Adultery is the only basis for an uncontested divorce in New York State but I can't prove you committed adultery. It's a matter of he said she said and no court would accept an unprovable act as the basis for divorce.

And I don't believe it would be in your best interest to admit the perfidious act. As for me, I am starting the process immediately ?"

"Is monogamy the end all of marriage?" she asked.

"No, George, but fucking a friend is a deal breaker."

"It takes two to tango."

"Yeah, but I'm not married to Barney Goldfine. I'm angry and I'm hurt and I don't have to ever see him again except in court. The shmuck still owes me $10,000. No. No. I'm the shmuck in this case for trusting him...and sadly, you."

She offered no explanation for her transgression if indeed it was a transgression.

It could have been a one nighter or it could have been one incident in an on going affair. Barney's former love Rosemary had dumped him and he was on the prowl. He wouldn't give her the satisfaction of asking.

As for Barney that son of a bitch, he was determined to collect his $10,000. Larry didn't care if the asshole had to declare bancrupcy, the traitorous fuck.

What a colossal joke he thought. Barney was wining, dining and bedding his wife on his dime. Georgeena was right. He lacked an inner toughness. He was an optimist like the little kid who got a bucket of horse manure for Christmas and said his pony must have run away.

Larry grabbed hs newly acquired British Air flight bag and began to stuff a few necessities in it, toiletries, socks, underwear and three clean dress shirts.

"I'll be back again on Saturday morning at 11:00, on the dot, for the rest of my things. Better make sure you're alone when I enter."

"You're keeping the keys?"

"Yes, maybe you should change the locks after this week. You know what sneak I can be."

He slammed the door, a little too loudly.

In the taxi on the way to Harold Freiman's Columbia University apartment, Larry took inventory off his past behavior. He was faithful to Georgeena in New York City except for Sheila Monahan and when he was separated, Agnes Doyle. He was not a serial adulterer.

On the road weeks at a time; the INDY 500, 10 days shooting a commercial In La Guna Beach, away from Manhattan at least 3 months each year, it could get lonely. Drinking with the guys is good for a day or two but what about all the nights alone in a cheap Motel in Gallop, New Mexico or the Mark Hopkins in San Francisco, too much quiet time is the devil's magnet.

Yes, he had a few one night stands for mechanical sex and unmemorable companionship.

A friendly fuck with a few laughs when you're lonely in a distant place, works both ways, for woman and man. Even the most avowed feminist would admit such actions puts both sexes on equal footing, no hypocrisy, no double standard.

Did his behavior make him a serial sex maniac or at worst a faithless Whoremonger? He used the word whoremonger figuratively since he never chose to frequent prostitutes.

The memory of betrayal wounds one's pride more than the heart and fades more slowly.

Larry liked women for all their many wonderful qualities; generousity, warmth, intelligence, protectiveness, humor, sense of responsibility, care giving to name just a few. Sex was just one of the myriad qualities a woman can offer a man to enrich his life.

The driver interrupted his reverie, "Here we are 116th and Broadway."

Harold's apartment was a one block walk from the Hudson River. He was home expecting Larry's arrival after receiving his phone call 3 hours earlier. Larry knew he could count on Harold, who had a few free hours before his 4:00 class.

Harold could absorb all the dicey circumstances of a divorce, with insights Larry's enraged state of mind might not see. There was no issue from the marriage. Although Georgeena claimed she would like to have a child, her general behavior belied that notion.

They had dinner after Harold's lecture had ended, at a west side restaurtant called the TIP TOE INN. It was the Jewish equivalent of the East Side Wasp eatery, SCHRAFFTS, which catered mainly to immaculately coiffed, blue haired ladies in their sixties and seventies.

At SCHRAFFTS women unaccompanied by men felt secure within the protective confines of its stolid walnut walls. At the TIP TOE INN women ruled. They didn't need a male companion to dine.

SCHRAFFT'S menu featured specialities which were free of garlic, onion or anything as exotic as curry. White bread was the favored wheat product, sometimes toasted. Grilled cheese was the sandwich of choice, cream of asparagus the soup of choice. For those who assiduously watched their calories the Waldorf Salad guaranteed a minimum. A mélange of apples, pineapples, chopped celery and pecans, rasins, lettuce and a splash of orange juice blended with a dollop of cream cheese, the Waldorf satisfied one's appetite, while protecting the waist line.

The TIP TOE INN catered to middle aged Jewish people who cared little about caloric intake. No one ever bothered to calculate the calories of a pastrami sandwich on rye or those of a slice of cheese cake topped with sugared strawberries.

Over matzah ball soup Harold and Larry discussed his need for a lawyer.

"I can put you in touch with a good lawyer. He's an adjunct teacher at Columbia law. Specializes in domestic law."

"That's okay, Harold, I have an aquaintance who is one of the best copyright lawyers in the city."

He laughed, "You going to copyright your divorce?"

"Not funny. He's a good lawyer."

"That may be, but has he ever handled a divorce case."

"Don't know. I'll ask him."

"Look, Larry, divorce is a nasty business and you need a nasty divorce lawyer who never heard of the Marquis of Queensbury rules of fair play.

Want some advice. Please call my guy. He the kind of aggressive ferret who'll make Georgeena's lawyer yell uncle."

"Thanks anyway. I'll get in touch with my guy, Marvin."

Harold shrugged and ordered an egg cream, indigenous to New York City, a simple mix of selzer water, milk and chocolate syrup.

The pre divorce proceedings were not lengthy. There was little negotiation. It was a resounding defeat. In a reversal of the natural order of things, Georgeena's asp-like counsel chewed Larry's guy, Marvin the mongoose to bits, in their contentious domestic drama.

The non-negotiable offer made to Marvin--more like an ultimatum— made retreat the only serious option.

1. Your client makes $26,000 per annum.
2. The apartment your client pays in rent each month is $250 or $3,000 per year. That is our starting point for alimony.
3. My client's household expenses: electric, water, heat, and phone are $200 a month or $2,400 per year.
4. My clients living expenses; food, clothing, medicines, entertainment and local transportation would be $200 a week, or $10,400 per year.
5. Your client would continue to pay for my client's health insurance under his current plan.
6. The total amount of alimony your client would be responsible for is: $3,000 + $2,400 + $10,400= $15,800.

Under the scenario offered by Georgeena's attorney Larry would be left with $10,200 per year, before taxes, on which to live. A reasonable split would have been 50-50, leaving each party $13,000 not great but liveable. That split would enable Larry to rent a small studio apartment and, if he lived frugally, could make it until his next raise.

Georgeena's lawyer unequivocally stated to Marvin that there would be no compromise. Take it or leave it.

Larry left Harold's apartment and returned to the lions den. Although If Georgeena was an animal, in Larry's mind she would be a cheetah.

Hat in hand, Larry entered his apartment somewhat cowed by his litigious loss. The announcement of his return home was greeted with silence.

"Okay, I'll be back tomorrow with my earthly possessions. Your lawyer stated it's my right to return with full conjugal rights."

He expected some kind of response. None came, although Georgeena greeted him with less than enthusiasm.

An hour later after unpacking, Larry said,"Georgeena, come join me in the living room, If you would.

This will not be easy for either of us, but let me try to clear the air with my concept of our future modus operandi. Please let me finish before any objections or additions you wish to make or maybe you have an agenda of your own. If you do, I would gladly listen to it."

She spoke for the first time since he entered the apartment. "That would be allright with me."

"Great. Let me begin with rule number one. And, oh by the way, I have a written copy to give you."

Larry cleared his throat to give his voice a more authoritative timbre.

"Rule one. I will continue to pay for the basic bills including groceries which you purchase. I will give you $100 each week for that purpose."

"What if I want to eat out?" she said.

"My best advice is find a meal ticket for eat outs."

He congratulated himself on restraint by not mentioning Barney Goldfine as a possible dinner patrone.

"Rule two. I will sleep in the small bedroom, keep it broom clean and will never entertain overnight guests whether you are here in the apartment or not. Regarding overnight guests I assume you will do the same. Lest you be alarmed, that's only an assumption, not a condition.

Rule three. I will not sleep over nights on most weekends. I will let you know about weekends when I plan to be here.

Rule four. I will prepare my own breakfasts. All other meals will be eaten out. That should help stretch your food budget a bit further.

Rule five. I will not receive telephone calls at this number. If any calls slip through, just gently tell the caller that I'm out and not expected back in the near future.

Rule Six. I will do my personal laundry in the basement laundry room including my sheets and towels.

Rule seven. Conversation between us is optional. If you feel like talking or asking questions, do so. If not, t here will be no problem.

If any emergency arises, we both are obligated to communicate with each other.

Rule eight. Many week nights I will be out late and will return as quietly as possible in my preparation for bedtime.

Rule nine. Provocative or insufficient clothing at any time in which we both occupy the apartment, is prohibited.

Rule ten. Your hegemony over TV watching is a given."

Georgeena smiled at his recitation of rule nine.

"Patience please. There's just a little bit nore to cover. The procedures for co-living as stated will be operative until:

1. You decide to re-marry at which time a divorce agreement will be actuated.
2. I decide to marry, although unlikely, considering the heavy financial penalties I would incur by initiating a unilateral divorce proceeding for the second time. You die.
3. I die.
4. You find the present arrangement unbearable and instruct your lawyer to accept a 50-50 split of my income.

Now is all that clear? Any part you want me to repeat or restructure?"

She offered no questions or suggestions, a silent approval he assumed.

So it went for the next 18 months, during which time Larry thought he found someone he wanted to spend the rest of his life with.

Meanwhile Larry's law suit, against Barney Goldfine for repayment of a $10,000 loan with 7% interest per annum, won a judgement in small claims court.

The final outcome was pre-ordained. Judgements without assets are worthless and when it came to assets Barney always was worthless.

CHAPTER 27

Olcott Changes The Game

Larry's after work life, while a room mate of Georgeena, became an odd distillation of frustration, doubt, guilt and yes, love. His anger was also directed at himself. They were both culprits in the no man's land of blame.

His less than monogamous behavior left him on no higher moral ground than she. And he could no longer maintain control of his fractionated life. It showed up in his work and social life, which consisted solely of Agnes Doyle. His dilemma was doubt about his relationship with Aggie. How real could it be if he still loved Georgeena?

At the office his relationshipwith Mike Olcott was quickly disintegrating.

There were no warning signs for the change from collegiality to outright hostility. One day he joked about Larry's enviable bachelorhood in the new era of sexual freedom. The next day his grim face said their friendship was over. Any friendship they ever had was at best a tenuous one. Mutual self interest had been the heart of their bonding and that interest was keeping HEFFERCO top management happy.

Mike excelled at editing facts for his own advantage. He was a man with no guiding moral compass. He showed the world his persona of the moment, instantly altered to accommodate the beliefs of the person he was talking to. He trusted no one. He loved no one. He was always scheming whether at work or play. He even postured as a loving father the one time Georgeena and Larry had dinner at his Long Island house. Love he felt was a weakness. It made you vulnerable. Thus his friendships were always transactional.

He never excelled at anything in college beyond a journeyman season of basketball at Dartmouth. His three year stint as a student did not include a diploma, yet he continually flaunted his Ivy League credentials.

Recalling that dinnert Larry was ashamed of his feigned interest when Olcott proudly showed his Dartmouth year book revealing his sixth man status on the team of 1957 or when he produced a 1954 High School year book which pictured Olcott amid 25 other uniformed teen age football players. Get a life Larry thought then.

Most women found Mike attractive from the neck up; blue eyed, with slicked down hair and a perfect left hand part, the look matinee idols sported in the 1940's anf 50's.

Mike was always scheming to gain an advantage whether at work or at play.

One Monday in early September he walked into Larry's office. No knock on the door, just an intrusion by the 210 pound jock with the odd shaped body. A frontal view of Olcott revealed no indent for his waist. He looked like a card board cut out that someone forgot to cut inward at stomach level. His profile revealed a stomach pushing hard on the lower button of his three button jacket. That exertion resulted in a lower jacket opening that revealed a tie and bits of a white shirt. Sartorially the effect was not pleasing.

Ten days remained before the agency was to present a new print campaign for HEFFERCO, one designed to complement the Thanksgiving TV commercial saturation blitz. Three days earlier

Larry gave Olcott preliminary rough layouts and copy, his first stab at the campaign.

"Did you get a chance to go over the first drafts?" he asked.

"Yeah, and they suck!"

Did Larry hear right? The belligerence in the voice said more than the toxic evaluation of the work.

"What's your problem, Mike? Tough weekend? And if it's not asking too much could you be a little more specific?"

"Specific? I'll be specific. You and the little Heeb Howie are becoming big buddies?"

"Not my type, big guy."

"Oh yeah, I'd say he's a lot more your type than you let on."

Whoa Larry thought. A bell rang in his head, a bulb lit above it. How's that?"

"You people always stick together."

You people said it all. The cat is out of the bag. Larry's six pointed star was showing.

"You have a problem with my personal faith?"

"Oh, so you admit it."

"Olcott, my religion has nothing to do with you or my work. I was hired to do a job and I'm doing it."

"Yeah, but would they have hired you if they knew it?"

"Teddy knew. Bob knows. My wife and Teddy's wife are best friends, old school mates. No secrets. You think I should wear a yellow star?"

"Now that I know your dirty little secret, you better watch your backside. I'm gonna make sure you're out of here in less than 90 days."

"Get the fuck out of my office."

He smirked, a final look of distain, turned and left the office.

They barely spoke after that morning except at meetings with Bob Steele and at client meetings with Howie and the Hassenfeffers.

When he looked at his roughs for the print campaign, he knew they had to be better than good. In their present state they were not.

Theirr social relationship ended abruptly. No more weekends in the Hamptons with his mistress, Jenny Diver, who once was one of General Clifton's girls. Clifton, the highest ranking military man in the Kennedy White House, had several assistants hired for their looks and congeniality. No one gave a rat's ass if they could type, take dictation or file.

Jenny's unfortunate surname gave rise to office jokes about Mike and the Muff Diver.

Prior to the deep freeze in their relationship a typical weekend, away from Georgeena, consisted of weekends in West Hampton with Larry's companion/friend/lover Agnes (Aggie) Doyle from STANDCO days. At his suggestion she left STANDCO for a new career in PR. Larry wrote her resume and she soon landed a job with Pearson-Marsden, an up and coming group who were making big news in the communication's world.

They liked Aggie's professional attitude and people skills. In a short time she became an account manager. For Larry she was the ideal companion. Her love of sports, politics, the Times Sunday Puzzles and sex neatly matched his top four. But most importantly, she was a friend who cared about his well being. They never talked about love. Too abstract, too imprecise.

He and Aggie shared most summer weekends with Olcott and Jenny in the summer of 1970. Competitive mixed doubles sets filled the mornings, beach time in the PM and cocktails at 5:00. The dramatic deep freeze between Mike and Larry ended those weekends after Labor Day.

Larry thought little of the rift with Olcott busying his days with new ideas for the upcoming print ads. Their work together on the day to day account problems was an awkward armed truce. Neither ever considered torpedoing the mission despite the falling out. Or so Larry thought.

Lunch with Agnes Doyle proved the optimism about his Mexican standoff with Olcott was a serious miscalculation.

"Larry, I have bad news. I think."

Could she mean she was pregnant he thought.

"What's up"?

"One of the creative guys I work with told me he has a great new free lance assignment."

"And."

"The assignment was for an account at Fremont-Richardson, your agency, Right?"

I nodded.

"I asked what account. When he said toys and the manufacturer was Hassenffeffer, I knew I had to immediately tell you."

"Holy shit! The guy blind sided me and, moron that I am, I never saw it coming." He pounded the table in frustration precariously jangling the table setting.

Aggie reacted quickly grabbing the two filled wine glasses, anchoring them until they were safe from his outburst.

"What do you mean?"

"We have a huge creative presentation to make to the client in 3 days. I've barely started polishing up my first drafts. It's a print campaign for SOLDIER BOY that will run nationally. It's aimed at both kids and their mothers. Different audiences, different media. You know Comic Books, National Scholastic and Ladies Home Journal.

The son of a bitch went behind my back. If you hadn't told me about your guy I would never about known about it until the last moment, when he will present an alternative to mine. I could lose you know. How good is your guy?"

"Very good."

"Thanks."

By the time you're in your mid thirties you should never be surprised by the misbehavior of close co-workers. By that age you should be able to read their tactics and be able to deal with anything tossed your way. If you can't you better watch out. As Tennessee Williams observed, 'There's a lot of mendacity in the world.'

He had ignored the warning signs. Mea culpa.

Back at the office, he called in Hal Del Blasio, his art director.

"I don't think we have the best creative yet." Larry said. "We need to pull a couple of all nighters to sharpen both campaigns; new layouts, maybe even new copy."

If you need free lance help. Get it. Forget the cost."

He said they should begin immediately. "This is very important. Get down to my office as soon as you can."

It was 7:30. He had just left Aggie. The assignment was two separate ad campaigns with a message tailored to each demographic; kids, 6-11 and mothers 28-45. Each campaign would consist of four different print ads. It was back to the drawing boards; revise or rewrite, revise or redraw. Larry wasn't kidding Deblasio. Both their asses were on the line.

Deblasio was a okay art director but not one who could make a good creative concept visually great. He was solid, but not inspired. What they needed was inspiration; dazzling words and visuals.

Three days later Deblasio and Larry carried eight layout boards as they walked into the Fremont-Richards conference room.

There were seven people in the room, of whom five were smokers. In less than ten minutes a thin blue haze drifted above.

The usual suspects sat around the agency's 16 foot long mahagonny table headed by Bob Steele. He was flanked by by Howard Politz, the HEFFERCO ad director, on his right and Brian Hassenfeffer, Marketing Director and heir apparent of the family controlled corporation on his left. Larry sat next to Brian and Mike sat next to Howard.

Also in attendance was Joel Stein, Media Director. Hal Deblasio's job was to run the carousel projector and pin up large scale versions of the eight ads he and Larry had created.

A sweating bottle of Perrier Water and a large glass ash tray had been placed before each occupant's place at the table.

Bob Steele started the meeting.

"Gentlemen, we're here to present the agency's recommendation for the print ad blitz to run beginning six weeks prior to Christmas.

As Joel said it will be a good complement to the TV saturation schedule we have planned for the period.

National Scholastic is the medium to reach our target 6-11 year olds. Our commercials are pitched to kid's desires to be first on their block to own the newest SOLDIER BOY equipment. The TV spot reveals how to get more play value from all their SOLDIER BOY accessories.

Our choice of Ladies Home Journal to reach women 29-45 is based on the fact that it offers us the largest female audience with appropriate age children from among all the women's service magazines. "

Now it's time for the creative. Okay, Larry, are you ready?"

Larry was puzzled. He made no mention of Olcott's alternative presentation. Did the son of a bitch have second thoughts? Not a chance. He's playing for keeps. Maybe Bob got wind of it and nixed a dual pitch. Dreamer.

"Larry, are you ready?" Bob said.

"Okay,"he replied with a forced smile of confidence. "Mike would you dim the lights?'

Reluctantly Olcott got up and did so. After his presentation, Larry knew Mike had dimmed his lights as well, even before a bravura performance presenting the work of the free lance guy. Aggie was right. The Marsden writer was really good.

CHAPTER 28

Has Anyone Seen Barney?--1972

Barney Goldfine fell off the face of the earth, a cause for concern because Larry Miller had still hoped to collect his $10,000. A recent phone call from Chip Manfreed, Barney's fraternity brother who had attended Larry's wedding, made him a little more optimistic about recovering the proceeds of the loans. Chip said Barney's sister had died and left him some money. How much? He didn't know.

If Chip was right, Larry might be able to pay off some of his divorce legal fees. His job was ending at Fremont-Richards and he was in a bit of cash flow bind. 10 grand would be a big help.

New negotiations were starting in the Miller v Miller divorce case. In desperation he decided to check around to see if any old friends had heard of Barney's whereabouts.

First he called Rosemary, Barney's alleged true love who got away, but she said hadn't heard from him in two years. And the son of a bitch owed her $3,000 which she needed now to help pay for her mother's nursing home.

"He's a rat and I'm glad I dumped him before I got involved in all his shit for brains publishing schemes which all turned to merde," she said."If you hear from him tell him to go fuck himself!"

Her gritty street talk belied the lofty air of her VOGUE editorial job.

"Okay, Rosemary I'll tell him. Let's get together for a drink sometime, okay."

"That would be nice," she said in a voice filled with feigned enthusiasm.

Next he tried Rod and Kate. Kate answered.

"No, Larry he hasn't tried to contact us. And if he did I think it would be about a short term loan which he would swear to return in 90 days. I think he needs new friends to prey on. Bye the bye, how's Georgeena?

"You better ask her. We see little of each other these days. You heard the divorce fell through?"

"Yes, we did. Too bad, I think you'd both be better off going your own ways."

"Me too, Kate. Here's hoping. Were in new talks and the attorney fees are getting scary."

"Let's try and get together. Rod would like that."

"You mean without Georgeena, I assume."

"Of course you're our friend as well. You know that and please bring whomever you fancy."

"Great. We'll talk soon."

He hung up feeling Kate was sincere in her efforts to keep up a friendship with or without Georgeena.

It was time to try Chip to see if he'd heard anything more about Barney's inheritance. Chip lived on West 75th street a few blocks from the Mansfield Hotel where Barney once maintained his New York prescence.

"Hey Chip how's everything going?" Larry said and before giving him a chance to reply continued. "It's about Barney, have you seen him or heard anything more about his inheritance?"

"No but one of our fraternity brothers, Al Shapiro, thought it might be true. He was close to Barney's sister. And oh, I had a call from the bartender at the VFW Lodge in Sag Harbor who said

Barney ran up a pretty hefty bar tab last summer. He wanted to know if I was in touch with him. I said no, but you know, Larry, I think he's still living at The Mansfield."

"I know he used to rent a room at the Mansfield Hotel," Larry said."

The Mansfield was a down at the heels Hotel that rented rooms by the hour, the week or month. Traffic was heavy mid-week at noon for those who sought recreational sex on their lunch hour.

Chip suggested they go there and inquire if Barney was still in residence. When they got to the hotel a gap toothed desk clerk told them,"Mr. Goldfine is not is his room but I expect him back shortly."

"We'll wait," Larry said.

In the dimly lit lobby the smell of stale cigar smoke vigorously competed with the nostril clearing smell of strong disinfectant. The disinfectant held a slender lead.

A dappled pattern of worn spots on the mohair arm chair, in which Larry sat, was a metaphor for the building's hopeless state of disrepair.

Thumbing, through a collection of eight year old magazines, one caught Larry's eye. It proclaimed that Barry Goldater was going to be the standard bearer for the Republican Party in 1964, an event that occurred eight years previously.

This dog-eared issue of TIME featured a smiling picture of the handsome Senator from Arizona on its cover.

In spite of his ultra-conservative views Goldwater was liked by many Democrats for his easy western charm. Unfortunately it was a fondness that did not translate into votes.

As Larry read past history, Chip kept pacing the Mansfield's worn marble floor, head down. He was so engrossed in his thoughts, worries, and fears he nearly collided with a heavily rouged 'lady of the evening' emerging from the two-man elevator. To be more precise the swaying bottom that passed Larry's chair on her way to the front doorway was in fact a 'lady of the early afternoon", her day's work complete.

"For Christ sake, Chip, sit down. You're making me crazy. Here read all about the 1964 election."

He tried to smile but all he could muster was a lopsided moue. Larry handed him TIME and Chip finally sat down in a ratty counterpart of Larry's woolly mammouth.

A vintage wall clock rang 3 bells. They'd been in the lobby for over an hour. As Larry fretted over the waste of an afternoon, a somewhat stooped man walked in wearing a baggy running suit. His eyes fixed on the man's his pathetically worn tennis sneakers bound by shiny grey duct tape. They flagged an unmistakeable mark of poverty.

The man walked straight passed them eyes forward. Did he see them? Was it his intention to avoid acknowledging them? They would never know.

The former Gucci clad GQ man smelled like the human scent of poverty. It followed him, like an undesireable companion. He nodded to the gap toothed desk clerk as he passed him to enter the cage-like elevator.

Gap tooth signaled to me that Mr. Goldfine had arrived. LarryI ignored him and grabbed Chip by the arm.

"It's time to go, pal, the game's over. Leave him in peace."

Three weeks later Chip called to say Barney had died. He had stopped by the Mansfield to check on Barney and gap tooth told him the bad news.

CHAPTER 29

The Madcap World Of Arnold Stanford

Arnold Stanford, nee Steinman, made his mark on Madison Avenue soon after leaving a family owned Super Market Chain headquartered in Elkhart, Indiana. The idea of selling ideas, big and small, had far greater appeal to Arnold than overseeing the sale of the endless package goods lining the aisles of every STEINMAN SUPER STORE in two mid-western states. None the less Arnold Steinman remained a dutiful son in the family business for over 6 years after college.

Arnold's German born grandfather, Leon Steinman, founded his first grocery store in Elkhart, Indiana in 1901. By 1921, the result of hard work and a modest living standard, Leon was the proprietor/ owner of 8 thriving grocery stores. Six were located in Elkhart, two in Indianapolis. Arnold's father, Sam, was handed the reins to the family business in 1926 at the age of 36. It was the second blessing bestowed on Sam that decade of the 20's. The first was his new son, Arnold, born in 1921.

Arnold, though small in stature, possessed an out sized ego, staccato-like gift of gab and a one million dollar trust fund availed to him at age 30. His diminutive size made for an unhappy childhood. The travails caused by of his physical short comings were compounded by another cross to bear, anti-Semitism. Midwestern America in the 1930's was a hot bed of bigoted Catholics, Lutherans and Nazi wannabes.

An only child, Arnold grew up a child of privilege who learned that money alone would not buy him sufferance from his school boy tormentors. Something else was needed. An agile mind and fruitful phantasy world offered Arnold his chance to stand tall against the bullies.

In 1936 at age 15 he hatched a guileful strategy. The first week of the school year at Elkhart Heights Junior High School, grades 7-8-9, a large banner appeared on the school's playground fence. In bold red letters it read:

```
ENTER THE FIRST ANNUAL STEINCO SUPERMARKET
                OLYMPICS

        Sponsored by Steinco Inc

   Sign Up Today! PRIZES FOR THE WINNERS—
   Giveaways to all entrants SITE: Elkhart
     Heights Junior High School Playground

DATES: Saturday & Sunday September 8ᵗʰ & 9ᵗʰ
```

The sign gave recognition to the metamorphosis of Steinman's Super Stores into **STEINCO SUPERMARKETS**. It was a nod to the marketing change that supermarket chains like A&P and KROGERS effected on the grocery store business. Larger was better.

Fifteen year old Arnold convinced papa Sam, that their company's name, STEINMAN, was too Jewish for the times. STEINCO sounded more contemporary American.

Unbeknownst to his class mates, Arnold, over the summer, had devised 4 unusual events. None remotely resembled a sporting event.

None tested the athletic prowess of a contestant. He deliberately made up events that required no inherent athleticism but could be mastered with adequate training. And train he did. All summer long in the four competitions that originated not in ancient Greece, but in his head.

THE BACKWARD BROAD JUMP. It was difficult for a first timer but doable for a boy who practiced for 80 consecutive days, the entire summer of 1936. The length of his jumps never exceeded four feet a considerably shorter distance than the 16 feet achieved by boys on the Junior High track team who jumped from a more favorable stance, forward.

THE WHIRLING DERVISH. It was an event that required an entrant to spin in circles for as long as he could. By the end of the summer Arnold could last four minutes, continuously, before spinning out.

THE FRIGID ARM ENDURANCE TEST. This competition tested the ability of an entrant to keep his arm in a vat of water filled with chunks of solid ice for as long as it was bearable. After many hours testing the frigid waters with his scrawny left arm Arnold's personal best time was 8 minutes. The family maid pulled him out after that time when she noticed his facial color tended towards an unbecoming shade of blue.

THE BREATH HOLDING MARATHON. How long can a young boy hold his breath? Arnold achieved 3 minutes.

On September 8th 200 school boys and girls showed up to compete amid a festive aura. The crisp, chilled air smelled of burning leaves. Burning leaves was a rite of the passage of time in 1936, long before ecological considerations were even a dream in the mind of the most fervid conservationist. Summer was gone in Elkhart early in September. The color spectrum of turning leaves was at its peak towards the end of that month. It was a time when every boy raked leaves resting on his family lawn into neat piles to be burned. Once lighted, the crackling reds, yellows, browns and tans of the shedding deciduous trees gave off their familiar welcoming smell of autumn.

Three tables manned by PTA volunteers handed out cups of steaming apple cider AND 200 Milky Way bars. Each white paper cup bore the legend, "courtesy of STEINCO SUPERMARKETS"

A fourth table was laden with 12 ribbons; 4 were Red, 4 were Blue, and 4 were Bronze, representing 1st, 2nd and 3rd place in the STEINCO OLYMPICS. Each ribbon bore a pewter medallion engraved with words: Winner in the STEINCO OLYMPICS,

A fifth table was manned by the Elkhart Junior High School Athletic Director, Ed Cummins, who wore a white sweatshirt with bright red lettering that read: GOVERNING OFFICIAL OF THE STEINCO SUPERMARKET OLYMPICS.

His job was to hand out printed entry blanks listing the events and boxes to be checked for entry. Later he would award ribbons to all 12 winners when they came to table number four.

Contestants lined up for entry blanks to sign up for those events they wished to enter. Up to this point no one knew of the four events Arnold had dreamed up. As far as the eye could see there were no hurdles, no discus or shot put circle in sight. One saw no lanes marked for running, no sand pit for the broad jump, no bar for the high jump. What's going on here many thought?

When the first entrant, Billy Blackbourne, looked at his entry form, he let out a primal scream, followed by, "What the fuck!"

Quickly the gathered 200 realized they'd been had by the little Jew weasel. The cockamamie events, that's the down side to this Olympic farce most agreed, but then the crowd in a mass murmur began to see the upside. Winners of the gold would get a year's supply of THREE MUSKETEER BARS. Two per day whether you need them or not, a total of 730 top name candy bars. Who wouldn't stick his arm in ice water for that?

Silver winners would get a case of PEPSI COLA delivered to their family's house every week for 6 months. That's 384 bottles of PEPSI. Not bad. I'm in, the crowd as one, silently assented.

Bronze winners were to receive one HERSHEY chocolate bar every day for a year. Okay! Okay! Okay! Let the games begin.

Watching Junior High Footballers perform their three backward jumps (their best attempt was recorded) was a hoot. The bigger boys, looking like teetering baby elephants, fell down most of the time. The puny nerds scored high, capturing silver and bronze but the Olympian heights of 3 feet 6 inches was achieved by the games originator, Arnold Steinman.

The whirling dervish competition left half the crowd in simulation of intoxication. Many threw up. A ramrod straight Arnold Steinman claimed the Gold. Trudy Guiford, in her fifth year of ballet, finished second, amidst a swirl of arabesqes. A plucky 7th grade gymnast took the bronze, having weathered the twisting and turning, often upside down in the high bar event of his sport.

Frigid arm competitors lasted far longer than anyone expected. It came down to the wire at 8 minutes and 40 seconds when Arnold reluctantly removed his blue arm from the artic tub. Three boys remained. One lasted up to 9 minutes. The last drop out was at 9 minutes 24 seconds. The winner of the gold, Fats Wallace, attributed his endurance to, "that extra layer of you know what, that, you guys always joke about."

The skinniest girl in class Donna Swenson, took the silver. One boy who dropped out but not before he accused her of being part reptile which caused Donna to burst into tears. There was a tie for the bronze which created a problem for Ed Cummins. He only had one bronze ribbon.

They flipped a coin for the ribbon after Arnold informed them they both would get the bronze prize.

Holding breath came naturally to all members of the school swim team so predictably all three winners in this category came from their ranks.

All non-winner participants lined up at tables one two and three to get their free prize, a six pack comprised of 1

SNICKERS Bar, 1 POWERHOUSE Bar, 1 BABY RUTH Bar, 1 BUTTERFINGERS Bar, 1 MOUNDS Bar and 1 MILKY WAY.

Arnold never suffered a moment of bullying the remainder of the school year and his popularity continued throughout high school where he was in constant demand by every entertainment committee in the school.

Father Sam was impressed with Arnold's ability to plant the largesse of STEINCO in the minds of over 1,000 teen agers who would become his next generation of consumers.

After college Arnold joined the family business where he enjoyed a few minor promotion triumphs, but there was one in particular that would foreshadow his flamboyant future. Spending a four years stocking shelves, building displays and studying consumer buying habits didn't satisfy his aching search for a big idea for STEINCO SUPERMARKETS.

The winter of 1952 in Elkhart, Indiana produced a record 110 inches of snow. Although one storm reduced the number of customers in STEINCO SUPERMARKETS to zero, it inspired an idea which launched Arnold on an exciting new career in New York City.

In the midst of a silent city frozen in place for nearly three days, Arnold came up with the idea that changed his life forever. In an intuitive flash he ordered all 8 supermarkets to close for two days and ordered all ambulatory and non-pregnant employees under 50 to go outside and make snowballs. The balls were to be the size of an 80 count grapefruit. (the size of a softball packed 80 to a crate)

At the end of two days the STEINCO work force had packed 9,000 eighty count snow balls. The balls were quickly shipped to a nearby cold storage house which had the facility to store them at 20 degrees below zero until July 1 of 1953.

The next day Arnold called the President of GLOBAL FOODS in New York and told him his plan. How he got through to this man will remain a mystery. He said that STEINCO

SUPERMARKETS would hold a SPECIAL BLIZZARD IN JULY SALE, in the coming year.

They would give away FREE frozen snow balls in the heat of the summer. He proposed a giant display for Global's popular frozen foods brand. In return for this exposure all he wanted was FREE prizes from Global to attract maximum store traffic. Snow balls in July and FREE prizes would guarantee a sales bonanza for both GLOBAL and STEINCO he assured the man.

At first GLOBAL balked at the idea of giving free prizes until young Arnold displaying a Chutzpah that would become his P T Barnum like trademark, said, "No deal without prizes. And furthermore I'll pull your entire product line from our eight stores permanently."

The other end of the line was silent for a moment or two,

"My Director of Marketing advises me that we at GLOBAL will gladly provide an array of suitable free prizes," the chagrined CEO replied.

On July 1, 1953 with the temperature in Elkhart a record 99 degrees, 9,000 frozen snow balls in Jiffy bags were delivered to eight STEINCO SUPERMARKETS. The allocation was 1,250 to each store.

The five day BLIZZARD IN JULY SALE culminated in record sales for both GLOBAL and STEINCO with over 40,000 FREE gifts distributed. Gifts ranged from a large bag of lollipops to a large Weber Grille.

At times the traffic was so heavy stores had to be padlocked to keep women out. The Elkhart Police Department assigned a special contingent of policemen to preserve civil order so that the adrenalin charged women could be allowed into the stores safely. A normally slack July sales period became the single largest week of sales in STEINCO's history.

After the overwhelming success of *Blizzard in July*, Sam thought that Arnold would be permanently rooted in the super market business, assuring its continuity for future Steinman heirs. Sam was wrong. He had not a clue about his son's desire for a bigger stage.

Young Arnold had bigger fish to fry, an ambition only New York City home of the exotic world of advertising could satisfy. His relatively short history in the world of retail commerce led Arnold to develop a unique business philosophy. Its two part mantra was: "Do put the cart before the horse" and "I'd rather have a client who is angry with me for pushing too hard, that a client who praises my manners."

In a pre-computer, pre-internet, pre social media world his simple, shrewd beliefs seemed to work, in practice, a startlingly large percentage of the time. It was faith over research.

Arnold Stanford nee Steinman went to New York armed with newspaper clippings, TV reels and magazine articles; kudos for his Blizzard in July triumph. His million dollar trust fund from STEINCO buttressed any lean period he might face in establishing his credentials in Gotham. The man who once described himself as looking like a Midwestern dentist had carefully culled a list of New York's five top ad agencies, all large enough and prestigious enough to accommodate an original thinker with big ideas.

He ultimately chose Young & Rickard after an interview with its executive vice president, John McCaffrey. Impressed with Arnold's creative chops, McCaffrey wondered if the arrogance of the man in front of him might be an obstacle to success at Young & Rickard.

"Mr. Stanford," McCaffrey began.

"Please call me Arnold."

"Yes, Arnold but I have one question for you. You appear to be a strong willed person. Now that's a good quality in this business but, and it's a big but, do you think you can be a team player here at Young & Rickard?

Arnold perked up a notch. "Sir, I go with what Frank Lloyd Wright had to say, 'If I had to choose between honest arrogance and hypocritical humility, I would choose arrogance.' "I fight for what I believe is right."

McCaffrey smiled. It was a smile which communicated his decision.

The brash young man from Elkhart, Indiana began his new career the following Monday.

After two years and a myriad of startlingly original promotions and events that made him the darling of top Young & Rickard's clients, Arnold's confidence in his creative skills accelerated beyond his imagination. He had reached a point where he could no longer work as a team player. He needed to be the final decision maker, the person calling the shots. Committee decisions could no longer inhibit his creative juices.

Arnold was sure his first new clients would include the blue chip ones of the agency he was leaving. They included such stars of the Dow Jones composite as TWA, General Foods, IBM, General Motors and Chevron.

The shrewdness in positioning his company as a fee-based think tank, that in no way competed with the advertising portion of Young & Rickard's clients, made him a potential resource of all large Madison Avenue agencies as well. Promotions and Special Events were never their profit centers. Their 15% commissions from billions of advertising media purchases would never be in danger from a motley crew of dreamers at Arnold Stanford Associates.

CHAPTER 30

Arnold Stanford & Associates --1971

In the spring of 1961 Arnold opened his doors for business in the new Seagram's Building, a much-praised creation of the renowned architect Mies Van Der Rohe.

His 24th floor suite was a departure from the traditional office look. Bold floral patterned couches anchored an ante room which looked more like a welcoming lounge.

A pretty young brunette, Sanford's secretary, his first and only hire the first six months in operation, personally greeted everyone who entered the inviting reception room. A marketing executive from Wilco Electric's Louisville office, often commented about the warm welcome he had received on his first visit as an Arnold Stanford client. He felt it was a stark contrast to the impersonal treatment he had previously encountered in the executive suites of Manhattan. Claudia Bellamy became more than a secretary/receptionist for Arnold Stanford. She quietly insinuated her way into his inner circle of one. Beneath her veneer of collegial friendliness she slyly operated like a Soviet style political commissar as the company grew over the years. She became the eyes and ears of Stanford. The Communists were known for their tight security, always seeking to find potential traitors and non-believers. Political commissars existed in every military unit, every university and every factory in the Soviet Union. The climate of fear engendered from such oversight created cliques and intrigues that struggled to survive. Such was the climate at Arnold Stanford Associates as perceived by the 20 working associates who made up the company's cadre of brain power when Larry joined them in 1971. After his dismissal at Fremont-Richards, Larry began looking for the kind of job that might invigorate his creative chops. Two years of SOLDIER BOY commercials had diminished them. He had run out of ways to put the little plastic doll in harm's way.

Upon departure Bob Steele wished him well, backing up his words with a generous severance package and a solid letter of recommendation. He was, indeed, an honorable gent, though surprisingly naïve—hoodwinked by the likes of Mike Olcott.

At J. Walter he turned down a senior copy writer's job on the IBM account. Flacking their line of products held little appeal.

After a few interviews he found one place that seemed more challenging than a conventional ad agency. One might have called it a creative think tank. It was not an advertising or public relations firm. The company's founder, Arnold Stanford, liked to call it a "big idea" factory available to America's blue chip corporations for an unexpected, unorthodox way to reach their consumers.

On his very first day he discerned that the staff at Arnold Stanford Associates was a fractionated one. He also observed that all hands were circumspect in conversation whenever in the presence of Claudia Bellamy. This sunny appearing woman, who warmly him welcomed him on arrival, turned out to be a one woman KGB who served her master well; quick to report disloyalty or the cover up of incompetence.

In a power struggle to service the most interesting clients competing cliques emerged within the company. They consisted of three factions. One was led by Rob Loeb, one of five Jews in the company. Arnold Stanford made sure his brain trust would never be saddled with the onus of being too Jewish.

45 year old Rob was married to a wealthy woman. He sought not riches but a small degree of power and prestige. Arnold recognized that Rob would never be a burden on his payroll and could be the perfect head of one the two warring factions he hoped to set up. He felt the best work could be achieved if two strong factions were continually competing to be the best.

Rob's group consisted of Betty Barbed Wire, a name assigned Jean Collins, sotto voce, by group number two led by an amiable lecher, Ted Van Oker. Ted was the perfect leader to head a group that contrasted Rob Loeb's caution with his go for broke style.

Jean earned her sobriquet through a prickly personality and sharp edged exchanges with peers in brain storming group meetings where ideas were uninhibitedly tossed around until one stuck to the wall. That one usually was the basis for the client presentation.

Jean was joined by Bill Bartlett, a suck up writer who also did his own color layouts. His dual skills barely masked the fact that, at best, he was an average writer and marginal artist. Sticking close to Joan and Rob at their morning breakfast meetings in Rob's capacious office offered him protection for his journeyman qualities in an office staffed with super stars.

Frank Metz, a 60 year old veteran of the agency wars who once was the advertising director of Westinghouse, was a Rob Loeb breakfast attendee. He joined the group for protection, having 5 years to sweat out before retiring. His role was defined, not by choice, but by the fact he was the most vulnerable if business ever dropped off. He stuck close to the Loeb faction.

There were 2 independents, those who chose not to join either of the two warring factions. Jacqueline Ferris was the one independent who joined the Rob clique for daily breakfast, primarily for any gossip she might glean about the progress of the ongoing internal war.

Jacqueline, a 39 year old virgin, was a stylishly turned out graduate of Wellesley. Her perpetual red cheeked face bespoke outdoor woman. She still attended reunions of her teen age camp days. Camp Sunapee would hold bi-annual gatherings in the hills of New Hampshire complete with color war games. Her sensible Peck & Peck tweed suits defined her unsuccessful attempt at femininity. Ted Van Oker's troops never talked male talk around Jacqueline.

The other independent was the executive art director, Dan Torgeson, whose imposing 6 foot 5 inch staure and grey haired crew cut made his presence as imposing as his talent.

Larry became a Ted Van Oker loyalist. Although hostentatious twirling of a Phi Beta Kappa key was a bit much, Ted was a man's man and a woman's man as well. He never met a woman he didn't want to screw. He was an eclectic predator and enjoyed both the hunt and the kill.

As in all his dealings he was direct. No pussy footing or mendacity. He told you where you stood. His loyalists knew Ted would always cover their rear.

The Van Oker clan included, little Sherman Berman, 20% of the Jewish quotient and Walter Mauer, a master of the numbers game that structured the boundaries of any promotion the staff might dream up.

Here's how Walter worked and hence his value to the firm. Let's say one had an idea for a Planter's Oats Brand Captain Crumbles. He knew that Planters was planning to sponsor a network TV program about Darwin's famous voyage to the Galapagos Island in his ship the HMS Beagle. The idea went something like this.

Planters Oats would feature a Sweepstakes on the back of every box of Captain Crumbles.

WIN A TRIP FOR 4 TO THE GALAPOGOS ISLANDS
FOLLOW THE ROUTE OF DARWIN'S SHIP HMS BEAGLE
AND 5,000 OTHER GREAT PRIZES! PLUS
DRAWINGS AT EVERY SUPERMARKET IN AMERICA
FOR A VIDEO OF THE NETWORK BROADCAST

That was not all. Each participating supermarket chain would give shelf space for displaying the promotion. For that they would get free standing displays announcing the promotion and directions for customers to pick up and send in entry forms.

After this structuring of the promotion the creator of it would go to Walter Mauer for what was affectionately called the "payout shit" needed to sell the promotion. Walter had to figure all costs ; number of potential participating stores, cost of the prize structure, cost of shelf space, cost of displays, cost of national advertising, cost of local city co-op advertising. Then he had to project what the sales of Captain Crumbles would be during the 60 day promotion period.

Walter would then reveal if the idea was a doable one from a cost effective point of view. Walter was far more valuable to Arnold Sanford Associates than any of the best of the creative associates. He was a powerful asset for the Van Oker faction. Loeb's group didn't have a numbers guy.

Ted had a secretary whose dexterous fingers could flick 100 words a minute on her IBM Selectric. Her thought process, however, ran at a far slower speed; intellectual range, A to B. Her name was Eleanor Munson, a graduate of Catherine Gibbs Secretarial School; second fastest typist in her class.

She performed beautifully under pressure but one had to be sure you gave her explicit instructions about every bit of minutiae for which she was responsible.

They had a new client, Sherwin Williams Paints, a company headquartered in Cincinnati, Ohio. Larry was the creative assigned to the account. After the first week he had developed a Fall Campaign, which he wanted the Ad Director to see.

In the pre-Fax, pre internet era everyone depended on the U.S. Mail for transmission of layouts and copy. Eleanor had brought him a large envelop addressed to Sherwin Williams into which he placed his handiwork.

"Mr. Miller" she said, "before you seal that envelop I should tell you there must be a mistake in the address."

"How so?"Larry said.

"Well look here. It says 420 Madison Avenue. And Madison Avenue is in New York not Cincinnati."

He looked into her vacant blue eyes wanting to choose his words with precision in a non-judgemental way.

"Eleanor, dear, James Madison was the fourth President of the United States and there may be as many as 1,000 Madison Avenues throughout America."

He then sealed the envelope.

"Here," he said handing it to her. "Send it Special Delivery. Please."

Larry and the two other foot soldiers in Ted's platoon shared the services of Eleanor Munson, always on guard for the next shoe to drop.

They were Jim McGregor, a talented 55 year old whose love of Johnny Walker Red always kept him on the outer reaches of Madison Avenue stardom. Fully sober Jim was the most prolific writer but, he was a morning guy. Three noontime bloody Mary's at P.J. Clarkes often made him a guy the Ted group would hide from Arnold Sanford at many afternoon brain storming sessions.

Ted's group was able to cover up and extend his stay at Sanford & Associates for over a year before the wily Sanford leader discovered his love of distilled products. Ted interceded on Jim's behalf to no avail.

Jake McDougal was the last man on the Ted team. He was a turtle among dexedrine-fueled hares but held his own like the winner of Aesop's fable by his unshakable steadiness. He was, by trade, an editor and fulfilled that function for Arnold Sanford, editing and polishing the presentations Arnold Associates gave to gain new clients and retain old ones.

Despite all the tensions and grievances that existed among competing alliances all creatives functioned as professionals, always delivering their best to the client.

Chapter 31

What Comes Around

Business was booming and Larry was now the brightest star in the galaxy of ARNOLD SANFORD & ASSOCIATES. One day Arnold Sanford called him into his office. He wasn't a man given to praise for a job well done. To him the associates were just hired hands, reasonably paid, doing a professional job. None the less two promotions Larry had created caught his eye. With no pomp or build up Arnold handed him a check for $2,000 while simultaneously uttering, "You now have a new title."

The new title—Director of Creative Management—was the pinnacle of success in the hierarchy of Arnold Stanford Associates.

Why did he choose him? When in doubt, look for the money trail. Easy answer, Larry brought him two cash cows, money makers that annually produced more revenue than the company's combined income from 14 clients.

The first, YULTIDE FAVORITES, was an album collection of Christmas Carols sung by artists such as Bing Crosby singing WHITE CHRISTMAS. That album sold one million copies at the 1,400 retail outlets of the RIDETRUE CORPORATION. The album's success raised RIDETRUE'S market share and sales to a new high in the tire industry. The revenues for both Sanford Associates and RIDETRUE: at $6.95 per disc were outstanding.

The album was a recorded collection calculated to appeal to American's large, generous, sentimental and mostly religious middle class.

Larry's second triumph consisted of, DO-IT-YOUSELF DECORATOR VOLUMES 1, 11, and 111. Overnight KHARMAN WALTER paint company stores became home decorating centers for millions of new home owners on a limited decorating budget.

That audience, nearing fifty years of age, consisted mostly of veterans of WW II and their families. It was the generation whose upward mobility was nurtured by the GI BILL OF RIGHTS, which accorded 16 million veterans a free college education. Twenty years after the ending of World War II veterans were living the American dream; new cars, new homes, new appliances and an outlook that said life would only get better.

The decorating books promotion ran for three years, a new one issued each year. Sales at KHARMAN WALTERS skyrocketed and Arnold Stafford watched his net worth propel on a parallel course. Three and one half million copies were sold in that period. At $3.95 per each edition; SANFORD ASSOCIATES was on a roll.

New accounts and renewal of old accounts highlighted the need for at least one new account supervisor who could complement the skills of the creative teams.

At the weekly staff meeting Arnold directed Larry to hire a marketing man who was long on tact, administrative skills and a finely honed contact ability; a heavyweight. He would be compensated accordingly, $40,000 per year. The equivalent of $250,000 per annum in 2020.

The first ads Larry ran in ADVERTISING AGE and AD WEEK resulted in 81 responses. That should have been no surprise as the country was still in the midst of the Carter/ Reagan recession of 1980-81 when unemployment reached 11%, the highest since the Great Depression of the 1930's.

The economic slowdown resulted in a 15% cut in advertising budgets, the first item large corporations slashed in slow growth periods. He would see many highly qualified people.

After reading 20 or so resumes, his eyes began to glaze over. None of them contained a super star, all well qualified, but nothing that made his nipples hard. Take a break he told himself. Well maybe one more. He picked up resume number 21st looked at the name and bingo he had struck gold.

Page one of the vitae curriculum led off with the name Michael Olcott. On further reading he knew it was his Mike Olcott. The thought of interviewing Olcott for a job he controlled? Delicious. It had been 13 years since they last crossed swords in a duel he had lost. Now he was in total control of the rematch.

The son of a bitch was looking for a job. Larry wondered how many he lost in the Intervening years. His two kids must be in college by now. Too bad, baby, that's life.

Larry set his resume aside. He wasn't interested in Olcott's self inflated achievements of the last several years. An hour later he finished reading the remaining applications in the pile, pleased at finding 5 real contenders—on paper at least—great references, big time account management and contact experience, and stability in employment.

Probably victims of the recession. Who in his right mind, with a decent job in this economic environment, would want to be out there looking to improve his lie. He placed the five in a small pile next to the Olcott resume which stood alone. Laura appeared seconds after his buzzer sounded.

"Laura, here are six resumes of people I want to see. Would you kindly send each one a note requesting him to call to schedule a date for his interview. For these five use my personal agency letterhead. For this one use general agency letterhead and sign off with your name."

"Fine, Larry. I'll get them off this afternoon. What days are you available next week?"

"This is a priority. I'm open for business any afternoon."

She left his office five resumes in one hand one resume in the other.

He could tell this was the beginning of a wonderful weekend. Aggie and he had tickets for a 1:00 pm game at Shea Stadium, Mets v Giants. What could be better than sitting in a spring afternoon sun overlooking a dazzling green field, its outfield grass a patchwork quilt of squares, seamlessly joined together.

Lithe young outfielders would be tossing high arc throws to each other, a timeless pre-game warm up while infielders insouciantly fielded grounders with practiced ease tossing the ball to the awaiting first baseman. Over and over, they repeated the motions; never such a thing as too much practice in the 'game of inches' called baseball.

Pitchers, loosening arms, leisurely played a game of catch with anyone willing to play, a prelude to throwing hard the fastballs, curves and sliders in their repertory when the real game began.

Mets were home so Giants were up first.

As fielders jogged to their positions, the Mets starting pitcher ambled to the mound for his six or seven warm-up pitches to a masked man wearing protective gear on his upper body legs and midsection 60 feet 6 inches away.

He watched Aggie check out the pitches tossed by the starter Craig Swan. She could tell a curve coming by the crook of a pitchers arm, a change-up by the slight hesitation of his release, a fastball by a longer arc of his body extension.

Some people would call her a man's woman based on her love of sports. But they would be wrong. If you really knew her you see she was nobody's woman. She was her own woman and that's what Larry loved about her.

Larry interrupted her fix on the pitcher's motions with a kiss on her neck. Smiling she turned to him.

"You're in a good mood."

"That I am," he said trying to sound mysterious. But the secret this day was his alone.

Mets won 3-1. It was a pitching duel between Swan, the 6'3" fireballer and the Giants Vida Blue, a former All-Star with the Oakland Athletics. John Stearns hit a winning 2-run double in the last of the 8th.

Sunday Aggie and Larry went for a bike ride in Central Park that ended with a picnic just a few yards off the croquet greensward leased by the U.S. Croquet Association.

"Come on what's really up?" Aggie asked when they were comfortably snuggled together under a tartan blanket she brought along for their outing.

"What do you mean?"

"You know. I know you're acting. I can always tell. You are just a little too smug with your secret, whatever it may be."

"Tell you what, Aggie, we've been seeing each other for nearly three years. Right?

"Right."

"Tommorrow night we'll have a special dinner at Café Des Artiste."

"That place with all the nudes on the walls?"

"Yes, but my dear, those are original murals done by a famous artist of the Art Nouveau movement."

"Yeah, but they're still nudes, T and A right?"

He ignored his little Philistine and continued.

"Tomorrow night I promise to tell you what's on my mind."

"I can hardly wait," she said with genuine enthusiasm.

Hmm, he thought that sounds like she might think I'm about to propose marriage. I'm not ready. No, hold it. Maybe I am.

At 4:00 pm on Monday, Betty buzzed his intercom.

"Mr. Olcott is here for his interview."

The moment had come.

"Please send him in."

13 years later and 20 pounds heavier a lumbering Mike Olcott walked into Larry's office. His rumpled navy blue suit fit too tightly around the waist.

Larry looked up and their eyes met. The startled look on his face said all he could have ever wished for. His jowls sagged even more as he recognized Larry.

"Have a seat, Mike."

He hesitated for a moment before shuffling his thick body the few steps to a chair facing Larry.

He settled his frame in the stiff back chair designed for posture not comfort, squirming to find a satisfying position.

"Well, this couldn't be a bigger surprise," he said, forcing a smile that immediately froze into carefully choreographed sincerity. Larry had seen that smile hundreds of times in the past they had shared.

"Mind if I smoke?"

He pulled out a pack of Marlboros from his jacket pocket. Larry pushed an ashtray toward him. He lit up. Larry waited until his first soothing inhale of nicotine. He did so with a desperate sucking sound holding in the smoke for at least 30 seconds,

"We've all had major surprises in our lives, Mike. The last one I recall was in the Fremon-Richardson conference room just before I left their employment."

His nervous laugh was a giggle, unbecoming a machismo man of 220 pounds.

"Well live and let live I always say," he said.

"Is that what you always say? When you leave this office you might want to try this one,'let bygones be bygones'. But the one I suggest you take to heart and use in the future is this one,'what goes around comes around.' I believe it is the most apt. Never know it just might work somewhere in your future."

He said nothing in response, just uncrossed his thick legs as though preparing for a quick exit. Larry waited for a reply. None came.

"Well, Mike it's been interesting seeing you again."

He reached for Olcott's resume and handed it to him.

"Here it might come in handy at your next interview."

He stood to accept the paper. His jacket seemed tighter now. His face reddened. His thin lips tightened. Reflexively he extended his hand which Larry let hang in mid air. Before he had a chance to turn toward the door, Larry reached into his in box and started to blankly read the first paper that lay there.

He looked up at the back view of this man whose stele shaped body had no indent at the waist. His creased blue suit sagged a bit more than when he entered. A further look confirmed his first glance. He was wearing dark blue and white running shoes. How odd.

Secretaries wore them for comfort on their commute to work via subway, bus or train but once in the office they switched to medium heeled black pumps for a more professional appearance.

Men in business suits never appeared in public wearing the casual foot wear of Nike, Reebok, Addidas or Keds.

Chapter 32

Eddie Callahan & That Oil Gang Of Mine

He was heavier now. The once youthful apple cheeks sagged, stuffed with the baggage of stress and the passage of time. He failed in the attempt to hide a perfectly rounded paunch. Brooks Brothers was never kind to an out of shape jock, not even their friendlier two-button model jacket.

As they drew closer on East 53rd Street and Park, just within the shadows of the Racquet Club, Larry wondered if he would look up. Five steps away the spring afternoon light hit his face, revealing dewlaps too large and too soon for a man in his late forties.

He stopped, looked up, eyes wide,"Lawrence," he said in a voice years younger than his years.

He smiled in as he always did, salivating slightly at the corners of his mouth. No one called him Lawrence in the fifteen years since he left the corporate side of advertising.

He was no longer the client being fawned upon.

After they shook hands Eddie Callahan, without any prompting, proceeded to verbally update his resume as they stood in the bright sunlight across the street from the Seagram's Building building now 45 years old.

In the intervening years their roles had switched. He now had the role of a client as a senior brand manager for a large Dutch brewing company. Larry was now an agency creative person on several blue chip accounts. After 15 minutes of catch up covering nearly two decades, plus his short infomercial on the efficacy of the art of brewing, they embraced, exchanged cards and vowed to have a reunion lunch with all the other players from their STANDCO days.

Eddie would be the point man contacting Bart Bassen, his old boss from the agency, Bob Dewey Larry's counterpart at STANDCO, and Warren Nelson his former assistant who had subsequently risen rapidly up STANDCO'S corporate ladder. He was now the VP Marketing of the 50 billion dollar giant.

Who else Larry wondered as Eddie receded into sunit Park Avenue. He might dredge up Dwayne Erickson the corporate slug who probably still toiled under the corporate security blanket, no doubt with a handsome nest egg from the company's matching stock purchase plan. Although at age 50 he might be feeling the grim reaper's hand that the Mckenzie Company and other downsizing consultants wielded in a new business climate that abandoned its benevolence of the 60's and early 70's.

Walking back to his office he wondered what toll the years had taken from Bassen, Erickson, Dewey, and Nelson. Physically he expected to see a quartet of flaccid, well tailored, battle worn warriors, suffering from too many twelve o clock tails, too many Bull & Bear ribs of roast beef and too many unfiltered Chesterfields.

Eddie was the youngest of the group, four years younger than Larry or Dewey. Bassen would be the oldest at 57.

They all probably still smoked. He felt a slight moral superiority having kicked the nicotine habit four years after the U.S. Surgeon General Dr. Koop turned thumbs down on cigarettes. But maybe he was doing them an injustice. Could he be the only one who discovered the benefits of regular exercise and moderation in alcohol consumption?

They really were not his friends. They were his associates. They never shared intimacies. What they shared was a post college male fraternity based on career aspirations, the need for companionship and someone to drink and chase girls with.

But then, to be honest, he was a closet Jew with that oil gang of his. Maybe it was a bad idea to exchange cards with Eddie. The anti-Semitic undertones and vibes he felt those many years ago were long gone. He was emersed in a new lifestyle no longer harboring a Jewish defensiveness. Was he looking for a lunch to be kicked in the ass again?

In his mind he recalled the first day he met met Eddie Callahan He was early. It was 8:45. He knocked on Larry's door.

He entered explaining he was Larry's he new junior account executive. He offered his hand. The shaking of hands began a friendly, three year working relationship.

Larry got along well with all the guys in the department except Dwayne Erickson who did not like him. He never knew why. Now looking back he realized Erickson was an anti-Semite. Why did he think Larry to be a Jew? Who knew? Larry never had a clue. It's was the only logical reason he could think of.

Erickson was a snob, flaunting his Williams College credentials a little too often. Larry was fully aware that he was an anomaly, a Jewish middle manager at a top three oil company. That just didn't happen in the early 60's. Not when the executive suites of the STANDCO building were regularly visited by burnous clad gentlemen shrouded by checkered scarves that discreetly revealed neatly trimmed beard and mustaches on faces that all looked alike. The Saudi Arabian ARAMCO partners were critical to America's oil access.

He didn't strike people as being Jewish with a name like Miller, regular features, reddish blonde hair and blue eyes.

Erickson, his inner Eichman working overtime must have known he thought. Larry couldn't accept not being liked for the person he was and presented to the world.

An occasional Jewish joke might be regarded as serious anti-Semitism by the more paranoid of his kinsmen but he was comfortable in his secular being. He also knew his job seeking had been freed from any hiring discrimination based on religion after the passing of the New York State Fair Employment Act.

During the period Eddie served as his account executive, Larry genuinely like him. It wasn't just the tickets, and event invites he freely offered. It was his good humor, candor and youthful vulnerability. What you saw is what he was. He gave you what he had to give with no strings attached.

He was ambitious and had a sly sense of humor. Eddie was the only person who could have twitted Dug Breitling and gotten away with it.

Doug with a thirty something second wife, hated being 54 years old. Age was a sore point with him. Once when he and Eddie were in his office to show him a new ad series for radial tires.,Doug rested his shiny black loafers on a paper free desk. It was a sure sign he wasn't quite ready to talk tires. His body language said let's talk basketball. It was March Madness time, the NCAA Tournament, the National Championship which was all 64 entrants hope.

Guys in every office in New York were busy working their ladder sheets, hoping to snare a share of the Daily News $25,000 prize money.

Doug liked Kentucky to win it all. After explaining the reasoning behind his pick, he quietly revealed that he once played on an NCAA championship team at the University of Kentucky. That winning team, in a time honored tradition, was invited to the White House to be congratulated by the President of the United States, an office then occupied by Herbert Hoover. Doug said he had the honor of shaking the hand of Herbert Hoover his last year in office.

Herbert Hoover?

That was in 1932 which to Eddie and Larry seemed light years ago. They simultaneously calculated Doug's true age. He must have been 22 years old at the White House 32 years ago. Eureka, he wasn't 48 as he claimed. His actual age was 54.

Without missing a beat, Eddie slyly asked, "Wasn't Hoover the president before Franklin Roosevelt?"

Doud acknowledged he was and all basketball talk abruptly ended. They segued swiftly into Larry's recommended media schedule.

As life with Georgeena was getting pretty dicey Larry spent more time away from the apartment. Occasionally he would crash at Eddie's modest studio pad on weekends to avoid the angst of spending two consecutive days in the same dwelling as with George.

To look at him you saw a choir boy in a Brooks Brother's suit. At 6 feet, weighing no more than 150 pounds, he wore clothes with style, close fitting but not too tight, garnished by the ever present triangular shaped white handkerchief in his breast pocket. Navy, grey pinstripe or tweed suit the handkerchief was his trademark at a time when guys didn't do white handkerchiefs. A daring few tried a matching tie and handkerchief combo but in the tight assed culture of the era, white oxford cloth button downs with a regimental striped tie completed the uniform of the day.

A blue oxford cloth shirt might be okay a couple days a week but on important meeting days WHITE was the only acceptable color. Every business guy looked a lot like a middle echelon FBI agent in 2020.

At their street side meeting Eddiehe looked like a slightly altered version of his youthful self. Maybe a little stouter but the muffin face smile still revealed his beaver-like front teeth.

Looking back Larry was sure Doug took a shine to Eddie not just for their symbiotic love of sports. He saw himself in some ways like Eddie; untutored in the ways of big city New York. Though born in the Bronx, Eddie was a New York provincial. Doug born in Valdosta, Georgia was a Southern provincial. You can take the boy out of redneck Valdosta but you can't take redneck Valdosta out of the boy.

Doug never did get the lingo of a French menu down pat and as long as waiters weren't black, his genially spoken racist slurs seldom erupted with one major exception.

At lunch at a new watering hole for ad men, Auereole, Doug observed the garish drapes that covered half its dining area. A large floral pattern utilized colors in day-glo red, orange, green and yellow.

"Damn, those are niggery colors,"he said pointing to the offending drapes Niggery? He sneaked a look at Doug's agency counterpart, urbane Princetonian, Hal McCallister. He saw Larry look but turned away quickly, wanting no part of any comment Larry might make.

Larry made none certain his boss was never aware that he just had converted the word "nigger", a deplorable noun, into a deplorable adjective.

Over the next few days Larry wondered if the STANDCO reunion lunch was for real or was it a "we must do lunch some time" fiction.

The more he thought about a reunion lunch the less viable it became. First of all, Dwayne Ericksion was a fucking anti-Semite and probably Dewey as well. Greenwich dwelling Bart Bassen's view of the world had a whiff of anti-Semitism. Anyone not acceptable at the NYAC was not in his orbit. Warren was genuinely a good person but one good guy vote was not enough. What should he tell Eddie?

The STANCO reunion lunch never came off. 10 days after their meeting Eddie called.

"Lawrence," he said.

Lawrence he called him. That much hadn't changed.

"I don't know how to say it but Bart and Wayne and Dewey said they'd rather not be a part of the reunion. Who knows what's with them?" he said.

He knew all right, but Eddie never was much for bearing bad news.

"Warren Nelson said he'd love to get together."

Good old Warrren. Nice man. Too bad couldn't break bread with him.

"Eddie," Larry replied, "you're a stand up guy. Always have been and I do have a warm spot for Warren but maybe it was a lousy idea for a reunion in the first place. Thanks for trying and good luck to you."

Before he could reply, Larry hung up.

CHAPTER 33

Time To Close The Doors Of Sanford & Associates

At some point even the canniest of promoters had to face the hard fact when, to move on. It was the time when the well ran dry. It was the moment when you exhausted your list of blue chip corporations, no longer enchanted by the cost of a big idea. Top managements no longer wanted to underwrite the output of wild eyed dreamers. PT Barnum knew the time to leave town. Arnold Sanford remained in denial, envisioning himself as latter day Aimee Semple McPherson, without the tent filled whooping and hollering.

Denial ended with Wilco Electric's decision not to renew their $125,000 retainer with Arnold Stanford Associates. It sent Arnold into a state of shock. His uncharacteristic response was depression, followed by a plan to reduce overhead. His new business model was premised on the quid pro quo: every client lost would result in the dismissal of one associate.

Wilco never gave a reason for their decision reason but the associates all knew that no great promotion goes unpunished by a greedy client. And greedy they were, the folks at Wilco Electric, a giant mid-western manufacturer of appliances. Sanford and

Associates had just given them their best Christmas Promotion ever for refrigerators, ranges and dish washing machines.

HAVE A DICKENS OF A CHRISTMAS!

For every purchase of a Wilco product in November and December a consumer would get an authentic reproduction of Charles Dickens' Book, A CHRISTMAS CAROL, complete with 4-color reproductions of illustrations from the original.

It was a masterfully produced book. The client loved it. Three hundred thousand copies were sold, representing three hundred thousand units of white goods that moved off the sales room floors of Wilco showrooms throughout America.

From the day the company was dumped gloom descended upon the 26th floor of the Seagram's building. It became a worrisome vigil waiting for the next shoe to drop or more accurately the next client.

The demise was more rapid than anyone could imagine. After Wilco the next drop out was Planter's Oats, which had been a client for eight years, a near record for client longevity at Arnold Stanford Associates. With their departure Mertz was the first man to be cut loose.

During the Black Days of personnel reduction Walter Mauer, the numbers guy, hung a wall chart in his office. It displayed his assessment of who would go next; the projected order of termination of each executive, himself included. His criteria were based on the following variables:

1. Estimated retention time of the client he or she serviced
2. Assessment of each associate's strength relative to those remaining, a decision made only by Arnold Stanford himself. Here Walter Mauer was second guessing the chief
3. The amount of his or her compensation

He would post his odds each week as conditions continued to worsen. Life became a surreal combination of "musical chairs" and "ten little Indians". The bunker mentality of the smartest group of people Larry ever worked with was heart breaking. The strongest paired with the weakest as alliances formed. It was a delusional bonding. Being part of a group offered no safety to any associate.

Larry lasted 28 weeks. Only 2 other associates hung on longer, Dan Torgeson, executive art director and Ted Van Oker, Director of Account Management. At week 35, when there was no one else to let go, Arnold Stanford closed his padded cloth doors for the last time. Goodbye Seagrams. Goodbye Mies Van Der Rohe.

The amenities of business courtesy eluded the self-absorbed little man from Elkhart, Indiana, who without the aid of a suit coat's padding he was a man with raglan arms, no shoulders just arms attached to his pot-bellied body, like Mr. Potato Head. In the end, like Mr. Potato Head, everything came apart for Arnold Stanford.

There were no goodbyes with Arnold; just as there were no Christmas parties, no office lunches, no real humanity toward the associates. They were simply hired guns with no back stories.

Stanford did not go quietly into the dark night. Larry witnessed his curtain call on network television. One day in January 1972 watching network coverage of the New Hampshire primary, he saw, George McGovern and Hubert Humphrey vigorously campaigning for the opportunity to unseat Richard Nixon, liberal America's evil incarnate.

On Channel 7 he saw a pretty, young Barbara Walters interviewing a familiar unexpected person. Thin faced, reddish hair graying beneath a ridiculous lumber jack's cap there he was old raglan arms himself. Oh my God. It was Arnold Stanford. Why was he in New Hampshire on the eve of that state's Democratic primary Election?

On camera standing next to Stanford visible, except for the extreme close-up shots, was 6'4" Dan Torgeson, an old associate at Stanford Associates. He had removed his hat revealing his traditional close-cropped crew cut, now more white than gray, looking like a modern dress spear carrier in BORIS GOUDINOV.

In an era of long haired hippies and long side burned business executives Torgeson retained his high school hair style of the early '50s. It earned him the designation Westmoreland by his peers at Arnold Stanford Associates. Dan, indeed, was a doppelganger of General William S Westmoreland, leader of U.S. troops in Vietnam. Larry knew Dan secretly enjoyed the celebrity of his nickname. There he was his usual towering presence over Arnold and the petite Barbara Walters.

"Mr. Stanford, are you aware that no one else has ever before run for the office of vice-president?" she said in a measured non-confrontational tone.

"I am, Miss Walters, but there's always a first time. Tell me why should I let precedence stop me from a run?"

The TV cameras zoomed in on a large campaign button pinned on Arnold's over coat. Red, white and blue it bore the words:

STANFORD FOR VICE-PRESIDENT Barbara patiently explained that the vice-presidential candidate historically had been selected either by nomination at the convention, after the president was nominated, or selected personally by the presidential candidate.

"Well," Arnold riposted, "I guess I'm making history."

You've got to be kidding me, he thought. Is he serious or is it a comeback for his company with free TV publicity?

Or could it be the last hurrah of a man consumed by unlimited self-esteem; a final attempt to gain recognition and praise. Larry was sure he chose this national stage for his valedictory, a venue large enough to satisfy his outsized ego.

During the attrition period at Arnold Sanford Associates, Larry did not spend his time wringing hands over the projected loss of a great job. He put out feelers for future employment. He credentials secure, he was a desireable commodity in the market place.

A small upcoming agency, Platt and Monk, saw the spark that Larry could bring to them. He was hired on the spot after a review of his sample book, with a signing bonus of $5,000.

CHAPTER 34

Freedom

Larry caught the "Freedom Flight" from New York to El Paso at 6:45 pm on a Friday night. He was but one in a homogenous group of 50 men and women whose common goal was divorce, Mexican style.

The destination was Juarez, Mexico, just across the Rio Grande from El Paso. There the machinery was designed to legally release unhappy spouses from unbearable marriages.

A Mexican Divorce was legally binding in New York State although a divorce agreement had to be negotiated and agreed upon by both parties before the Mexican decree could be actuated.

Larry met what he considered honerous demands upon acceptance of his promising new job and its financial rewards.

The 5 hour flight was a party which enabled the 50 to freely exchange past marital woes. The mood was one of tempered happiness. Freedom? Maybe for those who had no children but a future of the unknown ahead was daunting to most.

Larry wondered how many had a possible second marriage in mind as he did.

Leaving the past behind is almost impossible, yet life demands moving forward. The right direction, however, is most often a crap shoot.

The group appeared to be mostly in their 30's and 40's, both men and women, well dressed careerists.

Larry was amiable but shied away from anyone's attempt to engage in serious conversation.

The mass production divorce court in Juarez was presided over by Luis Guzman a soft voiced man in his fifties whose English was fluent, with just the trace of an accent. With efficient grace Guzman managed to release 50 men and women seeking a second try. In one case, a foxy blond woman pushing 50, it would be a third try.

The proceedings were solemn until the last person was handed an iron clad divorce, recognized in all 50 states. After the proceedings a raucous group headed for a celebratory dinner.

The next morning they flew back to New York, a six hour flight.

After the plane landed and came to a halt, the click of 50 seat belt could be heard, sounding a collective release from the state of matrimony.

As they debarked their comraderie morphed into a frantic hugging and kissing with solemn promises to stay in touch and above all a pledge of no returns to Juarez.

Date often. Date wisely but make no commitments for at least a year. Divorce to most was till an open sore. Larry wondered if he would be the first to break the no commitment promise.

His first stop was to see Georgeen and personally hand her a copy of the divorce papers. When the taxi stopped at 430 West End Avenue it would be his first visit to the apartment in nearly a year.

He wondered about what she would do with the next stage of her life as he approached the familiar door to unit 7B. He knew he should have been more considerate by calling before coming. He owed her that courtesy.

The door opened and Georgeena appeared, dressed in her any occasion sleeveless black dress, one strand of pearls and a Hermes scarf. There standing in the doorway was the person with whom he had first fallen in love. She hadn't changed in ten years. She was the same beautiful young woman, belying her 40 years.

"Hi," he said.

"Hi," she said. A moment passed. "Don't just stand there staring. Come in."

"You look as though you're ready to go out. I'm sorry I gave you no advance warning."

"I am. I have a job interview. A girl can't live by alimony alone."

Don't respond he silently warned himself. La guerre est fini.

"Are returning to the snap crotch crawler crowd?"

"No, I thought I'd look for something in your line of work. Maybe a very junior person in the art department. I can draw you know."

"Yes, I know you can and I thinks it's a good idea. But I must caution you. An art director's assistant is woefully underpaid."

"I'll take my chances."

Larry sat down on a chair across from Georgeena and removed some papers from his brief case. He handed them to her.

"Here's to your new life. I wish you well."

She glanced them over before setting them down on a metal end table, they had purchase on a trip to New Hope a few years back.

"I think best wishes go best with a cocktail."

"Sure, why not? We can toast to each other's future and even reflect on a bit of the past. Hard to believe 10 years have gone by."

She got up to prepare the drinks then stopped and turned to Larry.

"Tell me honestly, Larry what made you change your mind about accepting my Attorney's offer?

Waiting for his reply, she picked up a bottle of Beefeater's Gin and poured generously into a cocktail shaker. Measuring a pour was not In her nature. Adding some ice, she closed the sweating container, then shook a couple of times before pouring its clesr liquid into two long stemmed, wide brimmed glasses.

WE'LL ALWAYS HAVE PARIS

A substantial quantity of clear liquid remined in the container as she removed the ice, making sure not to water down its contents. A second and possible third round of drinks was assured.

Larry hadn't expected her question. Why did he have a change of mind? Did he really want to give an honest answer? Not completely. Too complicated.

'There are a couple of things, George. First of all, I got a decent raise. My new employer thinks I'm hot shit."

"So you can't plead poverty anymore?"

"Nothing spectacular but enough to keep me off the streets at night."

She took two olives from a jar and plopped them into his glass. He raised his it. She did the same.

"We'll always have Paris," Larry said, clinking her glass.

"Yes, we will but it's Rick whose leaving Casablanca in your scenario."

His second reason for accepting her lawyer's demand he put on hold. He was mellow. She was mellow. Sometimes, the whole truth should not be told.

Georgeena was different. She never lied. Regardless of the consequences, she never lied. You always knew how she where she stood.

He wish she had lied. Unfortunately, complete honesty in a marriage is often a path to divorce. People are not wired for complete honesty. He looked Georgeena in the eye, trying to read her response to his explanation. Without warning a black flash of fur leaped onto his lap with a purr of recognition. It was Mowgli. Half of the cat used to belong to him he thought.

"You should be flattered. He still likes you, considering how little he's seen of you this past year." As Larry scratched Mowgli's underbelly, he responded with a familiar purr.

Trying to strike a more collegial note Larry attempted to change the subject.

"We've had a pretty good run. George. Six years out of ten, not too bad a batting average."

"Oy, another of your dismal baseball references. You know I hate team sports, just a group of guys on a collective weenie wag."

Oops. Cool the sports analogies he told himself.

"You're right I am an unreconstructed sports nut."

"This is hardly a moment in our non marriage state to revive old likes and dislikes," she continued.

She was right.

"I apologize. I'm sorry I wanted this to be civilized."

"Larry, I want to tell you something. We both were not wise enough to see when we decided to become a couple. We were headed for trouble from the beginning. But we never bothered to talk about your Jewish hang up.

You know why? Because we had the hots for each other. And you know the hots beats cold logic every time."

She paused to drain half her cocktail.

"I agree with your analysis of the hots but what about my so called Jewish hang up. What are you talking about?"

"You were always looking for anti-Semitism. You saw injustices everywhere, but you never talked about them, to me or anyone else. A lot of it was real, not imagined. I'm not calling you paranoid.

You never dealt with it, always internalizing. Whether you believe me or not, I knew the pain it caused. I watched you carry all that baggage alone. You kept it all inside. You left me out as though I was a stranger. I thought marriage was sharing feelings, hurts, triumphs. You know closeness only can be achieved by leveling with your partner. You chose not to do that."

She paused. Her eyes were tearing. "I loved you. I know you believe that...and I believe you loved me. No. I know you were in love with me.

We could be so God damn good together. We had moments few people ever experienced. I know I fucked up but so did you. Why did we have to lose such a good thing?

A French poet once nailed the comsequences of failed relationships, but never the cause."

"The years wear down too fast,
Beware, Beware,
This sad brakage of the past."

Georgeena started to cry. She dabbed at her eyes with a handkerchief, then hid her face in her hands. The soft crying became an audible sobbing. Larry slowly got up from his chair and sat down next to her on the sofa. He put his arms around her. Tentatively at first, then committed. He started to cry. She wrapped her arms around him. They sat there in tight embrace. Not a word was uttered.

The next unexpected hour remained with him a lifetime. At the door he retied his rumpled tie and tucked in his shirt.

"We are getting sentimental," Georgeena said. "Now it's time to really say goodbye."

She adjusted his twisted coat lapels, pulled his tie up to meet his collar, then one final kiss. It was not just a touching of lips. It was meant to convey a remembrance of things past.

He turned and walked into the hallway, leaving one life behind to begin another. Astonishing, he thought, the melange of emotional complexity a couple is able to create.

In the ebb and flow of their relationship the tide always seemed to be going out. Now his only question remained unanswered. How could two decent people so damage each other's innate humanity?

The French are optimistic about partings. One can chose among:

A bientot—see you soon
A plus tard—see you later
A tout a l'heure—see you in a while

None seemed appropriate for their parting. Even au revoir seemed inadequate.

CHAPTER 35

The Big Question

After he left Georgeena Larry called Aggie to cancel their dinner date that evening.

"Aggie, I'm exhausted. I need a little time to get organized. Talk to you tomorrow, okay?"

He needed some time to reflect on his future, get things straight in his head. What did he really want to do with his life? Despite their unexpected parting, he knew Georgeena had now become part of his past. That chapter was over, but what was the next move. Or should he stay on an emotional treadmill where no end point needed be determined? The reality he needed to resolve was; what role would Agnes Doyle play in his new life?

He didn't call her back the next day. Five days passed before he called to set a new dinner date. She accepted the rescheduled dinner without questioning his delay in contacting her. Agnes Doyle was a pragmatic woman grounded in reality. Larry chose Café Des Artiste, his favorite New York restaurant, whose naughty, nubile, nudes adorned the six foot murals surrounding its spacious dining area.

The establishment, which opened in 1917, attracted the likes of Noel Coward, Charlie Chaplin and Cole Porter for both its food and ambiance.

Larry arrived early, directing the maître de to seat him at a table facing a mural called THREE WOMEN. by a famous American painter in the early 2oth century, Howard Chandler Christy.

He had taken Agnes to Des Artiste once before. She was less than overwhelmed by the place then. He hoped she would think better of it this time. Their usual eateries, the Bull and Bear and Madison Square Garden dining room were not known for their ambiance. When she arrived fifteen minutes later, she was escorted by a waiter who seemed pleased to be walking with a beautiful woman at his side.

Larry stood up to greet her. She remained standing staring at the THREE SISTERS.

"I see why this is your favorite restaurant. This mural is a six foot version of a SPORT'S ILLUSTRATED swim suit issue cover."

He ignored her negative tone of voice, took her hand and kissed her lightly on the cheek. "I guess your not into depictions of the human body."

"The only thing beautiful nudes arouse in me is jealousy," she said.

"You have nothing to be jealous about. I love every nook and cranny of your body. Top to bottom, especially the bottom."

She smiled, "You like my bum."

"Can't get enough of it."

Her smile said he was forgiven.

At that moment the waiter appeared. "The lady will be having what I'm having," Larry said, pointing to his half filled martini.

He turned to Agnes, "I suppose you're wondering why I called this meeting."

"Yes, I am."

"Let me start with show and tell."

He reached into is jacket pocket producing a small black box, which he placed on the table, gently pushing it towards her.

"Before you open it, I'd like to bring up a subject which could influence your reaction to this little black box. You are a good Catholic."

"I'm not that good. I don't go to mass."

"And I don't go to synagogue."

"Are you finished? Can I open the box now?"

'Yes."

She opened the box, stared for a moment, then took the ring out and proceeded to put it on.

"The answer is yes."

"That's the right answer," Larry said leaning in to kiss his new bride to be.

"Now let's get down to the nitty gritty," he continued. "My parents will not come east for a wedding to a "shiksah". Let them stew for awhile. I promise they'll come around soon enough. What about your mother?"

"She definitely would like to be present at her only daughter's wedding and my three brothers would kill if they were not invited."

"That's settled. It will be an eight person wedding at the Lotus Club with a Justice of the Peace presiding. The seventh and eighth persons would be my fraternity brother, Harold and his wife Dotty. Harold has seen me through all the craziness in my life. Do you approve?"

"Well I guess Madison Square Garden would be a little showy."

She paused for a moment, then stood up an hugged him.

"I guess you never were aware that I was in love with you when I was a humble secretary at STANDCO."

"You were never humble. That's part of your blarney charm."

They were married in a civil ceremnony at the Lotus Club, one month later. Her brothers each spoke, her mother uttered a few words and ginger haired Agggie recited a traditional Irish bit of folk lore which concluded with the cheerful wish for the future, "AND MAY THE WIND ALWAYS BE AT YOUR BACK."

For most of their 27 year marriage the wind was nearly always at their back.

CHAPTER 36

Georgeena Adieu

As was his early morning habit, Larry opened the New York Times to its obituary page the day of October 8th, 1996. Mortality was becoming an increasing preoccupation. His hunt for names of deceased he might know was interrupted that day by a lingering quote he couldn't quite get out of his head. it was George Burns reflection that, "everyday your name is not in the obituary column is a good day."

The comdian's observation offered but small comfort from one's awareness of the inevitable decline of those around him, including self.

He traced a wavering forefinger down the grey print columns of death, rarely finding a familiar face or photo. This day, however, halfway down column two, he abruptly stopped at a face he knew so well from a different chapter in his life.

The picture that looked up at him from the newsprint was accompanied by loving attributions about the deceased by grieving next of kin. He stared back. Could it be? The full lipped mouth and graceful neck line said yes.

Yes. Yes, it was she. The photo was circa 1961, as he recalled. It confirmed his Georgeena was no longer of this planet. Strange, 27 years had passed since their divorce and he still thought of her as his Georgeena. The smiling picture of a 30ish brunette, whose sensuous brown eyes could not be replicated in a grainy black and white photo, was Georgeena; his lover and wife for 10 years. Three of those years were mostly wasted in the long drawn out death of their marriage.

He continued to stared at the image that brought him into a world he'd never known before. She had opened doors for him into a social milieu, a middle class, mid-western Jew never thought attainable.

It was a heady and wild ride rubbing elbows with the best and brightest of New York's literary and theatrical communities.

She also brought him the pain of diminishment as a clueless cuckhold.

She was gone. Dead at the age of 65. Cause of death; cirrhosis of the liver. Surviving her were husband number three, John Mcgiver and a 26 year old daughter, Minerva. Oh, what a fucked up kid she must be, he thought.

Happily, husband number two, him, was not mentioned nor was husband number one revealed. Larry never knew his name. He did not exist in Georgeena's next phase of life, her 10 years with Larry Miller. He hoped she found peace with McGiver and Minerva. She was a woman/child in search of lasting unqualified love, something her Bohemian mother, Harriet was incapable of giving. Harriet was an alpha dog wrapped in intellectual narcissism, an early feminist, a libertarian, a collector of high profile lovers.

He knew nothing of Georgeena's life after Miller. Their lives never intersected.

The occasional Christmas card, over the years, from Teddy and Maria Serenghetti never mentioned her. Was that oversight on their part or did they want to spare him from the stormy past? Or was it just a case of losing touch with her. He'd never know.

At their best George and Larry reveled in magical moments; highs most people never experience; lows which scraped the nadir of perversity and humiliation. Love is never enough.

Could he have been a more supportive husband? Could she have been a more supportive wife?

Stop! No need to go there. RIP

The course of a marriage is never charted. There is no compass to keep it on a defined destination. It just unfolds; in ways often random. Once the ecstasy, danger and adventure of love is gone people try to examine what love really is all about. They discover, too late, that love at its core is negotiation; the surrender of two individuals to sharing the messy banal realities of living a life together.

He took one last look at the grainy picture before folding the obit section into the Times Op-Ed page.

His comforting farewell to Georgeena was a certainty that, "We always had Paris."